PRAISE FOR
CITY OF THE MUSE

"In *City of the Muse*, author Kate Hilton unites her deep understanding and passion for history, archaeology, literature, true crime, and academic one-upmanship in an all-encompassing and breathless tale. . . . Readers of historical fiction will revel in this wholly original, immersive, and gripping story."

NATALIE JENNER, INTERNATIONALLY BESTSELLING AUTHOR OF *THE JANE AUSTEN SOCIETY* AND *BLOOMSBURY GIRLS*

"Kate Hilton has accomplished the extraordinary—a masterful blend of a smart, propulsive whodunit and a fascinating work of historical fiction. As a present-day archivist uncovers the buried truths of a trailblazing woman archaeologist killed in 1903, the novel adeptly confronts the realities of forbidden ambition and survival in a man's world."

CATHY MARIE BUCHANAN, *NEW YORK TIMES* BESTSELLING AUTHOR OF *THE PAINTED GIRLS* AND *DAUGHTER OF BLACK LAKE*

"Ambition, greed, and privilege collide in *City of the Muse*. . . . Kate Hilton's richly drawn and well-researched novel reveals the all-too-often overlooked contributions made by women to archaeological research—and exposes the lengths to which some men will go in order to be the ones writing the history books."

BRYN TURNBULL, BESTSELLING AUTHOR OF *THE BERLIN APARTMENT*

"An accomplished and absorbing mystery set in two timelines, Kate Hilton's *City of the Muse* skillfully weaves together Egyptology, a hundred-year-old murder, and a present-day dilemma to deliver a story that kept me turning the pages to reach an immensely satisfying conclusion."

JANIE CHANG, BESTSELLING AUTHOR OF *THE PORCELAIN MOON, THE LIBRARY OF LEGENDS,* AND *DRAGON SPRINGS ROAD*

ALSO BY KATE HILTON

Widows and Orphans (with Elizabeth Renzetti)
Bury the Lead (with Elizabeth Renzetti)
Better Luck Next Time
Just Like Family
The Hole in the Middle

CITY OF THE MUSE

KATE HILTON

PUBLISHED BY SIMON & SCHUSTER
NEW YORK   AMSTERDAM/ANTWERP   LONDON
TORONTO   SYDNEY/MELBOURNE   NEW DELHI

A Division of Simon & Schuster, LLC
166 King Street East, Suite 300
Toronto, Ontario M5A 1J3

For more than 100 years, Simon & Schuster has championed authors and the stories they create. By respecting the copyright of an author's intellectual property, you enable Simon & Schuster and the author to continue publishing exceptional books for years to come. We thank you for supporting the author's copyright by purchasing an authorized edition of this book.

No amount of this book may be reproduced or stored in any format, nor may it be uploaded to any website, database, language-learning model, or other repository, retrieval, or artificial intelligence system without express permission. All rights reserved. Inquiries may be directed to Simon & Schuster, 1230 Avenue of the Americas, New York, NY 10020 or permissions@simonandschuster.com.

This book is a work of fiction. Any references to historical events, real people, or real places are used fictitiously. Other names, characters, places, and events are products of the author's imagination, and any resemblance to actual events or places or persons, living or dead, is entirely coincidental.

Copyright © 2026 by Katherine Hilton

"24a [you will remember]," "24c [we live]," "129a [but me you have forgotten]," and "129b [or you love some man more than me]" from *If Not, Winter: Fragments of Sappho* by Sappho, translated by Anne Carson, copyright © 2002 by Anne Carson. Used by permission of Alfred A. Knopf, an imprint of the Knopf Doubleday Publishing Group, a division of Penguin Random House LLC. All rights reserved.

"Sappho Fragment 58" was first published in the *New York Review of Books*. Reprinted by permission of Anne Carson and Aragi Inc. All rights reserved.

All rights reserved, including the right to reproduce this book or portions thereof in any form whatsoever. For information address Simon & Schuster Canada Subsidiary Rights Department, 166 King Street East, Suite 300, Toronto, Ontario, M5A 1J3.

This Simon & Schuster Canada edition April 2026

SIMON & SCHUSTER CANADA and colophon are trademarks of Simon & Schuster, LLC

Simon & Schuster strongly believes in freedom of expression and stands against censorship in all its forms. For more information, visit BooksBelong.com.

For information about special discounts for bulk purchases, please contact Simon & Schuster Special Sales at 1-800-268-3216 or CustomerService@simonandschuster.ca.

Interior design by Milly McKinnish

Manufactured in the United States of America

10 9 8 7 6 5 4 3 2 1

Online Computer Library Center number: 1523199687

ISBN 978-1-6680-6955-4
ISBN 978-1-6680-6956-1 (ebook)

For Jack and Charlie
May your lives be rich with the pleasure of discovery

but me you have forgotten

SAPPHO, FRAGMENT 129A
TRANS. ANNE CARSON

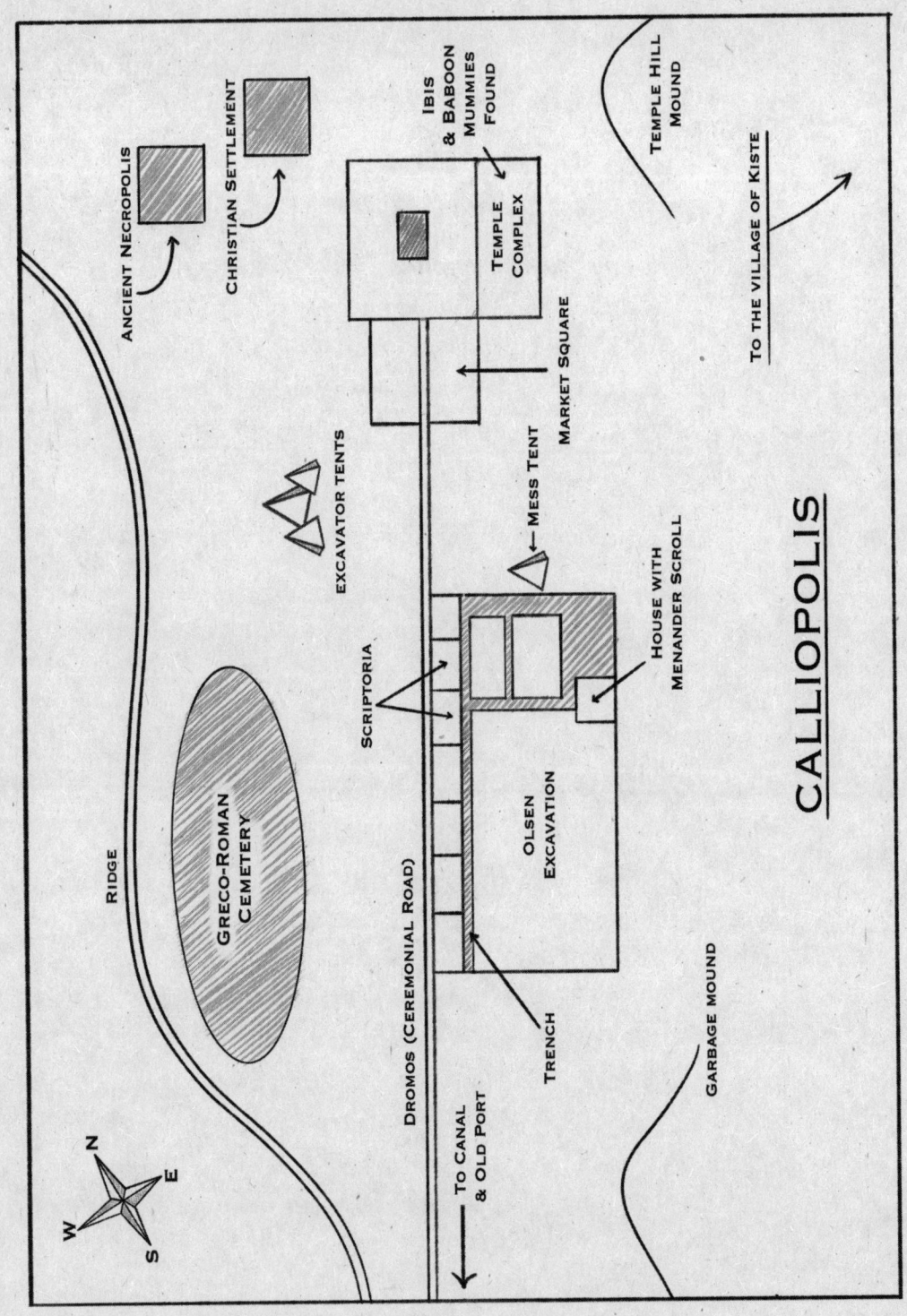

THE CURSE OF CALLIOPOLIS CLAIMS ANOTHER VICTIM

An inquest was held in Cairo, Egypt, on Monday, January 16th, into the death of Professor Emmett Olsen of the University of California, Berkeley, aged forty-eight. The verdict was death by natural causes. Testimony by Dr. Clive Hopewell, who examined the body, revealed that Professor Olsen's excessive alcohol consumption over many years had caused fatal liver damage.

Professor Olsen's death is presumed to be the fourth in as many years associated with the infamous city of ancient times. In 1903, Miss Alice Baker, aged twenty-four, departed from Calliopolis at the end of the season. She never reached her destination, and was never heard from again. In March of 1904, Miss Helen Gardiner, aged twenty-six, was discovered murdered in her lodging, an apparent victim of an attempt to steal priceless artifacts. Short weeks later, in April of 1904, Mr. Calvin Drake, sixty-three, of Berkeley, California, was killed by unknown raiders while bravely protecting the excavation site.

The history of Calliopolis is one of death and destruction throughout the ages. Indeed, its value as a site of archeological research is a consequence of its sudden abandonment around the year 180 AD. It is believed that Calliopolis was struck fatally by the Plague of Galen, which spread throughout the Roman world, destroying entire towns and scattering survivors who were forced to flee for their lives. Many believe that the Curse of Calliopolis lives on, blighting the lives of those who disturb the slumber of the plague's original victims.

San Francisco Examiner, January 19, 1905

ONE

Iris Wentworth found my body, which was unfortunate. I would have preferred it to be one of the men. Although now that I think of it, the men would have made an entertainment of it, a tale to be shared over a drink in rooms where women can't go. They would have made themselves the heroes of the story—my story.

So perhaps it is best that it was Iris. She was fierce, in her polite way. We all were. We had to be to survive the rigors of an excavation camp, to prove ourselves deserving of a place that might have gone to a man. We never complained about the scorching heat or the revolting food or the unsanitary conditions or the comments that belittled us and our abilities. We persevered. We shook out our bedclothes every night, making sure nothing had crawled in that might kill us in our sleep. In the small hours, we listened for hoofbeats that might signal a raid from one of the desert tribes. We kept secrets—our own, and the men's.

But Iris's guard was down that day. She'd come straight from a wedding in Cairo, surrounded by her old school friends, and stuffed full of fellowship and champagne and food served on fine porcelain for days. She hadn't had time to return to watchfulness. She hadn't put her mask back on, as all women in a man's world must do.

Rubi, the headman, took the donkey cart to Beni Suef to meet her train, along with a horse so that she could ride back on her own. Iris was an Englishwoman, and excellent on horseback, and Rubi knew that she wouldn't choose to jolt along in the cart when she could chase the wind. The track from the station was easy to follow; it had been a canal once, before it silted up, and it ran ten miles straight to the excavation house in the village, and another five miles on to the dig site. The ancient waterway had brought all of us to this place. Without the canal, there would have been no city to rise and fall on its banks, and nothing for us to find in the sand.

And so Iris arrived at our house alone, opened the door, and found what she could never forget. At least I assume she never forgot. I never saw her again, although I have thought of her often, many times.

I would have saved her from the shock, if I could, but even now, I don't have that kind of power. There are some that do. The desert is full of spirits, and not all of them are kindly disposed toward the living.

I have always been more interested in the dead.

TWO

TORONTO, 2019

In Maddie's cubicle at the Toronto Archeological Museum, the pale winter light illuminates a painting, one of her great-grandmother's. It dates from early in Iris Wentworth's archeological career: *Nora, Helen, and Rubi, Calliopolis, 1904*. It's been a favorite of Maddie's for as long as she can remember, although she is sometimes ashamed to say so.

In the left foreground, two women sit in front of a tent in a desert landscape. A distant ridge bisects the horizon, looming over a squat, rectangular structure the same color as the land itself. It's flagged by a single, lonely column, marking it as a temple, or the modest remains of one. The women are arranged on a Persian carpet, their feet tucked under them, drinking from dainty china cups. A man stands behind and to the right of the women, clothed in a white robe and a simple turban. This is Rubi, clearly. Maddie hopes the artist saw him as a subject, not an exotic element, of the piece. She knows it was more likely the latter.

One of the women—the one Maddie has identified as Helen Gardiner—is dressed plainly, in a long navy skirt and white high-necked blouse, her hair pinned in a severe, unflattering style. The other, Nora, wears an impractical pale pink dress, tucked and gathered and embroidered and puffed in a manner Maddie assumes is both fashionable and expensive for its time, and a hat with matching silk roses. This painting was once on the wall of her childhood bedroom, before her parents donated a set of Iris's objects and original watercolors to the Toronto Archeological Museum, ten years ago.

Inspecting it now, Maddie can't maintain a scholarly distance. She remembers how she loved this pink dress, coveted it, imagined herself swanning into school wearing it to the envy of all the girls who thought her odd. Here, in Iris's portrait, Nora is plausible as the irresistible mistress who wrapped Calvin Drake around her finger and made off with his fortune. Not like the Eleanor Alcott in the many photographs that exist of her in later decades: thickset and forbidding, glittering with gems and impatience.

In the painting, Nora looks at Helen with an expression of delight, as if she has discovered something welcome yet unexpected. Helen, on the other hand, looks out of the frame, straight at Maddie, her eyes bright and intelligent. Iris's skill as a portraitist emerges in Helen's coiled energy, her restlessness; she looks as if she is about to leap up from the carpet and begin doing something more constructive. It's a happy scene. And why shouldn't it be? These women are living a grand adventure.

Maddie is not.

Maddie is gigging her way to obscurity and penury—she's a part-time archivist at TAM, as the Toronto Archeological Museum is known, and a freelance contributor to its magazine (*tesTAMents*), as well as a sessional lecturer in the department of history at the University of Toronto. All the jobs are precarious, none are especially satisfying, and she's living in her childhood home, which provokes a daily sense of injury; after Ben left, she couldn't make rent on the apartment they'd shared.

"You are not stuck," her therapist has told her. "You are making choices. It may not seem that way, but you are." *She is right*, Maddie thinks. It does not seem that way.

Her phone rings. It is the call she's been dreading. Luisa Ortega, TAM's new CEO, wants to see her.

Luisa has been in the job for nine months, and so far, Maddie has managed to avoid her. Maddie is good at avoidance, and, let's be honest, Luisa's had bigger fish to fry: She's been brought in to repair public trust and soothe donor distress after a spate of successful repatriation requests have "revealed weaknesses in TAM's historical acquisition practices which the museum is eager to review and resolve under its new leadership," as Maddie herself wrote in a recent issue of *tesTAMents*. Maddie is inexpensive and as far removed from the corridors of power as she could possibly be, short of taking up residence in a utility closet. She is not a priority for Luisa Ortega.

But now here she is, in Luisa's office. "That fucking man!" says Luisa Ortega. Maddie is surprised by her employer's impropriety—it is, after all, their first meeting—but she understands Luisa's meaning well enough. "That fucking man" is Bill Hampton, who was the chief curator of the museum from 1969 to 1998, and a board member thereafter until his death in 2023.

In his prime, Bill was revered for growing TAM from a small regional outpost in the museum world to an internationally recognized collection representing the full scale of human civilization. "TAM wants one of everything," he announced upon his appointment, and he made good on his promise—mummies from Egypt, marble busts from Greece, temple reliefs from Cambodia, mosaics from Italy, ceramics from China, bronzes from India, ivory from Nigeria.

Luisa says, "He's trying to kill me from beyond the grave."

Maddie waits. She's been brought here for a purpose, one evidently having to do with Bill Hampton and his willful violations of the UNESCO 1970 Convention, a treaty intended to stem the flood of looted artifacts in Western museums. She is neither anxious nor excited, nor even particularly curious. She finds it hard these days to feel much of anything.

Luisa rummages through the papers on her desk, relocating one stack of file folders and shuffling the contents of another. "Ah," she says, "here you are." She extracts a document that Maddie recognizes as her own CV. "You have a PhD in history from the University of Toronto, yes?"

"Yes," says Maddie. She should be proud of her doctorate, she knows, but she can't separate her achievement from the catalog of disappointments connected to it. It feels like a financial and emotional boulder permanently strapped to her back.

Luisa flips a page. "And your dissertation was on gender discrimination in archeology?"

"In part," says Maddie. "I was mostly studying how patriarchal narratives about Mayan culture prevented Iris Wentworth's discoveries at K'abel from becoming—"

Luisa holds up a hand, indicating a complete lack of interest. Maddie doesn't mind. Her research barely registers with anyone in her field, so why should an outsider care? "And then you got a graduate certification in archives management?"

"Right," says Maddie.

"And what do we have you doing here, remind me?"

It's skillful, the way Luisa suggests she has any idea what Maddie does, as if it's momentarily slipped her mind. These are the kinds of management skills that Maddie is unlikely to need, given her current career trajectory. It seems to Maddie that Luisa would not allow herself to stumble, unwittingly, into a series of dead-end jobs (simultaneously!). She is a strategic plan, embodied. She will catapult this museum into the twenty-first century if it is the last thing she does, and it will not be.

What Maddie does at TAM is what all the archivists—five of them—do, which is review the documentary history of every object acquired during Wild Bill Hampton's reign and put the curators on alert to any potential issues of provenance. In those evening hours after five, when she ceases her labor for Luisa, she remains at her desk and continues her personal research in Iris Wentworth's archive. She tells herself that this exercise might generate enough material for an article or two and another shot at the academic job market, and this is faintly possible, but the truth is that she cannot think of anything better to do with her empty time.

Luisa closes the folder, having done her due diligence. "Can I count on your discretion?"

"Of course," says Maddie.

"Are you familiar with Peter Bahar?"

Like the millions of people who've watched his TED Talk, "The Cursed City of Calliopolis," Maddie is familiar with Professor Bahar's work. He is one of the best-known historians on the planet. He holds the most prestigious position in Egyptology in the US, the Emmett Olsen Chair at Berkeley. His last book, *Calliopolis: The Muse's City*, was a *New York Times* bestseller. "I am," she says.

Calliopolis has fared well by association too. Since Peter Bahar fixed his sultry gaze on it, it's become one of Egypt's greatest tourist attractions, although visitors tend to be disappointed. You need an imagination to begin to grasp what Calliopolis was at the height of its power. The temples, squares, grand homes, and processional roads are mere suggestions of what they were—indentations, ditches, stacks of mudbricks, and an unadorned and utilitarian temple structure that calls to mind a large storage unit.

To be cursed is to be erased.

"I want you to be his assistant for the week," Luisa says. "He's coming to evaluate one of the pieces in the collection." She purses her lips. "The documentation we have is inadequate, and we are hoping he'll be able to help trace the provenance for us. We found some suggestion in the files it might be from Calliopolis."

"Sure," says Maddie. "Happy to help." This is what she ought to say and so she does, but it underscores the point: Her PhD has qualified her for very little, other than being a real professor's temporary assistant.

She does have a fondness for TAM's Egyptian collection, though. It isn't the museum's strong suit; it's relatively small and contains nothing of international significance. The items with clear provenance are personal acquisitions made by Maddie's great-grandmother, Iris Wentworth, during her years as an artist on excavations in Egypt: a crocodile mummy from Tebtunis, a collection of *shabti* funerary figurines from Thebes, and an unornamented coffin from Deir el-Bahari. The Egyptian gallery at TAM is a fine place to sit undisturbed over the lunch hour. This will change, Maddie assumes, if any of the objects can be linked to the Cursed City.

"Trading one headache for another," says Luisa. "I'll be begging for another permanent loan, most likely." There's a knock at the door. "Come in," she calls, and they both rise to greet the media's favorite professor.

He is absurdly handsome. She has seen his publicity photos and watched his interviews and lectures. She has expected the strong jaw, dark hair, tan skin, and luminescent smile, but not the jolt of energy she feels in his presence. It's been a long time since she's been reminded that she's a creature with a soft body, not simply an anxious brain rattling in a bony cage. The last person she responded to this way was Ben, and that was months before he left.

He greets Luisa warmly, kissing her on both cheeks, before shaking Maddie's hand. "Please call me Pete," he says. "I understand we'll be working together while I'm here."

"Yes," she says. "Luisa was just starting to explain what we'll be doing."

Luisa gestures for them to sit down and then opens the folder in front of her. "This is the item we suspect may have come from Calliopolis, based on the former director's notes at acquisition." She extracts a page and hands it to Pete. "It's a statue of Thoth. I'm hoping that between the two of you—Maddie, because you are the one most familiar with Iris Wentworth's archive, and Pete because he's the North American expert on Calliopolis—we can get closer to figuring out where it came from before it ended up with Bill Hampton's dealer."

Maddie feels some relief to realize that she's been chosen, not because she is the most junior of the archivists and therefore the least likely to complain about redeployment, but because her specific knowledge is relevant to the job at hand. There have been moments in the past year when she has wondered if anyone would notice if she disappeared. ("That sounds like depression," her therapist said. "Studies show that depressed people have a more accurate perception of reality than normal people do," Maddie countered. "Fact." This was shortly before her therapist fired her for being resistant to change.)

Pete holds the door for her as they leave Luisa to her next meeting, billed as unpleasant: "They all are these days. Perhaps the two of you can change that." Maddie startles slightly at Pete's unfamiliar courtesy, and walks through.

"Our job is a lot more fun than hers," he says, nodding his head toward Luisa's now closed door, and the pandemonium presumably erupting behind it.

"Fair's fair," says Maddie. "She gets paid a lot more than I do."

Pete laughs, and Maddie realizes that Luisa's salary, enormous to her, must be a pittance to him. He has American research grants, and television contracts, if the rumors are true.

Curses, she is beginning to understand, are very good business.

THREE

ROME, 1903

I first met Emmett Olsen in Professor Wilson's greenhouse, at the American School of Classical Studies in Rome. He was coming for a consultation, according to the short note he'd sent to the professor, and we understood this to mean that he wanted to show us a papyrus find from Calliopolis. It would not be a social call: Professor Wilson's reputation as a papyrologist was unparalleled; and Mr. Olsen was notorious for his rough manners. Days earlier he'd offended practically everyone in the city with a blazing lecture at the German Institute, denouncing the archeological practices of every nation represented in the room.

I was jittery with nerves, and Professor Wilson's pacing made it worse. He was a stocky, red-faced man with a bald pate, which he mopped regularly and fruitlessly with a handkerchief. In the heavy, wet air, he wore his shirtsleeves rolled up to his elbows. Whatever relief this offered was surely counterbalanced by the heavy cotton gloves he wore to protect his forearms and hands from the rough stalks of the papyrus plants, and the leather smock that encased his round body almost to the ankles.

The greenhouse was filled not with raised gardens but with ponds, each one with a single crop of papyrus stalks topped with feathery tufts.

Every pond was at a different stage of growth; the youngest groupings were three feet or so in height, with stalks the width of my finger, while others reached toward the ceiling of the greenhouse, with stalks the width of my hand. I sometimes caught Professor Wilson talking to the plants, stroking their stalks, coddling them like household pets.

"How do the results look today?" Professor Wilson asked, stopping by my desk. Together, we were engaged in a series of experiments to restore badly damaged papyrus fragments and were making great advances in our rehydration techniques. The less brittle the papyrus, the easier it was to clean and, ultimately, to read.

"I like the results from the one-fifth papyrus juice solution," I told him. "With blotting and tweezing at the twenty-four-hour mark and brushing at the three-day mark." I showed him the samples I had laid out on my workspace. "You see? The papyrus is dry, but still supple."

"Extraordinary work, Helen," he said, using my Christian name for the first time. "The student has surpassed the teacher."

"Hardly," I said. "I continue to learn from you each and every day."

He blushed and harrumphed and walked over to the garden to tend a papyrus plant. "Still," he said, over his shoulder, "I cannot in good conscience keep you here, not indefinitely, as much as I would enjoy that. You belong in the field, Helen. There is no one working in Egypt now who comes even close to having your talent."

We heard the greenhouse door open. "Professor Wilson? Are you here?"

My teacher beamed at me, then called out, "Welcome, Mr. Olsen! I will come and fetch you. One moment." He hurried off to greet our visitor.

I thought about what he had said while I waited for them to return. He was right; I had become comfortable in Rome. But it had not been my dream to work in a laboratory, as pleasant as it was. I had wanted to be at the frontier of Egyptology, pulling works from the earth that had not been seen since Alexandria burned. I had wanted my discoveries celebrated in the newspapers, like Grenfell and Hunt's, or Olsen's.

When Olsen stepped into our work area, I could see that the papyrus garden had worked its magic on him. He smiled at me, wonder still alive in his face. "You must be Miss Gardiner. Professor Wilson has been singing your praises to the skies. I am very glad to meet you." He shook my hand firmly, one colleague to another. "This place is astonishing."

Professor Wilson offered him a seat and a cup of tea, which he accepted. "I'll get right to it," he said. "It is exceedingly rare for me to share any results from my excavations before I've had the opportunity to do my own study and publication. In this case, however, I admit—and this is not a regular occurrence either—that I require some help. You are somewhat aware, I presume, of present excavation at Calliopolis?"

"Of course," said Professor Wilson. "It is papyrology's best hope since Oxyrhynchus."

Olsen grinned. "Hope is the word," he said. "What I have brought to you may be the realization of that hope. My objective with this excavation has been to find evidence that Calliopolis was a regional, even national, center for the production of written materials on papyrus. If I'm right, Calliopolis at its height had many independent scriptoria, each of which generated a steady supply of literary scrolls for export. That being the case, Calliopolis is the best place in Egypt to search for complete literary works." He lifted his suitcase onto the table and removed from it a tin box labeled HUNTLEY & PALMERS SUPERIOR READING BISCUITS.

"Storage and transportation are a challenge in our field," he said, noticing my surprise. "Biscuit tins have an advantage over baskets. Do you have a spare pair of gloves? And a set of tweezers?" I handed him both, and then he lifted the lid of the box and reached inside.

I put a clean sheet of blotting paper down on the surface of the table, and he extracted first one, and then another, complete scroll. "Very little breakage," he said with satisfaction, showing us the tiny crumbs remaining in the tin. "A great relief, I don't mind telling you."

"Good heavens," said Professor Wilson. "These are not scraps from the refuse mound."

"They are not," said Olsen. "What they are, I believe, is the first concrete evidence of a scriptorium at Calliopolis."

Within a month, we had, if not proven him right, at least provided some spectacular evidence in support of his theory. Both scrolls were composed in an elegant, regular cursive, the lines evenly spaced, but obviously by different writers: The first scroll—the shorter one—had rounder, more sinuous shapes, while the second showed a taller, right-leaning hand. We had two individual scribes, for certain, highly trained and professional.

The first scroll had required none of the gifts which gave me an advantage over other ancient language specialists: an ear for poetry, and an intuition for the overall meaning of a passage that allowed me to bridge literal holes in the text with style. This was because the first scroll was not a literary text at all. It was a list of receipts: twenty-eight drachmae for ten thousand lines, including the *Plutus* of Aristophanes, and the third *Thyestes* of Sophocles; fourteen drachmae for *Sisyphus* and *Andromeda*, two plays of Euripides; twelve drachmae for *The Oresteia* of Aeschylus. It had been the first important signal that we were on the right path, and now the text of the receipts had offered definitive proof. I reached for my reference books to double-check my findings before summoning Professor Wilson.

"I'm embarrassed to tell you that I only know *Plutus* and *Oresteia*," he said. "And I thought *Thyestes* was by Seneca." He sighed. "At my age, you've forgotten more than you remember, apparently."

"No," I said. "That's not it at all. *Sisyphus* and *Andromeda* are lost plays. We only know they exist at all because they're mentioned in other classical works. But this receipt is evidence that they were well-known and circulated for centuries. And as for *Thyestes*, we may well be the first people since antiquity who know that Sophocles wrote a play on the subject. And not just one, but three! We must tell Mr. Olsen right away."

Professor Wilson sent a letter, and we continued unrolling the second scroll. It was painstaking work, but every section I transcribed made my heart beat a little more quickly. It was literary, without question; that much was apparent on the first day. But it was rolled from the top rather than the bottom, so the title (and confirmation of the author, we hoped) would be the last words to emerge. When we unrolled the final inches of the thirteen-foot scroll, tears came to my eyes, and to Professor Wilson's as well. *Dyskolos*, read the text at the top of the document.

"*The Curmudgeon*," I translated. "Menander won first prize for this play at the Lenaian festival, in . . ." I went over to my bookshelf and pulled the reference I needed. I ran my finger down the page until I found what I was looking for. "316 BC. There is no complete copy of the play in existence. Only a few lines here and there. Until now."

"Well," said Professor Wilson. He stared at the manuscript as if it had turned into something dangerous. "Well." He wiped his face with his handkerchief. "We must think what to do. I am unaccustomed to finding myself in possession of a priceless treasure. How long will it take you to finish the translation?"

"A day or two. No more."

"We must not let it out of our sight for a moment," he said. "We must tell no one. I'll send a telegram to Olsen, asking for instructions."

The return telegram advised us to expect the Pinkerton men. Two of them appeared in the greenhouse within the week, somewhat frightening in their size and efficiency, and spirited the box of papyrus away. A letter arrived from Olsen not long afterward, explaining that Calvin Drake, the funder of his excavation at Calliopolis, had been eager to take possession of the artifact for his planned museum in California and had no intention of letting the Egyptian Antiquities Service learn about the find until it was safely on American soil. The Pinkerton men would escort Drake and his treasure safely home across the Atlantic.

The letter also offered me a job.

"I must ask you to reconsider," said my aunt Margaret. "Egypt is no place for a young woman." We were sitting in a café on the Piazza di Spagna, across from the house where John Keats had breathed his last. My own mother having died of tuberculosis, I was less inclined than most to view it as romantic, in any sense of the word. Still, there seemed to be a steady stream of young women stopping at No. 26 to gaze up at the closed shutters with reverence.

"It is a fine place for an archeologist," I told her. "Arguably the best place on earth."

Upon receiving word that I had decided to travel to Egypt and join the excavation team at the beginning of the season, my aunt had booked a passage from New York to the continent to take the matter in hand herself. "I am speaking to you as a woman, Helen, not a child. You must consider what lies ahead. Not only this year and the next, but in the decades to come. Your currency is fading with every minute you spend on this folly."

"It is the life I want," I told her.

"You do not know what you are saying," she said. "Life as a single woman can be extremely bleak. Believe me, I know. It was nothing short of a miracle that I met your uncle Clifford. I had resigned myself to being a hanger-on in your household for the rest of my life. A burden to you. And I, at least, had a brother to take me in. You are an only child. Who will look out for you when I am gone?"

"You will outlive me," I told her.

"God forbid," she said. Her gaze passed over my shoulder, and she froze. "Oh dear. It is that tiresome man again, the one who was on the ship with me. The one who would not cease speaking of his desert fathers. Look away!"

But Reverend Banks had spied us, and charted a direct course to our table, his black robes flapping behind him. As usual, he wore a flat-topped black hat perched on his thinning white hair. He came to a stop next to our table and bowed, and as he stood up, he pushed his wire-rimmed spectacles up onto his long, bony nose with his equally long and bony fingers. "Miss Gardiner," he said. "What good fortune! I had hoped to see you in Rome, after Mrs. Cogswell told me of your scholarly endeavors here. And Mrs. Cogswell! I have missed our discussions over dinner. Your aunt and I were seated together for meals on the crossing. Such a remarkable coincidence!"

Reverend Banks had been one of my instructors at Barnard College, specializing in ancient languages. He had been more skilled in research than in teaching; he tended to wander from his subject and lose track of time. But he was a kind man and had been of real assistance to me on the several occasions when I had consulted him on a question that touched his own enthusiasms.

"I understand that you have received an offer of employment from Mr. Olsen at Calliopolis," said Reverend Banks. "A great tribute to your scholarly abilities, Miss Gardiner."

"Be that as it may," said my aunt, "her uncle and I are quite opposed to her going. Calvin Drake, of all people. Gallivanting around the world with a woman not his wife. Helen must think of her reputation."

"Mr. Drake will not be there often," I said. "He is a collector, not an excavator. And a dedicated philanthropist, like Uncle Clifford. He donated most of the papyri I studied at Barnard."

Aunt Margaret looked askance. "I've never understood this mania for scraps," she said. "Literal garbage, to hear you tell it, Helen. Jewelry, I can understand. Statues, artworks—these strike me as interesting. But shards of old pots? Bits of discarded paper? It is a mystery to me."

"My dear lady," said Reverend Banks. "That can only be because no one has explained their value to you. These scraps, as you call them, hold the key to some of the great questions of our time, of any time! Mr. Drake has assembled a very rare collection of cartonnage, some of which we were fortunate enough to use for the edification of our students at Columbia University and Barnard College."

"Cartonnage?" asked Aunt Margaret.

"It is a sort of papier-mâché, if you will, made with papyrus," said the Reverend. "It was used to create masks and breastplates for mummies." Aunt Margaret's expression was forbidding, but Reverend Banks leaned in, brimming with enthusiasm. "When you steam it, much as you might steam the glue of an envelope so as not to tear it, you can separate the layers of papyrus from each other. And when you do, if you are fortunate, you can find great treasures: historical records, plays and poems of classical antiquity, and even early versions of sacred texts. The developments in our field at present are thrilling."

"I hope I misunderstand you," said Aunt Margaret. "Your scraps of paper were used to wrap a mummy?"

"Not to wrap it, exactly," I said. "More to decorate it after wrapping."

"And you, Reverend, condone this . . . ghoulishness?"

"Ah," said Reverend Banks, realizing his error far too late. "It is in service of the highest possible purpose, Mrs. Cogswell, I assure you. Do you know that we have found fragments of the four original Gospels of the New Testament using this method? I see that you are astonished."

Aunt Margaret dabbed at her mouth with a napkin. "Indeed I am. I must tell you, Helen, that you are well on your way to becoming odd. It is most alarming. We will discuss this further, on our own. I bid you good day, Reverend."

FOUR

TORONTO, 2019

Maddie takes Pete directly to the Egyptian gallery. It's in the old wing of the museum, where the rooms are poky and dim, although elevated with ornamental plasterwork and the occasional sparkle of natural light filtered through stained glass. In the middle of the room, there is a table covered in plexiglass that houses a diorama of the Nile Valley. The plastic is greasy with the fingerprints of schoolchildren, and Maddie itches to scrub it down with sanitizer, but Pete seems not to notice. He sketches a sinuous line on the tabletop that follows the path of the river, tapping three times with his finger, top to bottom: "Alexandria, Cairo, and Luxor. And here"—he circles a spot some distance south of Cairo—"is Calliopolis. Named for Calliope, the Muse of eloquence and epic poetry. It's an amazing site, really. It has something for everyone. Have you been there?"

"No," she says. "I'd love to see it someday." She opens her mouth to tell him about the many places she *has* been—every museum in the world with substantial collections of Mayan art, and every Mayan archeological site in the Americas. She wants him to know that she isn't provincial. She realizes that this is exactly how she will sound if she begins reciting her passport entries; it will also provoke questions she does not want to answer. Instead, she says, "Can you tell me about the history of Calliopolis? It might help our research if I'm more up to speed."

He smiles, readies himself to win another fan. The story of Calliopolis, he tells her, begins around 300 BC, when the pharaoh realizes that his empire could be larger and more powerful if he can find a way to increase Egypt's arable land. He chooses a small natural waterway—Pete draws another line with his finger—and dredges it to make a canal that brings water from the Nile into the desert regions to the west. The canal branches throughout the area, like the veins on a broad green leaf. Before the canal system, Pete says, Calliopolis is a tiny farming settlement known by the local people as Kiste; as the waterway expands, the town rockets to fame as a publishing hub. At its height, dozens of scriptoria—workshops employing scribes—produce scrolls for export throughout Egypt. "And that," he says, pausing for effect as if practicing for his television series, "is why Drake and Olsen were there. They were papyrus hunters."

"Wasn't everyone in 1900?" Maddie asks, pleased that she sounds confident and informed. In truth, she knows very little about the field of papyrology. She hasn't studied the classics and can't read Greek or Latin. But she's a historian, and she can't help but feel a romantic shiver at the thought of Alexandria's great fire, a conflagration in which many of the ancient world's crowning works were lost to time.

Pete nods his approval. "Pretty much. It was another kind of gold rush, the mania for papyrus. There was an Oxford expedition in the late 1890s that started it. The British were at Oxyrhynchus, south of Calliopolis, on a site with remarkably similar conditions—abandoned, buried in sand, no rain, and well above the groundwater. They were excavating a trash heap out beyond the city limits when they found a set of scrolls. Can you imagine what they must have felt? They must have known in that second how famous they would be."

She has been asked this question, or a version of it, many times in her life. She grew up on an archeological site, half of each year of her childhood. It is partly why she herself is not an archeologist. She wants to understand history and the people who lived there. She doesn't want to plant her flag in it, claiming it as her own. She has known archeologists—her mother, for example—who see their role as custodians of culture, as educators. But more often she has seen a tempered version of the impulse toward conquest and self-enrichment. She wonders which camp Pete would occupy, given the chance.

He is still speaking: " . . . priceless, legendary works that no one had seen for almost two thousand years—Euripides, Aristotle, Sophocles—in a garbage dump! Front-page news all over the world. A global sensation. Everyone wanted to find one of the lost scrolls, and not only the literary ones. The Christians got in on the action, too, looking for early versions of the Bible."

It's easy to picture Pete at the front of a classroom, she thinks. His teaching reviews are probably off the charts. Her own are lackluster: high marks for preparedness, low ones for dynamism, and the occasional comment along the lines of "kind of defensive when asked questions." She imagines that Pete encourages feedback, maybe even appreciates departures from the syllabus. That he does not become flustered by overconfident undergraduates with one too many Google searches under their belts and a thirst for dominance.

He pauses. "Am I boring you? I could talk about Calliopolis all day, honestly."

"Not at all," she says. She banishes the dark thoughts that have been her downfall. "I'm thinking about how I can help. As far as I know, the only archival material we have relating to Calliopolis is from Iris Wentworth. She was much better known for her later career at K'abel, in Mexico, but she did spend a few seasons in Egypt, at Abydos and Calliopolis. We have some correspondence here, as well as sketchbooks."

"She was Olsen's resident artist for two seasons, if I'm not mistaken," says Pete. "I know that she assisted Nora Alcott in the early administration of the Drake Collection and the Alcott Library. I'm embarrassed to say that I don't know a lot more about her. My research has focused on the excavators: Calvin Drake, the funder; Emmett Olsen, the lead archeologist; and James Dunn, Olsen's second-in-command, who took over after he died. Although lately I've been looking at Helen Gardiner, one of the papyrologists." He looks reflective. "You know, the participation of women on Olsen's dig was unusually high. In addition to Helen, there was another papyrologist, Alice Baker, with Iris Wentworth rounding out the team. Plus, Nora Alcott, Drake's mistress, was fairly involved during the second season. Am I right in thinking that Iris was engaged to James Dunn?"

"Only briefly," says Maddie. It feels important to her that Pete understands this. "She never married, although she had a daughter." She pauses, and then says in a rush, "My grandmother. Iris was my great-grandmother."

Could it be that Pete doesn't understand the implications of this confession? The infamous interview, the public rift with her father? The family tragedy labeled by one magazine as "Shakespearean"? He simply says, "Luisa never mentioned it. I can see why she put you on the job, though. You must have taken a personal interest in Iris's archive. Have you written about it at all?"

Maddie feels almost giddy, as if she has been given permission to return home after a long exile. "Not as much about the material we have at TAM," she tells him. "My dissertation had more to do with her excavations at K'abel and how she and others interpreted their findings. I tried to get access to the Alcott Library, but the director said they couldn't accommodate me." Even accounting for awkwardness of tone in digital communications, Professor Field's message had been brusque, bordering on rude.

"Rebecca can be protective of her materials," says Pete. "Especially if she's working on a project of her own. She's been collaborating with Benicio Cupul from Stanford. Do you know him? He excavates at K'abel."

Maddie clamps down hard on the surge of grief and humiliation. She will not give herself away, not to Pete. She clears her throat. "Not really," she manages. It feels true. Ben is not the man she thought she knew. "Anyway, you were asking about Iris's archive here. I know it well. I cataloged it." She doesn't say that she cataloged it with her mother, while organizing it for donation.

"Excellent," says Pete. "That will be a great help. You know, Iris was one of the lucky ones. She escaped the curse."

"I should admit that I don't really know the details," Maddie says. "Calliopolis was like Tutankhamen's tomb, right? The members of the original excavation team tended to die early?"

"There's that aspect for sure," says Pete. "Alice Baker disappeared; Helen Gardiner was murdered; Calvin Drake was shot and killed in a raid on the dig site; and then Emmett Olsen died of what was most likely complications from alcoholism. If you're superstitious, you might conclude that the team at Calliopolis had more than the usual amount of bad luck."

"What do you think?"

"I think that archeology was a dangerous business then. It attracted extreme personalities. There was a lot of money at stake. You could get sick; you could get hurt. Then, as now, men inflicted specific kinds of violence on women, and these were women on their own in remote areas. Those are all factors that explain the modern 'curse.'" Pete paused, and then said, "Olsen was preoccupied with the circumstances that led to the destruction of the Greco-Roman city—the original 'curse,' you might say. Though Olsen would have rejected the idea of a curse as utter nonsense. He was looking for scientific evidence of what had happened around 200 AD to send the city into a fatal decline. Calliopolis was a major center during the Ptolemaic dynasty, one of the cultural capitals of the empire, and it remained that way for another two hundred years after the Romans took over. And then, suddenly, it wasn't."

This is the kind of curse Maddie can understand: watching your promise evaporate, leaving ruins behind. "What was his theory?" she asks.

"The Plague of Galen might have contributed; it swept through Egypt in around 180 AD. But Olsen thought it had been a more gradual decline. He believed that Calliopolis had been the victim of climate change." He scrolled on his phone and handed it to me. "Here," he said. "In Olsen's own words, as reported by the *San Francisco Examiner*."

OLSEN BLASTS BRITISH, FRENCH EXCAVATIONS AT CALLIOPOLIS

This evening, your correspondent attended an eagerly anticipated talk by Mr. Emmett Olsen, the lead excavator at Calliopolis, or the City of the Muse, as she is sometimes known. For decades, there has been a mighty contest between nations to unearth the treasures of Calliopolis, with our American team holding the concession at present.

Mr. Calvin Drake, who is funding the excavation, has promised results exceeding those of the French team in 1870, including a golden statue of Thoth, and an exceptionally preserved mosaic floor, both now residing in the Louvre. A British team scoured the site for papyrus in 1900, but left empty-handed. Of these efforts, Mr. Olsen said: "If you are one of those in our discipline who labors under the delusion that European excavators take more care than the local thieves do, I invite you to come and see the work of past excavations at Calliopolis. I put it to you that this was not the work of archeologists or scientists. It was looting, pure and simple."

Mr. Olsen's caustic assessment may not have won him friends among the French or the British, but his discoveries must be the envy of all. Mr. Olsen spoke tonight of his new methods of excavation, which have allowed for the preservation of strata closer to the surface; these contain more recent but perhaps equally significant structures. Said Mr. Olsen: "Where earlier excavations were attempted, nothing now remains of any early Christian or Greco-Roman structures that may have existed. And now we know, without a doubt, that these may be the periods in the history of Calliopolis that yield the greatest contribution to science."

Mr. Olsen astonished his audience by announcing that an additional complex has been found to the south of the great temple. In the catacombs of this structure, the American team has found ibis and baboon mummies, one hundred specimens in all, and each filled with papyrus of the highest quality. These papyri were revealed to be records kept by the priests of Thoth at the temple, including daily measurements of water levels in the canal over a twenty-year span.

Based on these documents, Mr. Olsen claims that Calliopolis was not destroyed by a sudden disaster, such as a plague, but was slowly abandoned through the Roman period due to a declining water supply. Moreover, he asserts that his excavation will show evidence of human occupation at Calliopolis much later than was previously believed.

"We must change our methods," said Mr. Olsen in conclusion. "We must seek to understand the evolution of a site through the centuries. We must rid ourselves of preconceptions and approach the site with the humility that is so often lacking in our profession. Only then may we begin to uncover the real treasure, which is the knowledge of our collective past."

Maddie fans herself, only partly joking. "A compelling character," she says.

"That he was," Pete agrees. "And way ahead of his time in the way he thought about excavation. Which isn't to say that he was indifferent to the finds themselves." An object in a glass case nearby catches his eye and he walks over to look at it.

It's a baboon, carved from black stone. It is about a foot high, with an elaborate medallion etched on its chest, and a strangely human expression. *Wise,* Maddie thinks. *Compassionate, even.* She knows the piece, a depiction of Thoth, and finds its proud and oversize genitalia amusing. "Do you think this fellow is from Calliopolis?" she asks.

Pete flashes her a broad smile. "I do indeed," says Pete. "And from my point of view, he may be the most interesting object ever located from the Cursed City."

"Really?" says Maddie. Baboon statues aren't unusual, and Calliopolis is famous for treasures infinitely rarer than this.

Pete holds her gaze as if he is entrusting her with a secret. "I may as well tell you, Maddie, I'm not just here to consult on provenance research for Luisa."

"I'm listening," she says.

"I want to solve a murder," he says.

FIVE

CALLIOPOLIS, OCTOBER 1903

"Helen." A hand was on my shoulder. "Helen, wake up."

It was still dark. "Iris? What time is it?"

"It's almost sunrise." I groaned, and Iris laughed. "You'll get used to it, I promise. It's a shock to the system at the start, though. We need an hour beforehand to wash and eat and get out to the site, but it's glorious out there before it heats up. You'll see."

I had met Iris Wentworth the evening before, having traveled from Alexandria by train, and then jolted in a donkey cart through a cloud of dust for hours. By the time I arrived in the village of Kiste, at the door of the house that was to be my home for the next six months, I was barely able to stand. Iris had greeted me with hot tea, a meal, a bowl of clean water for washing, and a bed to fall across. I thought her an angel. In fact, she was a British artist, and a graduate of the new department of archeology at University College London.

I had met ambitious women during my studies at Barnard, and at the American School of Classical Studies in Rome, individuals who valued intellectual pursuit and personal freedom as I did. Like me, they tended toward seriousness, even severity. Not Iris. She sparkled. She had been raised by aristocratic but unconventional parents and had traveled extensively throughout her life. She spoke six languages fluently—English, French, German, Spanish, Italian, and Russian—and was now in the process of adding Arabic. Only my abilities in Latin and Greek saved me from feeling utterly incompetent by comparison. She had thick blond hair, a button nose, and sparkling brown eyes, and was the prettiest person I had ever met.

"Khalid is making toast," she said. "Rubi will be here with the horses shortly." Khalid was our housekeeper and cook, a tall, cheerful boy of fifteen or so. He'd been hand-selected for the job by his grandfather, the headman at Calliopolis. He was determined to prove himself by anticipating our every need when we were at home, Iris told me. The attention was unnerving for one used to being alone. The lack of privacy, though, was a price I was willing to pay for the privilege of being in the field. I felt a shiver of anticipation.

"Tea?" I said hopefully, and Iris laughed.

"I'll make some at the site," she said. "You'll need it after your ride." After my bone-rattling trip from the station the day before, I'd agreed to try riding on my own. They didn't have sidesaddles out here, but Iris assured me that I could ride astride without having anyone bat an eye at my unladylike behavior or my unimpressive form, and that the horses could find their way to the site without any guidance from me.

We rode out as the sun was rising, saddlebags bulging, toward the pinking horizon. It was true, what I'd been told about the flies. As the sun came up, they were everywhere. I'd caught glimpses of the desert from the train, but being out in it, even a few minutes away from shelter, was an oddly vulnerable experience. I'd thought the sand would be soft, but it was gritty and rough, and when the wind got underneath it, it left marks on my skin. The vastness of the land felt primordial; humans had lived and died here for millennia, but there were no signs that they had ever been here. It seemed to me that we, too, our small band of people and animals, might disappear and leave no trace.

"There," said Iris, riding up next to me. "Do you see the mounds there? That's where we're heading."

"I thought you said it was a half hour away," I said.

"It is," she agreed. "It's an illusion of sorts. It's impossible to judge distances out here unless you're Rubi." The headman perched up on the driver's seat of the cart, swathed in a white robe and turban, pushing the donkey ahead with economical flicks of his whip. He was the most important man in the village, responsible for the hiring and firing of any local men or boys employed on the excavation. He was tall and lean but extremely strong; I had watched him load several heavy crates into the cart with no apparent effort. His face was lined, but his brown eyes were clear and sharp. It was hard to judge his age.

"Miss Helen," he said. "I hope you found your lodgings comfortable. Khalid has made you welcome?"

I assured him that his grandson was doing a fine job.

"Please tell me immediately if you have any complaints," said Rubi.

"Of course," I said. "But I cannot imagine that I will."

He nodded, satisfied, and we set off.

As we drew closer to the camp, Iris reined her horse and pulled alongside me. She pointed to two small hills on the landscape. "That's Calliopolis there," she said. "The mound on the right is fill from the first temple excavation. The temple is hidden behind it from here, but you'll see it when we get closer. The mound on the left is the rubbish dump. It's a mile out from the town center. James is dying to get shovels into it, but he may have to wait until next season. As you likely know, most everything of interest in Calliopolis is below the surface."

"How large is the excavated area?" I asked.

"Fifteen acres, give or take," she said. "And we are focused on a tiny fraction of that this season. Emmett believes it may have been one hundred acres at its peak, with forty thousand residents. Can you believe it?"

We gazed out across the sand together for a moment. "What's the condition of the temple?" I asked.

She sighed. "The wall paintings are fading by the day," she said. "I'm trying to sketch them as quickly as I can, but it's a losing battle. The French left it shamefully exposed, and once the process of deterioration begins, it is impossible to stop it."

We rode for another half hour and arrived on the outskirts of the site. The sandstone trapezium of the temple's inner sanctum now loomed over the mound I'd seen on the journey, along with a single column shaft. To my right, toward the second mound, I could see several partial mud-brick walls aboveground, and a large tent. "Are some of the excavators living on-site?" I asked.

"Yes," said Iris, "but not there. There's an encampment out by the cemetery. Emmett stays there, and James. Occasionally a guest. But it is an area for the men, not for us." She hesitated, as if tempted to say more on the subject, but when she spoke again, it was to continue her orientation tour. "The tent you see there is the mess hall. You'll find hot water for tea, and usually fruit and biscuits if you need a bite between meals. There's a horn at dinnertime, around one o'clock, and at suppertime around seven. You and I won't be here for the evening meal very often. I prefer to be at home."

We dismounted beside the temple. Rubi whistled, and with an answering shout, men appeared out of the earth beside the brick walls. Like Rubi, they were dressed in loose robes, but their faces and garments were smeared with dirt. "That's the trench for the scriptorium," Iris told me. "Emmett is spending most of his time down there, thanks to you. Your translation has given him new energy, not that he needed it. He is a force of nature, that man."

The village men came over to unload the supplies. Rubi introduced me to two of his sons, a nephew, and several other members of his extended family. Rubi's sons took the horses and the donkey and led them down a ramp next to the temple structure.

"That's where they found the ibis and baboon mummies," said Iris. "There's a trough of water down there, and shade, but nothing left for the horses to destroy. The desert took care of that years ago. Now, let's get you to the scriptorium. Emmett will be getting impatient."

As if on cue, a shout came from the trench where the men had emerged. "Where is she?"

I trailed Iris to a ledge where the earth dropped away. A ladder extended down into a series of trenches, which branched off into square pits; I could see five or six of them from where I stood. Iris gestured to a cloud of dust rising from one of them. "The men are working there today," she said. "James is supervising the digging. You'll see that part later. Emmett wants to show you the scriptorium first." She looked at me dubiously. "Are you comfortable on the ladder? We can go the long way down if you prefer. There's a ramp at the far end."

"The ladder's fine," I said, although it looked rickety, and I hoped my skirt wouldn't catch on it. But I thought there was a test implicit in the question, and I didn't want to fail it.

"Good," she said. "I'm right behind you."

I descended without incident. At the bottom of the ladder, I had the sensation of having arrived in another place entirely. It was cooler down here in the shade of the mudbrick walls on either side of the trench. The sprawl of the desert was gone, replaced with a narrow path, perhaps five feet wide and twelve feet deep. I could almost see merchants waving from each doorway, greeting their customers on a sunny morning two thousand years past. I caught myself before I could drift too far: Imagination was desirable in archeology, but only in small doses. You needed to retain enough detachment to see the objects in front of you as they were, and not as you hoped they were. Many good excavators had damaged their reputations by falling too much in love with a story of their own invention, only to be tripped up by contrary evidence that had been in plain sight the entire time.

We passed two doorway openings, each marking a separate address connected by a common wall. Two workers were installing a supporting frame consisting of three wooden planks in the first opening, while another man spread plaster along the base of the wall close by. "Mudbrick is horribly fragile," Iris told me. "We excavated here at the end of last season and it's already flaking. We do what we can to protect it. Emmett favors filling the whole thing in when we are done with our study. It seems a shame after so much effort."

It was a significant difficulty, I could see. Calliopolis had been constructed almost exclusively with mudbricks, except for the *dromos*—the major highway and ceremonial road leading from the port to the market square—and the temple, which were both made of stone. Leaving aside the question of preservation, it posed a problem for identification: In the absence of stone pediments or other identifiers, any single collapsed structure resembled another, and excavators were hard-pressed to guess the purpose of a building unless it contained abandoned objects that could aid interpretation. Mr. Olsen's theory that Calliopolis had been the scriptorium capital of Greco-Roman Egypt relied on the discovery of papyrus scrolls. The two he had brought to me in Rome were a start, but they would not make the case on their own.

We continued past the remains of several more buildings before reaching the end of the trench, which terminated at another open doorway. "And here he is," said Iris. "Our fearless leader."

Emmett Olsen sat at a rough desk in a shady corner under a canvas awning. He stood up as I came into the space, stepped out from behind the desk, and clasped my hand.

"Welcome," he said. "I hope Iris has taken good care of you?" In a loose linen shirt, open at the neck, his hair grown out, his forearms flecked with dust and scratches, he seemed larger, wilder, and more comfortable than he had in Rome.

"Very much so," I said. "And Rubi and Khalid. Everyone has been most helpful. I'm grateful for the opportunity, more than I can say, Mr. Olsen."

"Emmett," he said. "We operate on a first-name basis here."

"Then you must call me Helen," I said, and we shook again.

"Right," he said. "Iris, can you go and see James? He's pulled some pottery shards out today and I want a sketch for the excavation diary, please."

"I'll see you for luncheon, Helen," she said. "Have fun."

"Do you have water with you?" he asked. "I want to walk you around the site first, so you understand what we're doing, and then I'll get you set up. I've got a tent for you in one of the cleared rooms so you can keep the wind and sand away from your papyri. It's cooler down here, as you've no doubt noticed. You'll want to do most of your restoration in the village, where you can control the elements, but you'll need a place to do preliminary identifications, at least."

"That sounds sensible," I said. "How have you fared this season? Are you finding any papyri of consequence?"

"It's been slow," he said. "I have a box of fragments for you, but they are in poor condition, to be candid. I don't have high hopes for them. I have a feeling our luck is about to change, though. James is digging out a section that looks promising. We'll see it shortly, but I thought you'd want to visit this room before any other. Based on your translation this summer, we believe this was a scriptorium, one of several in the city."

He led me to the west wall, where the bricks were marked with imprints of ascending boards. "There was a staircase here to the second floor, do you see? A two-story building means housing for the wealthy, or a merchant's premises with living quarters above the storefront." He pointed to the corner of the floor. "We found two intact ceramic jars here, in what would have been a storage room under the staircase. One of them contained the scrolls I brought you in Rome."

Standing inside the room, I wondered if Emmett had enough evidence to conclude that he'd found a scriptorium. I thought it more likely that he'd found the personal collection of a poetry lover from the upper classes; even in Calliopolis, there were bound to be more consumers than producers of literature. I was not going to say so, at least not on my first day. I could tell him, honestly, that it was thrilling to see the place where the scrolls had been recovered.

"Now to your office," said Emmett, showing me to an adjoining pit. This one had a tent erected inside, the flap open to reveal a simple desk and chair. "Close enough to the action, but far enough away to allow for some peace and focus. That's precious around here, believe me."

"Shall I set up?"

"Not just yet," he said. "Come and see this." He led me over to the side of the pit, which was supported with scaffolding. The original brick walls were gouged with heavy tools; the excavation here had been reckless. "Shocking, isn't it?" he said.

"The French?" I asked.

"Not even the French are that incompetent," he said. "No, that's the work of the *sebâkhîn*. They got onto the site in between concessions and made a colossal mess. Who knows what they destroyed in the process. It doesn't bear thinking about."

Sebâkh was a mineral-rich fertilizer produced by the decomposition of mudbrick architecture. As population and development had increased in the region, more land was required for cultivation, and *sebâkh* extraction had become big business. In addition to its uses in commercial farming, *sebâkh* could be used to manufacture gunpowder, and huge factories had sprouted up near some of the well-known sites in the region. A desert mound might announce a buried settlement to an archeologist, but it signaled a cache of fertilizer to a local farmer or factory. In some places, excavators and *sebâkh* diggers—*sebâkhîn*—might cooperate, with the latter removing the earth after it had been thoroughly examined for finds. But more often it was a fierce competition.

"Tell me about the spot where you're digging today," I said. "What made you choose it?"

"You know about *afsh*?" he asked.

"I read Grenfell and Hunt's paper on the subject."

"Then you know it is earth with potential," he said, shaking some tobacco out of his pouch and tamping it in his pipe. "So much of what we do out here is about instinct. Training helps, and so does experience. But you have to be able to feel the earth under your boots—the straw and the clay—and to know by its color and tone that it's dry but not too brittle or too hard. And you have to know your site, so you don't waste your time, time you can't afford, by digging in places where there's nothing worth finding." He lit his pipe and puffed. I waited. He struck me as a man who liked to set his own pace. "Let's walk," he said.

He exited the room and turned eastward, walking along the trench that I was already beginning to think of as a street. He turned north, into a dead end. Another ladder was propped against the dirt wall. His gesture was a challenge, and I took it. The heat was brutal on the surface, and I stopped to take a drink of warm water from my canteen as I waited for him. He gave me an appraising look, and then said, "I saw a water dowser once in California. Old fellow took a divining rod out on the driest patch of land you ever saw and hit water on the first try. That's the closest comparison I can find to what we do."

He turned north to face the ruins of the temple. "There's the heart of the city at its height," he said. "Imagine, Helen, a traveler coming up from the canal to the south, bringing clean rolls of papyrus for the scriptoria. It's an active port, and a wide, busy road that runs for half a mile, leading right into the market square and the great temple of Thoth. Forty thousand people live here, in the city proper and on the farms to the south. It's a wealthy town, and the rich build homes to the east, where the air is fresher. The poor live to the north, closer to the burial ground and further away from the water, and also to the west, closer to the garbage dump. On the streets right here, he unloads his goods at each scriptorium, where the head scribe examines the quality of each roll before offering refreshment and payment. Can you see it?"

I could see it, through Emmett's eyes, and I told him so. He smiled and was about to speak again, but he was interrupted by a shout that came up from a nearby pit. He broke into a run and I followed him toward a cloud of dust rising from the desert. "Stop!" he called, waving his arms. "Everyone stop." The dust slowly dissipated as I came to stand beside him. Below, I could see twelve Egyptian men and boys, many with baskets on their heads, and a single white man, shading his eyes as he gazed up at us.

"Is that Miss Gardiner?" he asked.

"It is," I said.

"James Dunn," he said. "Emmett's second-in-command. Welcome to Calliopolis. Perfect timing. We just hit a vein of papyrus. Let's put you to work."

SIX

TORONTO, 2019

"A murder?" asks Maddie. "Which one? There are a few to choose from, it sounds like."

Pete grins. "Fair point. Helen Gardiner's. There was much more to her death than was reported at the time. There was a robbery, and then several days later, there was a murder. And this statue was at the center of it." He seems to hesitate, and then says, "I'm working on a proposal for a television series based on my book. The feedback from my agent is that the pitch needs more of a mystery narrative, and Helen's story has the best hook. Ideally, we'd want to suggest a theory of the case."

Maddie observes again how much Pete likes telling stories. "Consider me hooked," she says. "I love a true crime documentary. What do you think happened to Helen?"

"I'm not sure yet. I do know the police got it wrong."

"Tell me what you know about the crime," says Maddie.

"Helen and Iris were living in a village house that doubled as a storage facility for the excavation," he tells her. "One evening they came home and found that a number of objects were missing: a brooch, a necklace, a pair of earrings, a papyrus scroll, a box of papyrus fragments, and a baboon statue of Thoth. Immediately, everything of value was moved to Calvin Drake's steamer and put under twenty-four-hour guard. When Helen was killed, several days later, there was nothing in the house to steal."

"Maybe the thieves didn't realize that," says Maddie. "Or maybe they wanted to get rid of evidence they'd left behind. Maybe Helen was there when they returned, and they killed her so that she wouldn't identify them to the police." Maddie has told Pete the truth: She loves crime stories, and not only the ones based in fact. She finds real satisfaction in the detecting process, with its inexorable march out of chaos and into order. There is justice in a classic mystery. It is not like life, not at all.

"That's what the police thought," he says.

"You disagree?"

"I don't disagree that the crimes were connected. I think they were. But I think the wrong person was accused. The police targeted Helen's cook, a teenaged boy from the village called Khalid. A statue—likely this statue—was found in a basket in his family home. It confirmed his guilt as far as the police were concerned, and that was that. No uncomfortable questions for the rich white people. But it doesn't make sense, not to me at least. The villagers were well aware of how to dispose of stolen goods, and it wasn't by hiding them in their one-room houses. And then, why take the excavation diary? You'd only do that if you wanted to erase the record of what had been excavated. That points to someone with a sophisticated plan to conceal the crime."

"Did any of the other stolen items ever turn up?"

Pete shook his head. "Not a one. Vanished, like so many other artifacts. I assume into private collections. That's where this statue was for eighty years before the owner approached Bill Hampton's dealer."

Maddie looks again at the little baboon. "Why are you so sure this is the statue that was used to frame the cook? You haven't examined it yet."

Even she knows that there are thousands of these baboons in museums and private collections around the world.

"I was pretty sure before I arrived," he says. "We have an excellent description of the statue from the robbery. It was found earlier in the season and recorded in an excavation diary that still exists in the Alcott Library. I did a call with the curator when I took the contract and had her send me the file. The measurements of this statue match the measurements taken in 1903. And lastly, a section of the hieroglyphics on the medallion is replicated in the excavation diary. I'll want to have a closer look, but so far, I'm optimistic."

Maddie is quiet for a few moments, thinking about Helen Gardiner, the papyrologist. Papyrology, she imagines, is as risk-free a specialty as you could find in archeology. But then again, papyrologists had access to information that no one else could read. They were codebreakers, and that was an occupation with a whiff of danger to it. "Do you know anything about the stolen scroll?" she asks.

"It was found underneath one of the mummies, but it hadn't been identified before it disappeared, as far as we know. There may have been details recorded in the lost excavation diary."

"And the box of fragments?"

"Same problem," he says. "We only know that it was labeled as Box 27. Olsen shipped hundreds of boxes of fragments out of the country, and most of them were full of papyrus pieces the size of cornflakes. If someone chose one particular box to steal, it suggests that the thief knew something about what was inside, and its value."

Maddie looks again at the baboon. It feels familiar to her, and not only because of the hours she has spent in this room, reading mystery novels, and eating wilted sandwiches from the cafeteria in the basement. You aren't supposed to bring food here, but the security guard looks the other way if the room is otherwise empty. "Iris drew it," she says.

"The statue? That's likely," says Pete. "She would have drawn most of the finds."

"I mean that I've seen it in her sketchbooks," says Maddie. "They're downstairs in the archive. Would you like to see them?"

They are waiting for Claudia, the curator of the Ancient Egyptian, Roman, and Greek collections, who, due to cuts, is now also responsible for textiles and decorative arts. Maddie has found her irritable and unhelpful in the past, but Claudia lights up when she sees Pete, and agrees to do a search for any other items they have in storage relating to Calliopolis.

While they wait, Maddie retrieves Iris's sketchbooks, and begins looking for the image she can only vaguely recall. She can feel Pete's impatience as she searches, and it sparks a small burst of resistance. She fears wanting a seat at the table badly enough to go hungry for it, serving him the portion that is rightfully hers. The archive, Iris's materials: She has a greater claim to them than he does. She knows more about Iris Wentworth than anyone else in academia. She has made a hash of her career, certainly, but suddenly she wonders if it can be saved, if the tide of good fortune that Pete anticipates can carry her little boat as well.

She turns a page and sees it immediately. It is a sketch of Helen Gardiner, in the same plain dress and practical boots that she wore to pose with Nora Alcott. Here she sits foregrounded at a writing desk, with cluttered shelves on the wall behind her. A sarcophagus leans against them. Perched on one corner of the desk, next to an inkwell, is a statue of a baboon. "Do you have a magnifying glass?"

"I have a phone," he says, opening the camera and increasing the size of the image. "Welcome to the twenty-first century." He is quiet for a few seconds, and then says: "Oh, you genius." Maddie does not think he is speaking of her. "Look at the medallion. And the expression on his face!

She's captured it exactly." He looks at Maddie. "These sketchbooks are a gold mine. You know what? I'm going to request a loan from Luisa. I'd like to have all the reference sources on hand at the Alcott-Drake when I write up my report."

Maddie opens her mouth to protest but nothing comes out. It's not as though she has any legitimate grounds to argue against him taking the materials—no eagerly anticipated work in progress, no academic status. And who would care about her opinion? As of this morning, Luisa couldn't recall Maddie's role at TAM, the institution she leads. Pete, on the other hand, is a star, whose CV lives on a shelf in Luisa's brain. But once the sketchbooks are gone, the tiny flicker of hope Maddie has will blink out. She'll be sitting at her cubicle again, but poorer even than she was. Before Pete came, she could at least boast of having some distinctive knowledge of Iris's archive. Now Pete will have that too.

"Are you all right?" Pete asks.

Claudia's entrance saves her from having to answer. She's carrying a large jewelry box, bright red and covered in hieroglyphics. Maddie recognizes it as part of her family's donation to the museum, the twin of an object that remains in their possession at home. "It belonged to Iris," she tells Pete.

"It did," says Claudia. "We had someone here a few weeks ago doing research on the Egyptian revival movement. He loved this box, and said that the hieroglyphics on the top correspond to the sounds that make the name Iris." Maddie looks at the symbols: a reed, a mouth, a reed, a piece of folded cloth. She has seen them many times, and it has never occurred to her that they spell a word in English. "This box was manufactured in Egypt around 1900, specifically designed to appeal to Western tourists. Your timing couldn't be better. We cataloged it a few weeks ago."

Maddie listens, astonished, as Claudia tells them that the box has hidden compartments. "Here, I'll show you," she says. She removes a drawer, exposing the bottom of the interior, and shows them how to press on the rear inside right corner to release the spring-loaded floor. When the floor is lifted out, another compartment is revealed underneath, with its own removable box.

"I had no idea," says Maddie. It feels slightly magical, the idea of a hidden container.

Claudia smiles. "That was the point," she says. "A lady might need a place to keep her secrets. Iris Wentworth kept correspondence in here." She hands Pete a folder containing a single sheet of paper. He reads it slowly and then hands it to Maddie.

Dear Iris,

Miss Alcott has given me your letter. I admit that I am surprised you felt unable to communicate your decision to me in person. I believed our relationship was such that I had earned that courtesy. I am disappointed—very much disappointed—that I have been mistaken.

I am not writing to persuade you to alter your views on marriage as an institution. I well understand that there are women who prefer to retain their independence, and feel that matrimony is a tax on their freedom. I did not think you were one such woman, but if you say it is so, I cannot but accept it.

What troubles me—aside from the loss of your companionship, present and future—is the sense that you may hold me responsible for the unspeakable events that ended our season at Calliopolis. Perhaps it is simply that the shock you experienced upon finding Helen murdered altered your feelings about many things, including our plans with each other. If that is so, I understand. No woman could be expected to recover quickly from such a discovery. But if there is another reason, if you harbor doubts as to my reliability or morality, I would ask you to give me an opportunity to hear your reservations and to explain myself to you.

With my deepest respect and affection,
James Dunn

Maddie studies the box and the letter, half listening as Pete sells his plan to Claudia.

"This is a treasure," Pete says to Claudia. "Thank you so much for bringing it to me." He explains that he hopes to arrange a temporary loan of the sketchbooks and would now like to include the letter in the request. "It's directly relevant to a project I'm completing this year."

"A book sequel?" asks Claudia. "I hope so. I loved *The Muse's City*."

"I so appreciate hearing that," says Pete. "I can't give you any details yet, but I can promise that you'll be included in the acknowledgments."

"Really?" says Claudia. She looks thrilled. "That's very generous of you. I can't see why there would be any problem with the loan. It's not as if we're organizing new exhibits right now. Tell Luisa you'll do a reciprocal agreement with the Alcott-Drake so that we receive some objects from their collection next year. She'll sign off."

"You're a real gem," says Pete. "I promise we won't add to your workload. Maddie and I will take care of everything."

Maddie watches as Claudia departs with a flirtatious wave, exiting through a metal door marked ENTRANCE RESTRICTED. She wonders if she is as malleable under the right conditions of attention and praise. She hopes not, but suspects she might be.

Pete turns to her. "What do you think of the letter?"

"Iris thought that James had something to do with Helen's death," says Maddie. "That's how I read it." Maddie feels closer to Iris now. She is familiar with the disappointments of love, paramount among them the discovery of a stranger in the place where your future once stood.

"This trip to Toronto gets more useful by the minute."

"Wait till you hear this," says Maddie. "There's another box, identical from what I can tell, at my apartment. It was my mother's."

Pete raises his eyebrows. "You're kidding. Does it have a hidden compartment?"

"I don't know," Maddie says. "Up until this morning, the idea had never occurred to me. But I'd say it's very likely. I need to get home and open it."

SEVEN

CALLIOPOLIS, NOVEMBER 1903

My first weeks at Calliopolis were both overwhelming and exhilarating. I was doing precisely what I had come here to do, and the rightness of it sang in my bones. The men were restless and impatient, Emmett and James most of all, but I insisted on marking each section of earth carefully with stakes and string, forcing the diggers to remove the dirt one layer at a time, sift it, and bring it to me so that I could record, evaluate, and store the papyrus fragments from each area. I asked Iris to make a map of the pit which showed the origin of each numbered storage box; it was our only hope of reassembling documents spread across adjacent excavation plots. I had Emmett move my tent into the active pit, and my constant instructions to the men earned me the moniker the Dictatress. I didn't mind. Filthy, hot, surrounded by cranky men and donkeys and the occasional camel, up to my elbows in ancient scraps of paper: I was in heaven.

During those long days, collection was the only priority: Preservation and translation, apart from the largest and most intact pieces, would have to wait for the off-season. Between April and September, conditions in the desert were too inhospitable, the heat impossible, and excavators returned to their home institutions in far-flung countries to evaluate and write up their results. I was not troubled; our vein was exciting for what it represented, as much as it was for the quality of papyrus fragments it was producing. There were thousands upon thousands of them, the vast majority no more than a half-inch square; puzzling them into a set of coherent documents would take years, perhaps decades, if it could be done at all.

It would have been useful to have a second papyrologist, but I understood that Alice Baker, who had worked on the site for the past two seasons, had elected not to return. There seemed to be some mystery attached to her, but I was not interested in gossip, and respected Iris's obvious desire to avoid the subject. Meanwhile, we dispatched Rubi to Beni Suef each week for another load of tin storage boxes from the metalsmith, and as I filled them with fragments, I assigned each one a priority color as well as a number. This way, I could focus on the most promising boxes from the beginning and hope to have results to share with Emmett and the others sooner rather than later. I had repurposed some of Iris's oil paints for this purpose, and she assisted me over several evenings in the storeroom, painting red, yellow, and blue dots on the boxes: red for urgent priority, yellow for intermediate, and blue for low.

I wondered how long it might take for a scholar to crack open the final, blue-dotted boxes. Would I be that person? I found the idea oddly attractive. I didn't need the sort of material comforts I had known growing up. A desk, a comfortable chair, a friend to share a pot of tea with, and the opportunity to make a meaningful contribution to my field: These were the satisfactions I desired from life. If I ended up cataloging the Calliopolis papyri from start to finish, over a long career, I wouldn't complain.

I did, however, need some assistance in the present day, and I found it close to home. Khalid was a bright boy, and eager to learn. I discovered that his grandfather had sent him to school in Beni Suef, and while it seemed to me that his education had focused mostly on languages, I was satisfied that he understood the basics of the scientific method. I invited him to be my apprentice in papyrus restoration. He accepted with great enthusiasm, and I could see that Rubi, also, was gratified.

Our village house was made of mudbrick, like the structures that had once housed the population of Calliopolis. It was a single square floor, divided into four rooms: two small ones in the rear, each outfitted with a simple wood bedframe and thin mattress, along with a packing crate serving as a makeshift bedside table; and on the street side, a small pantry and eating nook, and a large open room that served as both an office and a storage area—and now, a laboratory.

With Khalid's assistance, I moved Iris's desk and my own into the center of the room and commandeered the vacated area for a row of tables built to my specifications. I was ready to begin teaching my first student.

"Did you know that papyrus used to grow in this area?" I asked him.

"Yes," he said. "Miss Iris showed me the paintings inside the temple. She told me that I could use them to see what life was like in the village in the old days. There is a picture of men fishing at the river, near the papyrus plants."

"Very good," I told him. "*Cyperus papyrus* is a freshwater reed that requires large quantities of water to thrive. It hasn't grown here since the canal ran dry, and maybe even earlier. Some say the papyrus crop was destroyed by overharvesting, which would have been a tragedy for the city's commercial interests. As to that, we can merely speculate. What I do know is that it is the most useful and beautiful of plants."

"Have you seen it?"

"Yes, indeed. Would you believe that before I came here, I studied in a greenhouse in Rome? A huge glass building with ceilings tall enough for trees to grow. My teacher, Professor Wilson, acquired samples of papyrus plants from a botanical garden in Paris and cultivated them over many years. He wanted to understand how the ancient Egyptians had made their papyrus scrolls, and so he set out to make his own."

Khalid's eyes were wide, I assumed at my description of my beloved greenhouse. He asked, "Is it true that you can still see the building in Rome where the gladiators fought to the death?"

I reminded myself that he was still a boy, with a boy's attraction to tales of battle and bloodshed. "The Colosseum is there," I told him. "Perhaps you'll see it yourself someday. But the gladiators were hardly the most interesting of the Romans." Khalid looked doubtful. "Have you ever heard of Pliny the Elder, for example?" He shook his head. "He was a Roman writer with a special interest in the natural world. His book, *Natural History*, contains the only known account of the ancient Egyptian method for papyrus manufacture. During my studies, I spent many months trying to replicate his recipe, only to find that it didn't work."

"Pliny's book was wrong?" asked Khalid.

"It seemed so. It was most perplexing," I told him. "Pliny never visited Egypt himself and was likely misled by a papyrus producer who didn't want to reveal his secrets."

Khalid nodded knowingly. "There are many shopkeepers in Beni Suef like this," he said. "They will cheat you if you are not on your guard. It is a shame that Pliny was fooled." I realized that I was not making a compelling case for Pliny as a subject more worthy of fascination than gladiators.

I changed tack. "It was a riddle," I said. "One that my teacher and I were determined to solve. Eventually, and with great patience, we found the right formula." I explained how we had selected plants for harvest, sawing the stems into usable lengths and peeling the rind away, before soaking the reeds in tubs to soften them. Thereafter, we would slice strips from the inner pith of the plants and lay them in a lattice form of vertical and horizontal fibers. "Can you guess how the layers were held together?"

"With paste?"

"A good guess, and probably what was used to join the completed sheets together to create the long rolls. But no: It seems that it was the sap of the plant itself. We spent hours with mallets of different sizes, pounding away at the papyrus fibers until they bonded. As the papyrus broke down, it released a natural glue. A most satisfying discovery. Then, of course, we had to figure out how to polish the surface to render it smooth enough for writing."

"Did you succeed?" asked Khalid.

"As far as I know, Professor Wilson is still dedicating himself to that particular experiment," I told him. "My own research in the laboratory had to do with restoration techniques, and this is what I will be teaching you here."

I lifted a dark green bottle out of a crate. Nothing about the move to Egypt had prompted as much worry in me as the fate of these bottles. They were irreplaceable. "This contains a solution that we distilled from the live papyrus plants," I told him. "When we soak the old papyrus, we can rehydrate it. The solution strengthens the fibers and increases the elasticity of the papyrus, literally infusing it with fresh life. This allows us to clean the fragments without having them break apart." I looked around the modest room. "This is where we will see what it can really do."

Khalid helped me organize a modified laboratory with wet and dry areas. In the wet area, we filled a soaking pan with clean water and papyrus solution, and then put two yards of plain white cotton fabric in it to soak. In the dry area, we cut stacks of blotting paper so that they were ready for use, and set up a personal station for me, where I unpacked my microscope with tender care. Khalid had never seen such an instrument, and I allowed him to look through the eyepiece at a strand of his own hair.

His astonishment was a pleasure to behold. "You have the curiosity of the true scientist," I told him. "But you must promise me that you will not touch the microscope yourself. It is essential to our work and cannot be replaced. Do you understand?"

He nodded vigorously. "Yes, Miss Helen. I swear it."

"I'll use the microscope for the final stage of restoration," I told him. "When I can see the surface magnified, I can use tweezers and dry brushes to remove any pollutants, such as sand, salt, or dirt. I can also see how to realign the fibers if they've been twisted. And when all of that is done, we put the treated fragments back between two sheets of blotting paper under a light weight, until all the excess liquid is absorbed. Then, and only then, can I begin my translation. So you see, if you perform well in your role, it will allow me to report my results to Mr. Olsen much more quickly. Shall we begin?"

I reached for a box marked for urgent attention with a red dot. I knew that it contained a relatively small number of fragments—fifty-six in total—and five of them were large, roughly the size of my palm. I had high hopes that, taken together, they might form a complete document, since the handwriting and the quality of the papyrus appeared consistent. The papyrus was brittle, however, and I hoped that my rudimentary laboratory would be adequate for its restoration.

"In scientific inquiry, it is often wise to be cautious," I told Khalid as we wrung out the cotton cloth and spread it over a table in the wet area. "Consequently, we will start with three fragments only, so that we can test our methods before proceeding further." I took my tweezers, holding my breath as I grasped the edge of one small piece of papyrus and placed it on the cloth. "No breakage. Excellent. Twice more and we're away to the races." I moved two more fragments without incident, and with Khalid's help, placed a second damp cloth on top of them.

"Well done," I told him. "Tomorrow, we'll check them, and if I'm content with the results, we'll hydrate more fragments. These ones will likely need to stay in place for three days—that was typical in my last set of experiments—although the conditions here are drier, so we will have to see."

Khalid seemed disappointed. I understood his impatience. "We might also decide to use wet blotting paper instead of cloth, or even a weight at the soaking stage," I told him. "Until we settle on the best method to use in this environment, we must be ready to shift our strategy. Which reminds me that we need a weight." I cast my eye over the storage shelves and spotted a carved statue of Thoth in the form of a baboon. I walked over and took it down. "This should serve, I think."

Khalid looked concerned. "Are you sure, Miss Helen?"

"What do you mean?"

He seemed to squirm, appearing younger than his years. "I wish to be respectful."

"To the statue? It won't mind being put to use. Thoth was the god of writing after all."

"I'm sure you know what is best," he said. "But my grandfather . . ."

"Your grandfather is a sensible man," I told him. "I cannot believe he is superstitious."

"Not superstitious," said Khalid. "He is cautious. He says that we should never make an enemy when we could make a friend." He eyed the statue warily. "The old gods were terrible enemies."

EIGHT

TORONTO, 2019

Pete comes home with Maddie to examine the jewelry box. If he's surprised that she lives in a large house near the university, he doesn't say so, but she explains anyway. "It belongs to my parents. Well, my father. But he lives in Mexico most of the time. I'm house-sitting."

She doesn't bring guests here any longer. She's learned, from bitter experience, that most people find a tragedy irresistible. Do they think that knowing every detail of someone else's misfortune will protect them from a similar fate? Whatever the reason, she can't tolerate being an object of pity or curiosity in her own home. Or anywhere else, but that part is outside her control.

She has Pete wait in the living room while she retrieves the box from her bedroom. She returns with it and places it gently on the coffee table. It's full of her mother's things: Mexican turquoise and sterling silver, a strand of pearls, an antique locket, a tangle of hoops and chains. She's rarely opened it since her mother's death, when she wore the pearls to Silvia's memorial service. "This one stayed in the family. My grandmother used it, and my mother inherited it when she died. It's not in the same pristine condition as the one we donated."

She runs her hand over the lid, tracing the symbols through a fine layer of dust. It is not, it turns out, identical to the box at the museum. The cartouche contains five painted characters, not four: a piece of twisted flax, a reed, a lion, a reed, and a ripple of water. Maddie opens the search engine on her phone, finds a hieroglyphic typewriter, and taps on the symbols.

The translation appears, letter by letter: H-E-L-E-N.

"Hello, Helen," says Pete. "Let's see what you've been hiding."

Maddie opens the lid and proceeds one step at a time, as Claudia has shown them, lifting out the top tray and removing the empty middle drawer. From here, she has a clear view down to the base of the box. Gently, she feels her way along the right edge of the floor, feeling for a bump under the silk lining near the hinge plate. She freezes as she makes contact.

"Do it," says Pete.

She exhales and presses down, feeling rather than hearing the release. The bottom panel eases upward, offering no resistance as Maddie extracts it. Together, they lean forward and peer inside.

They are looking down on a flat wooden box without any ornamentation. Maddie lifts it out, placing it gently on the coffee table. Her hands shake as she flicks the simple latch open and cracks the lid.

"Do you have a pair of tweezers?" he asks.

"In the bathroom," she says. "Don't do anything while I'm gone." She races upstairs and rummages through her makeup bag, returning in triumph. Exhilaration races across her skin like a charge.

"It's a cloth bag," he tells her. "Linen, I think." He takes the tweezers from her and pokes gently at it. Maddie thinks fleetingly of her childhood game of Operation, half expecting a buzzer to sound as he reaches in and seizes the top edge of the fabric, lifting it away from the contents.

Maddie hears the rustle of dry leaves, sees the layers crumbling like

French pastry. "A papyrus scroll," she says aloud. Blood pulses in her throat as if she's run a long distance.

Pete gazes at her as if she has morphed into another being entirely: an alien, or a goddess. "Who owns this box?" he asks.

"I guess I do," she says. "My father told me to take it when my mother died. Of course, he had no idea about the secret compartment."

"Well," he says, "if you want to change your life, this would be the moment."

"I wouldn't mind," she says. She keeps her tone casual, to match his. She has no idea how to change her life, but it sounds as though he might.

He retracts the tweezers and closes the box. For what feels like a long time, they sit and stare at the object on the coffee table as if it is an unexploded bomb. And in a sense, it is. The familiar landscape of Maddie's life is about to crumble to dust. Whatever rises from the destruction will be different from what was there before.

"We need a plan," he tells her.

Her brain is moving more slowly than she'd like. Her first thought, which she snaps off the moment it blooms, is to call her mother. Her second is to call her father, but they aren't speaking to each other. "We should maybe take it to TAM?" she says, hesitantly. "It would be safest there."

He shakes his head. "Forgive me for saying so, Maddie, but TAM is a disaster right now. Luisa is barely keeping her head above water. Donors are fleeing. And TAM doesn't have the expertise to evaluate the scroll, in any case."

"What do you suggest?"

"It should go to Berkeley. Rebecca Field is the best papyrologist in the US. She may not be the warmest personality, but she's extraordinarily talented at what she does. If this scroll is what I think it is, she's the one to prove it."

She can feel that there is an opportunity here, but also no shortage of risk. She doesn't trust herself. She doesn't know if she trusts Pete, either, but he seems to know how to build a career.

As if reading her thoughts, he says, "I can help you. You're talented, Maddie. You're a good researcher. You see connections that other people miss. You shouldn't be locked in a basement pushing paper. This scroll is going to generate publications for years. Why shouldn't your name be on some of them?"

"How?" she asks. "Tell me how to get from here to there." Whatever he proposes is bound to be an improvement over what she's managed on her own.

He leans back on the sofa, his posture relaxed. "What if we started by giving you a fellowship at Berkeley? I have some funding available. You'll be part of the investigation into the scroll; it belongs to you, after all. It's part of the story of the women of Calliopolis. We could work on a proposal for a coauthored book, divide up the research. You'd have access to the Alcott Library. Those are some ideas off the top of my head; what do you think?"

Maddie's heart races. Could it be that after so much regret and disillusionment, there might be a reason for hope? That someone like Peter Bahar sees what so many have missed? Even if she cannot completely believe it, she won't let her doubts scupper this reprieve.

"Yes," she says. "I'm in."

Two weeks later, she is landing in San Francisco.

Pete has arranged everything, as promised. He's taken care of the insurance, the customs forms, the permissions and releases, the signatures from both institutions. He's sorted out a deal whereby she gives Helen's box and the scroll to TAM on a temporary loan, and TAM in turn loans it to the Alcott-Drake for assessment and valuation. All she's had to do is sign a few contracts, and even that has been painless; he's marked the signature pages with flags and placed them in front of her. The force of his enthusiasm leaves no room for pause; there is only action. And why should she hesitate? She has been stuck in life's waiting room for too long. She wants to travel beyond her disappointment.

Pete is waiting for her in the arrivals area. She is surprised at how relieved she feels. Part of her still suspects this reversal of fortune is some elaborate cosmic prank, with her shame as the payoff.

"May I take that for you?" he asks, reaching for her suitcase. He is in an expansive mood. The museum loan—Iris's notebooks and James Dunn's letter, along with Helen's jewelry box and the scroll—had arrived earlier that day without incident. At Maddie's request, Rebecca is waiting to open the box until Maddie is present. Maddie is determined to stay connected to the process at every stage. It would be terrifyingly easy, she knows, to be left behind again.

In between spates of packing, Maddie has read most of Rebecca's published work, and it is undeniably excellent. Her research is exacting and her prose elegant; her book *The Literary Life of Calliopolis* examines documents found in the three scriptoria, letters found in the garbage dump outside of town (part of a later excavation led by James Dunn in 1910), and literary scrolls found in various locations on the site. According to the National Book Award committee, who shortlisted it, Rebecca's book provides "definitive evidence for Calliopolis's near-mythical reputation as the publishing capital of Greco-Roman Egypt, while re-creating, in meticulous detail, the day-to-day life of the doomed city's literary community."

"Rebecca's keen to get going," says Pete. "You might find her . . . impatient. Don't take it personally."

"Okay," says Maddie. "I'm sure we'll get to know each other. My office is in the Alcott Library, right?"

"Small glitch there," says Pete. The demand for faculty offices is ruthless, he tells her. But she won't need one. He's arranged for a library pass and made an appointment for her to meet the next day with the curator of the Alcott-Drake Museums. He believes a designated carrel in the library is doable. He is sure she'll find it adequate. Maddie is breathing hard as she almost-runs to keep pace with Pete's long stride through the parking complex. Pete clicks his key fob and a sleek, dark gray Audi sedan chirps in response. He loads her suitcase into the trunk and opens the passenger door.

"I brought you a present," he tells her, pulling a book from the glove compartment and handing it over, before starting the car. "Something related to our research."

She's touched by the gift, and by his use of the word *our*. She turns the book in her hands: *Travels in Egypt* by Julia Melton Dunn. "I've never heard of her before."

"She was never a runaway bestseller like her former boss," he says. "She was Hortensia Musgrave's personal assistant for several years. *Miss Musgrave's Advice for the Lady Traveler* was the go-to guide for female tourists on Thomas Cook holidays, so Julia rubbed shoulders with all the big characters in Egyptology. She talks about Helen Gardiner's murder in there; Julia met and liked her, and was quite upset about what happened. She knew Calliopolis too; she spent a season there after she married James Dunn. It's one of many references that I haven't had time to read. I can't tell you how pleased I am that we're going to be collaborating."

Their project is a book, tentatively titled *Murder in the Cursed City*, centered around the death of Helen Gardiner. Pete's publisher is excited, he tells her, and wants a full proposal, which Maddie is going to write; this is the focus of the three-month research fellowship Pete has secured for her. When the project is done, he says, she'll get a writing credit, maybe even her name on the book's cover. Luisa has grudgingly agreed to a leave for three months; if the fellowship is extended, which Pete tells her is a possibility, she will have a tough decision to make. But right now, cruising down a California highway with her sunglasses on, Maddie begins to feel her shoulders drop. She's wanted access to the Alcott Library and the Drake Collection for over a year—and now she has it, along with a revitalized research agenda, a powerful friend, a potential book deal, and what is likely a priceless scroll as leverage. She does not need to be intimidated by Rebecca Field.

"Do you know Rebecca well?" she asks him.

"You could say," Pete says. "I used to be married to her."

NINE

CALLIOPOLIS, NOVEMBER 1903

We would return to the village during the hottest part of the day, from noon until around three o'clock, and during these hours Khalid and I would nurse our fragments, making small adjustments as we moved them from the wet area to the dry. We were a good team, with Khalid's boundless enthusiasm tempering my impulse to be overcautious. Aside from the scroll that Emmett had brought to me in Rome, I had been accustomed to handling the most degraded, illegible specimens, the ones that had no value to collectors and wouldn't be missed if they were destroyed in the name of research. These papyri, usually from garbage mounds, had been soaked by rising groundwater, or tossed out with food waste, and were corrupted with mold and wormholes.

Our current objects of study were in the opposite category. They were dry but not particularly stained, and the ink was responding well to treatment with my papyrus solution; I had feared that it might prove unstable when exposed to water, as had sometimes occurred during my research in Rome. However, Khalid and I had now hydrated all the papyrus pieces from the first box without incident, and they were moving through the drying and cleaning stages of our system. A few were ready for translation, and I laid them out on a sheet of blotting paper, puzzling them into a coherent pattern, and keeping careful notes. I longed for more time to spend in the laboratory, but it felt that within moments of arriving at my worktable I was departing again for the dig site. It was maddening.

Emmett tried not to exert too much pressure on me for results, but I could feel frustration emanating from his skin like the heat that shimmered above the sand. One day he called me to the mess hall, and I prepared to make a spirited defense of my methods. "You should return home," he said.

"You are making a mistake," I told him, bluntly. "You will not find a papyrologist better placed to decipher your fragments. Not in Egypt, not anywhere, and certainly not in the middle of the season."

"I'm not giving you notice, Helen, for heaven's sake," he said, laughing. "I'm telling you that I want you to focus on restoration unless it's necessary for you to be on-site. I promise I'll send Rubi to fetch you if I find something for you. But Iris says you don't sleep, and frankly you look like you're going to fall over. You're more use to me in your laboratory than you are here."

"Oh. Very well," I said, with as much dignity as I could muster. "In that case, I should have a translation for you by the end of the week."

———

"I should be annoyed with you," I told Iris over dinner. "I hate feeling weaker than the rest."

"Weaker? What nonsense," said Iris. "You are doing two separate jobs when the rest of us are doing one. It is right that Emmett should recognize it. It is not in his interest to have your attention divided; he simply needed to have it pointed out." I knew without asking that Iris had done so, far more subtly than I would have been capable of doing.

"Thank you," I told her. "You are a good friend." Iris and I had been living together for six weeks by this time, and I trusted her implicitly. I had been told by other students in Rome that the bonds formed on excavation were like those forged in battle. Allies could be essential to survival. But my relationship with Iris was far more than utilitarian. She was keenly observant and witty, and her experiences studying archeology at University College London in its first years as an academic department—the epicenter of British Egyptology, led by the great Flinders Petrie—had given her enough material for a lifetime of stories. I looked forward to our evenings together.

"Margaret Murray called us Petrie's Pups," Iris told me, referencing the woman who had trained the current generation of British Egyptologists. While Petrie made his mark in the field, Professor Murray stayed behind in London and taught his academic courses for him. She was one of the few unmarried women in archeology who commanded widespread respect. Iris and I idolized her. "We were a mixed litter for certain," said Iris. "Men and women side by side, studying together as equals. The field was so new that they hadn't got around to excluding us yet."

I knew from other conversations that the curriculum at UCL was extensive, covering topics ranging from anthropology and pottery to history and languages to human anatomy. Students had to pass eleven examinations before being cleared for field training with Petrie, whose prodigious achievements were evidence of both an exceptional mind and a legendary work ethic. Iris had been sent to Abydos, an immense site between Amarna and Thebes that contained two major New Kingdom temples to Seti I and Ramesses II. "I started out cataloging potsherds," she told me, "but eventually Petrie figured out that I could draw the stelae more accurately than anyone else." Her sketches had been published in Petrie's 1901 study of the royal tombs at Abydos and led to a job offer at Calliopolis.

"You have no idea how well we are served here," Iris told me over a simple dinner of stewed chicken and rice. "At Abydos, Petrie would store leftover cans of meat in the sand until the following season, when he dug them up and threw them against rocks. If they didn't explode, we ate them." She shuddered, and I knew she was thinking about the bout of food poisoning that had sent her to the hospital in her final season with Petrie. "As for housing, the men slept in the rock-cut tombs. I counted myself fortunate to have a tent. I asked about a toilet, and Mrs. Petrie pointed me to the desert." She laughed. "When I got the letter from Emmett, I thought it was Christmas come early. He may be tyrannical in his own way, but Americans insist on a higher standard of living."

When Khalid returned in the morning, I advised him that we would be accelerating our work, and that he would be taking more responsibility for handling the fragments while I concentrated on translation. He thanked me profusely for my confidence in him, but I assured him that I, too, was grateful. It was a joy to watch an apt student progress.

"We have more than one scribe here," I told him. "Once the papyrus is clean, our next task is to gather like fragments with like."

"That is easy, Miss Helen," he said. "There are four writers. It is not hard to tell them apart." He showed me samples written in four styles, pointing out the characteristics that made each one distinct.

I was astonished. Khalid could not read Greek, but a lack of comprehension did not hobble his powers of observation. "That is exceptionally well done," I told him. "I agree with your conclusion. So let us set out four pieces of blotting paper and you will help me fit the documents together." I gave Khalid his own set of tweezers to mark his achievement, and from that moment on, we advanced quickly, and my excitement grew.

"Will you not tell me?" Iris asked, as we rode to Calliopolis one morning. "You are vibrating with anticipation. If you are coming to the site, you must be ready to make a report."

"You are right, as always," I told her. "But Emmett deserves to hear it before anyone else. Well, excepting Khalid. I'll come and find you as soon as I've told him the news."

"It must be good," she said. We dismounted, and she held out her hand for my reins. "Go. I'll see you later."

I burst into the mess hall and found Emmett drinking coffee and peeling an orange. "I wondered when I'd see you," he said. I took a seat across from him. I realized I had been so distracted that I hadn't noticed Emmett's decline. There were deep shadows under his eyes, and he smelled faintly of alcohol. "So," he said. "What do you have to tell me?"

There were four commercial documents, I told him. There was a contract for the sale of a donkey, and another outlining the particulars of a dowry. There was a census declaration. And there was a personal letter from a man to his brother, providing an introduction and recommendation for a friend. The letters were all in distinctive hands, elegantly formed and phrased. "Taken as a whole," I said, "and considering the documents I translated in Rome as well, I feel confident in saying that Calliopolis contained at least one scriptorium. There was a group of professional scribes here, producing commercial documents for customers. Congratulations, Emmett."

Emmett stood, his chair tipping over, and hollered for James. He came around to my side of the table, took me by the waist, and swung me around in a circle. My feet were still in the air when James ran in. He stopped abruptly, muttering apologies, and made to leave, but Emmett dropped me and grabbed him by the arm. "She's done it," he said. "She's found the scriptorium." He gave James the details of my discovery.

James shook my hand. "Thank you, Helen," he said. "We needed this. Now go and find Iris; she's beside herself with anticipation."

I found her working on the lower level of the temple, where the digging was complete. In the morning, the position of the sun allowed for a shaft of natural light that illuminated her subject. She was reproducing a set of wall paintings depicting Thoth, which had been exposed during the French excavation but were already beginning to fade from exposure to the elements. Her paintings were exquisite, works of art in their own right, although Iris didn't see them that way. "I'm a mere copyist," she insisted, and I had stopped arguing with her. I sat on a low wall close to her easel and told her about my findings.

She dropped her pencil and embraced me. "You absolute genius," she said. "You should ask for a pay rise next season." It was an unusual statement for her; in my observation the English were more reticent than Americans were when it came to discussing the practicalities of money, even though Egyptology was a business as much as a science.

"I will," I said. "I'll ask your advice when the time comes. I think you are one of the few women out here being paid what you are worth." It wasn't a fair competition, though, since most of the women working in the field were wives and therefore unpaid, despite their multiple roles managing staff, organizing meals, documenting finds, and corresponding with funders; they were usually highly trained archeologists to boot. For all of this they rarely received credit for their contributions, except occasionally on the dedication page of a husband's book. On the other hand, they would never be forced out of the field and into a life of domesticity unless they preferred it. "James says you are the most sought-after artist in the Nile Valley."

Iris's cheeks seemed to pink, but it was hard to tell in the poor light. I worried that she and James were forming an attachment. There were many women in our field who sought marriage as a way of remaining involved in excavation. I would be disappointed, I realized, if Iris chose to follow this path. She had more than enough talent to succeed on her own merits. I could also admit to myself that I had become comfortable in our little household and didn't want to see it change. My professional ambitions might be vast, but our modest arrangement matched my domestic needs perfectly.

Learning to tolerate loss: This was the key to endurance. Whatever happened, I knew, I would have my work. I determined to give it my entire focus instead of fretting about events beyond my power to change.

"We have done excellent work, but we can't rest on our laurels," I told Khalid. "We must bring the same attention to each new box that we gave to our first one." During the translation process, I had taken a second box from the queue and asked Khalid to begin hydration. "Let us see what we have."

Now Khalid lifted the damp cover layer of blotting paper from the new set of fragments, and I could see that the fibers were plump and flexible, although some ink was beginning to flake. "We'll need some paste," I told him.

I had taught him to make a simple wheat starch paste, a formula I had devised at the greenhouse in Rome. Flaking ink needed a fixative, but one that could be reversed; I'd seen many fragments destroyed by compounds intended to preserve them. As Professor Wilson's student, I had spent hours cooking paste on my Bunsen burner to arrive at the right formula—one that yielded a thin paste with enough adhesive strength to preserve the text, but without lumps that would occlude the surface.

I selected a large fragment with my tweezers and placed it on a microscope slide. "The ink is holding on this one," I said. "But I can see debris on the surface. I'm going to remove it now before it dries completely." I carried it over to my station and began the delicate process of removing sand particles. As I did so, a notation caught my attention, and I adjusted the magnification so that I could read it. It was a number: 1320. I heard myself gasp and began rubbing my palm across my chest to settle my breath.

Khalid was by my side in a flash, and Iris—who had been at her own desk, adding color to one of her sketches from the temple—was close behind.

"What is wrong?" she asked. "Are you ill?"

"Not at all," I said. I explained the significance of the notation, which sat beneath the main text on the fragment. "1320 is the number of lines. It suggests a literary text. A poem, or a play."

"And that is good?" asked Khalid.

"Literary papyri are the rarest finds of all," I told him. "The most prized."

"And the ones Miss Helen loves above all others," said Iris.

"We will not get ahead of ourselves," I said, sternly. "It is a process. It will take the time it takes. Is the paste ready?"

For the next two days I immersed myself in transcription and translation of the numbered fragment, pausing only to clean the other pieces from the same batch. This was the only one with a line notation, and I had an instinct that it represented the final lines of the text.

"You are very tense," Iris said, on the second evening, bringing me a cup of tea. "Are you disappointed?"

"No," I said. "Not that." I was checking my translation from the previous day and beginning to accept the enormity of the find in front of me.

"It is something extraordinary, then," said Iris. "It has to be the one or the other. You don't have to tell me. But let me know if I can help."

I was grateful not to have to explain. The dialect was Eolic, with a stanza formation typical of the most celebrated lyric poet of her age. I forced myself to linger over each individual symbol, and gradually, the words took shape, as if surfacing from a lake:

you will remember
for we in our youth did these things
yes, many and beautiful things

I did not realize I was weeping until Iris pressed a handkerchief into my hand. "What is it?" she asked.

"It is the voice of the Muse herself," I said.

TEN

BERKELEY, 2019

Calvin Drake is a household name in Berkeley, Maddie realizes. So far, she's seen a Drake stadium, a Drake commercial building, and a Drake Boulevard. She stands now before Drake House, the famous man's own neoclassical mansion turned local landmark, sought-after wedding venue, and occasional meeting place for heads of state.

She admires the white marble slabs and columns glittering in the California sun as she climbs up to the entrance. Calvin Drake's primary home during his life, the building became a museum under the terms of his will. After his fatal encounter with the raiders, his wife (rarely mentioned, Maddie notices, without the adjectives *sickly* and *reclusive*) relocated to a Drake family home on the East Coast and promptly disappeared from history. Nora Alcott took her place in the mansion, ostensibly to oversee the renovations, and remained there, in an apartment on the top floor, for the rest of her life. In time, she added her own stamp to the property, creating the Alcott Library to house her collection of historical books and documents.

The Alcott-Drake Museums (comprising both the Drake Collection and the Alcott Library) are now part of UC Berkeley, which is why Maddie can access them on a Monday, despite their closure to the public. She has a faculty pass. Somewhere in the basement, she pictures Rebecca in a proprietary crouch over the papyrus scroll. She hopes that Ben has finished whatever brought him here and has returned to Stanford.

The problem with freedom, Maddie must admit, is that it manifests (at least in her) as restlessness and worry. She woke early this morning, paced the length of her Airbnb, went for breakfast and too much coffee, and ultimately, having read the same sentence of a journal article five times without understanding it, decided to use the power of her faculty pass to tour the collection on her own. She has an appointment in an hour with the curator. She's hoping that a deep dive into Olsen's excavation diaries might offer some clues about the identity of the scroll.

The Drake Collection represents the personal whims of an extraordinarily privileged, curious, and somewhat undisciplined mind. The Americas Wing has West Coast totem poles, an Aztec sun stone, and gold figurines from the Mayan and Incan empires; the European Wing has paintings by old masters, some particularly ghoulish reliquaries, two Linear B tablets from Crete, a Roman bath with intricate mosaics—removed piece by piece from a country house in the South of France and reconstructed in a purpose-built solarium—and a preserved bog man from Ireland with a garrote knotted around his neck.

Egypt has its own wing and over twenty thousand objects; Drake spent his last eight winters on the Nile, recruiting an extensive network of agents throughout the country, and growing increasingly creative in his attempts to circumvent the Egyptian Antiquities Service, a government organization which was inclined to cherry-pick the best finds before permitting export. One famous story reads like a French farce, involving bumbling customs agents in Alexandria opening boxes of oranges, while Drake loaded the true booty onto the Atlantic steamer and set sail. In addition to the artifacts from Calliopolis, there are amulets, statues, chalices, bowls, collars, and temple reliefs from many of the leading sites in the Nile Valley, along with the main attraction: a pair of mummies complete with painted wood coffins. Maddie wonders if the CEO's desk is as littered with repatriation requests as Luisa's is at TAM. She suspects the situation here might be even worse.

But Drake's piratical habits are not her concern today. She has the luxury, for once, of concentrating on her own project—and even enjoying the beauty of the objects on display in the Calliopolis collection. They are magnificent. The papyri aren't in this building—they are in the Alcott Library—but here are Iris's original watercolors of the temple of Thoth; a heavy gold bracelet in the form of a snake, with delicate scales rippling around the band, a tongue at one end and a rattled tail at the other; and a whole case of animal mummies, mostly ibises and baboons. The mummy portraits are the centerpiece of the exhibit, and Maddie stands in front of them, reading each face, imagining their lives in the bustling city of Calliopolis in the first century of Roman rule.

"Oh, there you are," says a voice, and she turns to see Pete. "Are you ready to dive into the excavation journals?"

"You didn't have to come," Maddie says, but she's glad to see him.

"Don't be silly," he says. "If you see something in the journals that I've never noticed, you'll be doing me a favor. And it's our best bet at figuring out what that scroll in Helen's box is."

He joins her in front of the portraits. "They're amazing, aren't they? As if they were painted yesterday. I feel like you could leave this building and see them walking on the street outside, maybe minus the togas and wreaths." Maddie understands what he means; the naturalism of the artist's hand is exceedingly modern. There is depth and honesty in the ruddy complexions, misshapen noses, and hulking brows, and also in the depictions of striking beauty, the kind that wouldn't be out of place on a newsstand magazine cover. "These were probably some of the last residents of Calliopolis. They've carbon-dated this set of portraits to around 200 AD, around the same time the plague hit. Gather ye rosebuds, Maddie."

A woman appears, introducing herself as the curator, Marielle Joseph. "Thank you so much for arranging access," Maddie says.

"It was no trouble," says Marielle. "I'm happy to help."

"I'm forever asking Marielle for favors," says Pete.

"True words," says Marielle, with an indulgent smile. "This was one of the easier ones to accommodate. Let me take you into the staff area. I have the excavation diaries set up for you there."

"Being chair of the board of the Alcott-Drake Museums has its privileges," says Pete, as they pass through the secure doors. "And if you find something, you'll be helping us. I've read the journals a hundred times. It's quite possible I can't really see them objectively anymore."

Maddie settles in with the journal from the second season at Calliopolis, the year Helen arrived. As recently as last week, Maddie would have described her problem as a dearth of primary sources. Now she is literally surrounded by withered notebooks from an excavation about which she has little knowledge and no expertise. She is navigating by starlight, in a lifeboat.

The excavation diaries are a collaboration between various members of the dig team, each one a presence on the page. Olsen's cursive is thick and spiky; Dunn's tall with an exaggerated slope to the left; Iris's elegant and embellished with garlands; Helen's clear, sharp, and upright. The system, as far as she can tell, involves a daily note made by either Olsen or Dunn, recording what got pulled out of the ground each day in real time, along with some personal observations about the progress of the work. Detailed descriptions of the finds are listed at the end of the day's entry, including the assigned catalog number. In the case of objects, there are often sketches, and Maddie recognizes Iris's distinctive style. For papyri, the identifying characteristics include the type of document, and occasionally a line of Greek text in Helen's script.

The early diary entries record Olsen's mounting frustration. Having cleared the building where he'd found the Menander scroll the year before and moved to the structure next door hoping for more of the same, Olsen is empty-handed after two full weeks of digging. He then changes tactics and puts the diggers closer to the main road in and out of the city on the theory that a major business like the scriptorium would have had a storefront there. Alice Baker has failed to report for the season, and he is anxiously awaiting Helen's arrival in October, still a couple of weeks away. Helen's arrival, when it comes, is the harbinger of a major find, a rich vein of papyrus fragments. An accounting of their storage containers is the first entry recorded in her crisp handwriting.

"When was the Sappho papyrus found?" Maddie asks. "The one you have here at the museum."

Pete looks up from his laptop. "During the second season."

"But I can't find a record of it in here."

"Well, no," he says. "You remember that the theft included the excavation diary in progress at the time? My best guess is that Olsen and Dunn couldn't re-create the details in the stolen book from memory, or else they didn't want to take the time to do it, so they made a list of the objects they had in storage that weren't described anywhere else. You'll find the list in a separate book in that pile somewhere."

This makes sense to Maddie. Based on what she sees in the journals, the old division of hunting and gathering applied on Olsen's dig. Men drove pickaxes into the dirt and pulled mummies out; women cleaned, measured, categorized, recorded, sketched, and stored. But the consequence of this is extremely annoying from Maddie's point of view: The surviving records include a volume covering the autumn period, finishing at Christmas; a volume covering the period from the end of March until the conclusion of the season; and a volume consisting of one extraordinarily long and boring list. *Papyrus fragments, 20 boxes: high priority; papyrus fragments, 47 boxes: medium priority; papyrus fragments, 106 boxes: low priority.* She flips quickly through the pages, reading every entry, finding none for *unidentified scroll, suspected literary significance.* "Let's say I was trying to figure out when the scroll in my box was discovered?"

"If there's no specific entry for it, I think we would have to assume that it was found in the period after Christmas and before Helen died, and since it was hidden in her box, it didn't make it into the catalog that Olsen put together later."

"You know," says Maddie, "Helen vanished when that book was stolen." She blushes at Pete's expression. "Aside from being murdered, obviously. I mean the loss of the record effectively erased her role in the excavation. No one else there could understand the significance of the papyrus fragments. The interpretation was part of the discovery. She must have translated and identified the Sappho poem. It's one of the most famous finds of that season. It's one of Sappho's best-known works now. My roommate in college had it on a poster in our common room." Pete laughs. "My point is, she was cheated out of any credit."

"Helen died," says Pete. "The books were stolen. Olsen and Dunn did what they could to fix it and moved on. Did they fail to ascribe credit to Helen Gardiner? Perhaps so, but it will be a hard argument to prove, Maddie. To me, what's compelling about the theft of the excavation diary is that it points to the crime being committed by someone inside the dig team, who knew the precise system of recordkeeping and wanted to make it difficult, if not impossible, to identify what was missing." He glances at his phone. "Rebecca wants to meet with us. Can you tear yourself away from the journals for a bit?"

Pete leads Maddie through the ornamental garden that connects the two buildings. They enter the Alcott Library, a smaller structure constructed of white marble, with a portico at the main entrance. "You haven't been inside yet?" asks Pete, and when Maddie shakes her head, he beckons her over to a side hall. "Rebecca can wait a few minutes. Come and see the Calliopolis papyri."

There are no windows in this gallery, and the effect is that each specimen seems to bask in its own gentle spotlight. The Menander scroll is displayed in five panels, with a full translation provided alongside each one. The translations are attributed to Professor Percival Wilson and Miss Helen Gardiner. Maddie touches Helen's name furtively, embarrassed by her own sentimentality.

Pete calls her away. "The Sappho," he says, pointing to a standing case in the center of the room, where forty-eight fragments—from the size of a postcard to the size of a stamp—are mounted like puzzle pieces between two layers of glass so that they can be seen from either side. "She's the real celebrity of the collection. Over a million visitors a year."

Maddie stands in front of the case and reads the translation, attributed to Emmett Olsen. There are several poems here, incomplete but precious. When this scroll was revealed to the world, Maddie knows, it caused a sensation: an incomplete edition of Book One of Sappho's collected poetry. To recover even a fraction of what was lost in antiquity seemed miraculous, then and now. She smiles to see the lines that she once knew by heart. She is straddling her own lifetime now, a foot anchored in an undergrad common room, a foot stretching toward the edge of whatever comes next.

> *you will remember*
> *for we in our youth did these things*
> *yes, many and beautiful things*

"There you are," says a voice, and Maddie turns to see a tall woman, with dark, wavy hair cropped short, standing next to a man with thinning blond hair. She is formally dressed by California standards, clad in a crisp cherry-red pantsuit. She wears an expression of irritation. "Rebecca Field," she says, shaking Maddie's hand without warmth. "I thought you were coming right over."

"She needed to see the Sappho," says Pete. "Hello, Brett. It's been a while."

The blond man extends his hand to Pete and then to her. "I'm Brett Cooper," he tells her. "It's good to meet you, Maddie. You've brought a remarkable specimen to us."

"I asked Brett to come and review my preliminary findings," says Rebecca. "We've worked together on damaged documents in the past. He's the world's leading expert on digital restoration of ancient manuscripts."

"Okay," Maddie says. She's never heard of Brett Cooper and feels uneasy. The circle of people who know about the scroll is widening, and she is losing control of it. She glances at the Sappho fragments again, her eye landing on another line this time: *But me you have forgotten.* She stiffens her spine and ventures a question. "What's the next step?"

"We're going to have to take the fragments to Sacramento," says Rebecca.

"Sacramento? Why?"

"The equipment I use is in a purpose-built lab at Resurrection College," says Brett. "We need to take the scroll there to analyze it. And I think the sooner we get a handle on what we have here, the better. I'm suggesting that we leave in the morning."

"I . . . okay," Maddie says. She has heard of Resurrection College, a small, private Christian university known for its collection of biblical materials. "I'll have to figure out accommodation. And a car as well, I guess."

"You'll drive with us," says Brett. "And I'll take care of your accommodation. Not to worry."

"Wait," says Maddie. "Hang on. Can everyone slow down for a second and explain to me what Brett is going to do with the scroll?"

Brett considers the question, and then says, "Rebecca's genius is that she can read the letters on a very old page and make sense of them. But what if the letters or symbols aren't visible because the document is damaged? That's where I come in." He explains that he designs computer programs that surface the text when traditional methods of restoration fail. "Let's say your manuscript caught fire and then got doused with water in an effort to save it. From the point of view of digitization, you have two problems. One, your paper is charred, and there's no contrast between the black ink and the black surface of the document. And two, your paper can't lie flat because it's buckled from the water damage. If you try to digitize it in two dimensions, you're going to be replicating all of the textural defects."

"I'm with you so far," says Maddie.

"Okay, then," Brett continues. "To deal with the charring, we use multispectral imaging. By using infrared or ultraviolet filters—depending on the type of ink—we can separate the black letters from the black background and begin to read them. That's relatively easy. It gets much more complicated when we need to return an object that is now three-dimensional—a crumpled piece of paper, for example—to its original two-dimensional form. To do that, we need to have a de-skewing algorithm that simulates a force pressing on the geometric structure of the document and converting it to a planar structure."

Having lost the thread at *de-skewing*, Maddie puts up a hand. Brett apologizes. He tends, he says, to get overexcited about the possibilities of computer modeling. But the basic point is that he's figured out how to replicate a two-dimensional version of the document as it existed before the catastrophic damage was sustained. That isn't even the best part, he adds. The next frontier of his work is virtual unwrapping—a technique designed for scrolls like the one Maddie has brought. They're going to try to unroll it digitally before they attempt to do so manually.

"I didn't dare touch it," says Rebecca. "The scroll started to crumble when I separated the linen bag from the first layer. I'll tackle it again after Brett scans it. But it's going to be a painstaking job, and we may decide it isn't worth it. Papyrus starts to deteriorate as soon as it comes out of the ground, assuming that it was well-preserved at the outset. Your scroll was exposed to moisture at some point. It's extremely delicate. I'm hoping that mold isn't a big issue, but it's possible."

"I hear you saying that you believe the scroll has value," Maddie says. "Is that right?"

Rebecca raises an eyebrow. "We've got two full-time faculty members on this from two universities, plus whatever time Pete's putting in between television appearances. We have travel expenses, your fellowship money, and at least a couple of weeks in Brett's state-of-the-art lab."

Maddie chooses to ignore Rebecca's tone. "That's a yes, then?"

"In my opinion?" says Brett. "What you've brought us falls somewhere between precious and priceless. So that's a yes."

ELEVEN

CALLIOPOLIS, DECEMBER 1903

I waited to share my discovery. I wanted to be sure I was right. I wanted, for another few days, to be the only person in two thousand years to hear the voice of the tenth Muse, the towering female genius of the classical world. I wanted to be alone with her.

But then Calvin Drake arrived.

I was out at Calliopolis late one afternoon, overseeing the extraction of a new vein of fragments, when a stranger on horseback blasted into the site, dust flying, bearing a dinner invitation for Emmett.

"A week early, at least, the bastard," Emmett said, scowling. "And when we were making progress too. Now you'll see, Helen, how it all goes to hell when the hobbyists arrive."

"Calvin Drake funds the excavation, does he not?" I asked.

"On very hard terms, as you will see. Meddlesome, ignorant of our methods, impossible to please. I could say more, but I'll restrain myself in the presence of a lady. James!" Emmett shouted across the pit.

"He'll be pleased with the papyri, surely?" I asked.

Emmett rolled his eyes. "Don't count on it. He thinks we should be finding a museum-quality treasure every week. The Menander scroll—a once-in-a-lifetime find—was acceptable. He won't think much of your flakes, I can tell you, even if they do prove the existence of a scriptorium. *James!*"

"About the translation," I said. It was past time to share what I knew with Emmett.

"It will have to wait, I'm afraid, Helen. I can't exempt you from excavating indefinitely. Especially not now that Drake is here." He had misunderstood me, I realized, assuming that I was asking for more time away from the site. I tried again. "There have been some developments—"

"Boss." James stepped into my tent and gave me a half smile.

"I've been summoned to dinner," said Emmett. "I'm heading into town for a bath and a shave—I'll stop by your house, Helen, so don't be alarmed if you see a disturbance in the storeroom. I keep a good set of dinner clothes packed away in there, but I'll have to ferret them out. James, you know what to do."

"I'll take care of it," said James.

"I'll stay overnight in town and ride in with them in the morning," said Emmett. "Give them the royal treatment."

"Have a nice dinner," I said.

"Bah," said Emmett. "Not bloody likely."

James and I watched him clamber out of the pit. "Are they so bad?" I asked. "And who, exactly, are 'they'? Does Mr. Drake travel with an entourage?"

"He travels with an entire steamer," said James. "At least twenty staff plus a stable and a henhouse. And a full-sized carriage that rolls on and off for day trips. And more often than not, parties of guests. But Olsen's talking about Miss Nora Alcott, Drake's cousin and companion."

"Oh," I said. "I've heard the name."

James raised an eyebrow. "You've heard more than that, if you've heard her name." I blushed, remembering my aunt's unkind comments.

"Your expression gives you away, Helen. But don't underestimate her. She's much more informed than the average sunseeker. She's clever and she has Drake's ear. We make sure she enjoys herself while she's here."

"Is that why Emmett's annoyed? Do we have to drop everything to entertain her?"

James laughed. "To the extent we do, it's a minor distraction. If they've brought a party with them, we'll have a day or two of guiding duties. No, the annoyance is Drake himself. But since he's the reason we're here at all, it's a cross we have to bear." He held up a hand to stop my question. "I won't spoil the surprise. You'll have to see for yourself."

Mr. Drake and Miss Alcott arrived the next day in a shaded carriage with red leather benches, one for the driver, one for the pair of them, and one for an array of picnic baskets that were unloaded by the staff members who arrived in a separate carriage altogether. "How big is this steamer?" I asked James.

He shook his head. "You have to see it to believe it," he said. We had lined up the entire excavation party to greet them, as if we were the household staff of a great European country house. James, Iris, and I stood in front, while the local men stood behind us, several rows deep. "If you play your cards right, you'll get an invitation to tea." I wasn't sure I wanted one, having come to the far side of the world to avoid precisely these sorts of social obligations. But this was wealth on a scale I'd never seen, let alone experienced, and I was intrigued.

The group spilled out onto the sand, Mr. Drake in a waistcoat and boater; Miss Alcott in a delicate dress of embroidered lawn, a parasol, and a broad straw hat decorated with silk flowers; and a clean-shaven Emmett wearing a tight smile. Emmett led them over to us. "You know Mr. Dunn and Miss Wentworth from last season," he said. "And this is Miss Helen Gardiner."

"We are pleased to make your acquaintance, Miss Gardiner," said

Miss Alcott. "But where is Miss Baker? I had understood that you would be collaborating on the papyri."

"She fell ill at the end of last season," said Iris. "We had hoped that she would return, but evidently she decided against it."

"Have you had any correspondence from her?"

"I haven't," said Iris. "Which was, to be candid, unexpected. But I imagine she has resumed her life in England and this all seems rather far away."

"Nora, my dear," said Mr. Drake. "Miss Baker left us high and dry. We were fortunate that Olsen was able to get Miss Gardiner out here on short notice. I hardly think we should spend our energies fretting about her when she abandoned us so readily." He turned to me. "Welcome to Calliopolis, Miss Gardiner," he said.

"Thank you," I said. I'd been resident at Calliopolis for over a month now, and had felt entirely at home, but with Mr. Drake's greeting, I understood my position anew. We had been left to our own devices like schoolchildren in a playground, and now the headmaster was calling us into the classroom to produce our assignments for marking.

"Well, Olsen," said Mr. Drake, "I think we have time for a bit of digging before lunch, no?"

"Certainly," said Emmett. "Rubi, James, please prepare the site for Mr. Drake. Miss Alcott, I thought you might enjoy a tour of the temple with Miss Wentworth?"

"Has anything changed since last season?" she asked.

"I've done some cleaning and preservation work on the wall paintings," Iris said. "And we've had some hieroglyphic translations done in the off-season, so I'm better placed to explain the images to you than I was last year."

"That sounds lovely," said Miss Alcott. "Thank you. Perhaps we can have a cup of tea in the tent afterward." While we had been carrying out introductions, the staff had erected a silk tent nearby, swept the sand flat, unrolled a Persian carpet, and scattered pillows on the floor. A genie from the tales of the Arabian nights could not have conjured a more romantic spot.

I beckoned to Emmett, stepping away from the hubbub at Miss Alcott's tent. "Will you be needing my assistance at all?" I asked. I had no idea how these visits normally proceeded. Would we go about our business on the margins, or was the entire stay a performance? And if so, what was my role?

"Most likely," said Emmett. "Stay close by."

I returned to the scriptorium site, as I now thought of it, with James and half the men, and we continued to harvest papyrus fragments. We were getting to the end of the vein, and the specimens were fewer and poorer. It had been several weeks since we'd filled a red box.

Meanwhile, Emmett led Mr. Drake into a second, adjoining pit, along with the rest of the crew. "Why is he going down there?" I asked James. It was an older pit, one that we had scoured and deemed to be exhausted.

"You'll see," said James, and within a half hour, a great shout went up.

"They can't have found anything, surely?" I said.

"By the sound of things, I'd say that Mr. Drake has uncovered a cache of valuables in what was likely the scriptorium's equivalent of a vault," he said. "We suspected it was there, so we waited for him to arrive. We knew he'd want to be present for the excavation." His eyes never left mine. "A poker face is a real asset in this business, Helen," he said. I took a moment. "Much better," he said. "Shall we go and congratulate him?"

We climbed up and saw that Emmett and Mr. Drake were already on the surface. Emmett shaded his eyes and scanned over to us. James waved. Emmett pointed in the direction of the picnic area, and beckoned. "That's our cue," said James, and we climbed the ladder closest to us. "Praise and enthusiasm, Helen, are the only skills required today."

"I understand," I said. These were skills that every woman had in her survival kit, even one with unnatural ambitions.

"Please join us," Miss Alcott called to us as we approached. "Sit down. Would you like some tea?"

I took a cushion next to Iris. "Yes, thank you," I said, and a maid prepared a cup for me.

"Do you like my new bracelet?" asked Miss Alcott. She extended her wrist, around which was coiled a gold bracelet in the form of a snake, the head meeting the tail. "Or should I say my old one?" I tempered my expression as James had taught me to do, but it was shocking to see a museum-worthy treasure reduced to a lover's token.

"It's a magnificent find," said Iris. "I'm not expert enough in Greco-Roman jewelry to date it precisely, but this style was popular from around 300 BC until the end of the first century."

"Worn by one of the elite of Calliopolis in its heyday," agreed James. "Museum quality, absolutely."

"Just needed a bit of polishing," said Drake. "It's as if it was underground for a month, not two thousand years."

This, at least, was true. "You've brought good fortune with you," I said. "Long may it continue."

Mr. Drake beamed and my colleagues seemed to exhale together. Miss Alcott cocked her head and gave me a slight smile, as if I'd exceeded her expectations. "You must join me for tea on the boat," she said. "Iris is coming on Sunday. We'll make a party of it. You don't mind if the ladies take a day off, do you, Mr. Olsen?"

"Not at all," said Emmett, who looked as though he minded very much.

"I'd be delighted," I said.

"Excellent," said Miss Alcott. "You know, Miss Wentworth was telling me something of your background, and it turns out that we're acquainted with your aunt, Mrs. Clifford Cogswell."

"Cogswell?" said Mr. Drake. "He let you come out here on your own? I'm astonished."

"Mr. Cogswell is married to my mother's sister," I said. "He is not my guardian and never has been. My father, on the other hand, was a keen amateur archeologist, a professor at Columbia University. In fact, he introduced me to your papyrus collection there. In that sense, Mr. Drake, you were the catalyst for my adventure in Egypt."

Mr. Drake chuckled. "Well said, Miss Gardiner." He held out a small silk bag. "Do you know anything about Roman coins?"

"No more than the basics—only what they teach in the standard archeology curriculum," I told him. "I'm a specialist in papyrus restoration and translation. I've devoted myself exclusively to that subject for many years now." I opened the bag and a handful of heavy coins fell into my palm, bright as a promise. "I'm sure Mr. Maspero at the museum in Cairo could provide some guidance." Gaston Maspero was the director-general of the Egyptian Antiquities Service and the conservator of Cairo's famous museum, but he was no mere functionary; few could match his achievements as a scholar and excavator. His translation of the Book of the Dead alone would secure his position in history. I very much hoped to meet him when I found my way to Cairo.

"Oh, I think not," said Mr. Drake, taking the coins back with a frown. "You should tell Miss Gardiner how it is, Olsen." He turned back to me. "I'll find an expert when I'm home in the United States. I can say goodbye to half of anything I show Maspero, and it'll be the best half, you can be sure of that. He'd like nothing better than to stash my finds in that leaky pile he calls a museum, and then sell them out the back door at the first opportunity. No, we'll take him a selection at the end of the season, and then only what we're prepared to part with." He was sitting on a low bench, which placed him higher than the rest of us, and he lit a cigar which filled the tent with smoke.

"We have another guest joining us next month," said Miss Alcott, "and I think you'll be very pleased to see him. He is a great booster of yours, a former teacher as I understand it."

"How lovely," I said. Professor Wilson was here in Egypt? What a joyful reunion that would be. How excited he would be to see the papyri.

"He plans to stay for several weeks," said Miss Alcott. "He's secured some generous funding to excavate the Christian settlement on the west side of the site. Of course, Calvin was delighted to give him access to our concession. It seemed to make sense to combine our efforts."

"Yes, wonderful," said Emmett, with the expression of a man barely containing his rage. "I'm sure Reverend Banks will be most helpful."

Although disappointed to realize that I was not to be reunited with Professor Wilson, I was not displeased. I felt glad for Reverend Banks; his arrival must signify advances in his research, which I knew was as essential to him as my own work was to me. I wondered if we would have reason to collaborate at Calliopolis.

"Miss Gardiner," said Mr. Drake. "You are the papyrus expert here, so tell me: Have I made a good investment? Are we digging up anything of value?"

"It's too early . . ." Emmett began, and I said: "Our chances are good." Emmett stared at me and shook his head slightly.

I continued: "I think we can be confident at this point that there was at least one major scriptorium, and it's likely that there were others. It's also likely, given what we've found so far, that the residents of Calliopolis achieved a high level of literacy in relative terms. From the point of view of a papyrologist, the site holds a lot of promise."

"I'm not interested in promise, Miss Gardiner. Not after what I've spent in this godforsaken desert. I want results." He jangled the coins in his hand. "Don't talk to me about the historical value of city records. I don't care about that. You can keep your contracts and your tax payments. I want literary treasures. You're the only one who's examined what's come out of the pit so far. What was in there?"

I felt Emmett's eyes on me, but I looked only at Drake. "A lost poem by Sappho," I told him.

TWELVE

SACRAMENTO, 2019

"Welcome to the lab," says Brett, opening the door to a large white room that looks like a medical facility. It occurs to Maddie that she hasn't been in a lab since high school chemistry, although Brett's workplace is a far cry from those scarred tables and mostly functional Bunsen burners. He tours her around the room, explaining the purposes of various machines: "We'll test the ink first," he says. "If it's iron gall ink, we'll do ultraviolet imaging. If it's carbon, we'll do infrared. I'm hoping for carbon, I'm not going to lie. With the infrared, we get better penetration. I can usually see both sides of the page." He grins. "I'm getting ahead of myself. All will be revealed in time."

The door to the lab opens and a tall, lanky man with a shock of white-blond hair enters. He looks to be around her age, Maddie decides. "Oh, excellent," says Brett. "Maddie, meet Gareth Anderson. He's the curator of early books and manuscripts at the Cogswell Library. He'll be part of our team in the lab on the preservation end of things."

Gareth smiles and shakes her hand. His gray-blue eyes are friendly behind tortoise frames. "This is going to be fun," he says. He explains that the library will take custody of the scroll for security purposes while it is on university premises. "Every now and then, you hear about a papyrus fragment that somehow ends up at an auction when everyone thought it was safe in a university lab. We don't take any chances. We'll photograph and catalog it, and we'll lock it in the library vault when we're not studying it actively. No one will be left alone with it, at any time."

"You can trust him," Brett assures her. "He's borderline obsessive about security. In the best possible way."

Gareth laughs. "It's been said," he agrees. "But you all knew what you were getting." Gareth tells her that he's a provenance expert, specializing in written materials. He came to Resurrection College as a consultant, hired to examine a fourteenth-century illuminated manuscript that had been donated to the university anonymously. "The bindings were from the mid-twentieth century and there was very little documentation with it, so the chief librarian was worried that it might have been stolen at some point in its past."

"Was it?" asks Maddie.

"Unfortunately, yes," Gareth says. "We were able to trace it to a private collection in Paris that was looted by the Nazis in 1940."

"How awful," says Maddie.

"People don't realize how many books disappeared during the Second World War. Millions of them, and many are still hiding in plain sight on library shelves around the world. I run a project here, mostly powered by graduate students, that tries to reunite descendants with their family collections." As he talks, Gareth rummages through the satchel slung across his body and pulls out a slim volume. "Brett thought you might want some reading material this morning. There isn't much to see during the computer modeling stage of the proceedings."

It's an old edition, clothbound and musty, bearing the title *Mersis of Calliopolis: His Life and Times*. The author is Alistair Banks. Gareth continues, "You're welcome to anything in our collection, but I understand you want to spend some time in the Alistair Banks archive."

"I wouldn't put it quite like that," she says. "I'm working with Pete Bahar at Berkeley." She feels a small thrill as she says it. "We're collaborating on some research on Emmett Olsen's excavation of Calliopolis. It's a long shot, but Pete thinks it's possible there are some diaries or letters in the Banks archive that contain his observations of the dig."

"I don't want to get your hopes up," says Gareth. "I don't have a strong handle on what's in there yet."

"My expectations are low," Maddie tells him. "I promise."

Gareth seems relieved. "Music to my ears," he says. "You'll see why when I take you over to the library. Give me a couple of hours?"

She thanks him and takes the seat Brett has offered her in his office. *Mersis of Calliopolis* isn't scintillating reading, but it's a useful introduction to the Christian history of Calliopolis and its place in the larger context of monasticism. Starting in the second century, she learns, small numbers of early Christians in Egypt left nearby cities for the isolation of the desert to experiment with the ascetic life. Some had become hermits, some had formed brotherhoods of equals, and still others had gathered around a religious figure as disciples. The most famous communities had been established in desert outposts in northwestern Egypt in the middle of the third century. The leaders of the movement became widely known and sought out for their gnomic droppings of wisdom, ultimately collected as *The Sayings of the Desert Fathers*.

Maddie doesn't have to read beyond the first page of *Mersis of Calliopolis* to glean that Alistair Banks believed the history books had got it wrong. He proposed an alternative origin story which placed the first Christian monastic community at Calliopolis under the leadership of Mersis, a monk who eventually migrated north and carried his well-established ideas with him. Banks's argument rested on a brief mention of Mersis in *The Sayings of the Desert Fathers*, in which Saint Agapius of Scetis was recorded as saying: "A group of strangers came up from Calliopolis where they had lived for many years. One of their number, a man called Mersis, said that they had walked for many days in the desert having been harassed by demons with visions of cool water, but God had pulled him safely from their grasp and delivered him to this place."

Banks's narrative is thick with descriptions of Mersis's heroism and virtue, including the assertion that Mersis performed a miracle by predicting the destruction of Alexandria by tsunami in 365 AD. The case for the miracle is pretty thin, in Maddie's view, although necessary to make the case for sainthood, which is clearly Banks's larger objective. It's another quote from Mersis's second-biggest fan, Saint Agapius, who enjoyed telling a story about two young men who came to Mersis for guidance. "They said to him, 'Would it not be a greater test of faith to live in Alexandria, surrounded by every temptation known to man?' And Abba Mersis said to them, 'I have lived in the two greatest cities of my age or any other—Calliopolis and Alexandria. I saw one destroyed by God's wrath; and so the other will be one day.'"

Maddie leans back in her chair, feeling the effects of a rich serving of purple prose.

She's curious, though, about how non-agenda-driven scholars view Calliopolis's Christian history. She turns to Wikipedia and learns that there is some support for the idea that an early monastic community resided at Calliopolis, based on the wall painting (described at length in Banks's book) of a female figure in a head covering dated to the late second or early third century. In Banks's telling, the painting is an image of the Virgin Mary, and the building which houses it is a place of worship—the first Christian church. Other art historians, the internet advises, are divided.

"Ready to go?" Gareth taps on the glass wall of the office. She wonders if he has deliberately cultivated a sexy librarian look. She doubts it; she's guessing that a girlfriend (or boyfriend?) chose the glasses for him.

"Any news?"

Gareth shakes his head. "This part of the process takes ages. They're doing some preliminary modeling. Brett will call when there's something to share. He isn't territorial about this stuff." She hasn't been either, but she's beginning to notice how often people are certifying the trustworthiness of the research team. She has a sense of being managed behind the scenes. What are they afraid she'll do? Take her papyrus and go home?

Gareth leads her out of the lab and walks her across the small, charmingly designed campus. It doesn't take long to arrive at the centerpiece of the plan: a long rectangular building in the classical style, constructed from sand-colored stone and topped with a white balustrade. There is a colonnade on the ground floor, mirrored by high arched windows across the second story. "Welcome to the Cogswell Library," says Gareth.

"It's spectacular," she says.

"It was modeled on the Wren Library at Trinity College at Cambridge," he tells her. "Amazing, isn't it?" Inside, a soaring white ceiling, stained glass, and a marble checkerboard floor give the impression of a cathedral, but instead of pews, carved bookshelves stretch along each wall. "It was built in the 1920s. Before the stock market crash, obviously. Although the Cogswell Company came out of that all right in the end. People kept on eating chocolate."

"Wasn't the Cogswell family based in Boston?" Maddie asks. She visited their chocolate factory as a child; it's as famous in Boston as Ghirardelli is in San Francisco.

"It was. But Mr. Cogswell and his wife wintered in California in their later years. They felt strongly that modern universities were leading young people astray, and that Christian teachings should be part of higher education. As I understand it, a young woman in their family had met a bad end, and they felt she had been encouraged in unhealthy directions by her teachers. They put a lot of their fortune into establishing Resurrection College as an alternative." Maddie wonders what sort of bad end the young Cogswell relative met, and feels a pang of sympathy; if she survived her disgrace, the heavy and permanent judgment of the senior Cogswells must have been a kind of death in itself.

Gareth guides her past the circulation desk and into the staff area. "My colleague is away this month, and is fine for you to use her office," he says. He stops at his own office and ducks inside, returning with a security pass and a key. "The key is for the office, and the pass will get you into the building and the stacks. You're a couple of doors down." Maddie follows him as he unlocks a nearby office. She takes in the view over a peaceful quad. She's planning to use her time here to concentrate on a section of the book proposal that highlights Iris's contribution to the Olsen excavation; this lovely setting is an unexpected gift.

"Thank you," says Maddie. She puts the Mersis book on the desk along with her backpack.

"You can take some time to settle in now, or I can show you where you can find the Mersis materials," he says.

"Let's do it," she says.

In the staff elevator, he says, "I'll be honest: They're in a state. The cataloging is approximately eighty years overdue." He catches her eye. "I'm not joking. These crates arrived at Resurrection College in April 1940." The doors slide open onto a large, austere room. "Here you go. The shame of the Cogswell Library." A series of dusty crates of varying sizes are stacked against a wall, a crowbar resting beside them, along with a heavy pair of gloves. Maddie counts seven crates.

"When did Banks die?" she asks.

"December 31st, 1929. He left his archival material related to *Mersis of Calliopolis* to Resurrection College but instructed his executor to release the bequest ten years after his death. That part seems to have gone according to plan, at least. But then, in May 1940, there was a huge earthquake that damaged the basement. One of the storage rooms caved in and was sealed off. During the war years, there was enormous disruption, and several staff left to fight in Europe. By the time normal life resumed, the crates were forgotten. Then last year, we did a huge renovation down here to create temperature-controlled storage for our ancient manuscripts and take care of some long-overdue earthquake-proofing." Gareth gestures to the boxes. "They opened a wall and found the boxes, pretty much as you see them. Life being what it is, they haven't made it to the top of anyone's priority list yet. So I have a favor to ask."

"Ask away."

"I'm told you're a trained archivist. Would you be willing to start on a catalog of the Banks archive? I'll happily pay you for your time. I'll have my summer interns complete the detailed work, but a basic accounting would be great."

"Not a problem," says Maddie. "Any thoughts on where I should start?"

"Why don't we pick a couple of crates and move them upstairs? I don't want you to have to work down here."

"Seconded," says Maddie.

They return upstairs with two large crates in tow. Gareth gives her directions to a decent lunch spot and promises to check in before the end of the day. Alone in her office at last, Maddie cracks open the first box and finds a collection of monographs about monasticism. She opens a file on her laptop and lists the titles and basic descriptions, as she has promised to do, and then moves on to the second crate.

This one is filled with correspondence, mostly letters between Reverend Banks, his academic colleagues, and his funders. The papers reveal a collection of strange bedfellows united in a quaint passion for a marginal desert cleric: religious figures, both Catholic and Protestant, European and American; academics and hobbyists obsessed with sainthood or monasticism, or both; and moneyed backers with a range of demands and motivations.

Then, halfway through the stack, she finds the last thing she expected: a letter from Clifford Cogswell to Reverend Banks.

December 15, 1903

Dear Reverend Banks,

Further to our earlier correspondence, I write to confirm my pledge of five thousand dollars toward the excavation at Calliopolis. A cheque for half of this amount is enclosed, and may be used for the purpose of Christian study at the site during this season. The second half will be made available for next season, provided that certain conditions are met.

I understand that you are familiar with my wife's niece, Miss Gardiner. It has long been Mrs. Cogswell's wish that her niece return home and take up her position in society.

Consequently, we are placing our trust in you to exercise what influence you can to persuade Miss Gardiner to quit Egypt and sail to America at the earliest opportunity. Should you fail to do this, and should Miss Gardiner determine to remain overseas, the remaining funding will not be forthcoming and I will consider our agreement to be at an end.

Sincerely,
Clifford Cogswell

Helen Gardiner, then, was the Cogswell relation with the unfortunate fate. Maddie wonders what Helen would think of her uncle's establishment of Resurrection College, a monument to her shame. Maddie feels sure that it could not have been the legacy Helen envisioned for herself.

But Maddie cannot know what Helen would have wanted; believing that she does is a simple projection of Maddie's own longing to be seen and understood. She is aware of this. And yet Helen is a presence, appearing unexpectedly, leaving cryptic messages behind. If Maddie believed in ghosts, which she does not, she might imagine that Helen is trying to draw her in. *I am here*, she seems to say. *Find me.*

THIRTEEN

CAIRO, DECEMBER 1903

For the Christmas holiday, Iris invited me to join her in Cairo for a reunion of her University College London classmates at Shepheard's Hotel. The dining room famously produced a ten-course meal on December 25th, she told me, with turkey and plum pudding and other delights like champagne sorbet. And since the ex-pat community was alone in celebrating Christmas at the end of December—the local Christian community observed the holiday on January 7th, on the Julian calendar—the city would be open for business, and we'd have a chance to do some sightseeing.

Olsen agreed to spare us for a long weekend, and that settled it. I took it as evidence that he had finally forgiven me for announcing the Sappho find to Mr. Drake. He considered it a personal affront that I had not consulted him before speaking, perhaps even a deliberate strategy to undermine him, and it had taken all of my persuasive powers to convince him that I had no such intention. The episode had taken an emotional toll on me, and as much as I loved Calliopolis, I was glad to get away for a few days.

I'd bypassed Cairo altogether when I'd arrived in Egypt, seven short weeks ago. The journey had been so arduous—a long day on the railway from Rome to Brindisi, and another three and a half days on the steamer to Alexandria—that I opted to book a sleeper berth on the train and took it all the way to Beni Suef without disembarking. Cairo's distractions, I knew, were innumerable, and I was needed in Calliopolis. I was already late for the beginning of the season, having taken a couple of extra weeks to complete edits on a paper that Professor Wilson and I intended to publish together.

James accompanied us on the train north but left us at the hotel to carry out some business for Emmett. He said he would see us at dinner. When we arrived, it was the middle of the day, and the hotel's activities were in full swing. The building itself was an absolute beauty, its creamy walls glowing in the late sunlight, its broad staircase adorned with ornamental palms in pots. But it was a mere backdrop for the spectacle playing out around it: ladies in extravagant hats eating finger sandwiches and pouring tea on the terrace; carriage drivers jockeying for position at the foot of the stairs; local men in long robes and little red hats hawking souvenirs and being waved off by hotel staff; guests arriving and leaving in a cacophony of languages including French, German, Arabic, and at least two others I didn't recognize; a monkey in a green jacket on a golden lead; and on the roadway itself, bicycles and donkey carts whizzing past at breakneck speed.

Various staff greeted us, took our luggage, and escorted us up the stairs into the lobby. I felt the curious gaze of other travelers lighting on me as I signed the register. There was a giddy atmosphere of high spirits and familiarity, as if we were all guests at the same exclusive party. I had been warned that the rates at Shepheard's were astronomical—it operated at full capacity during the excavation season from November to April and was shuttered for the rest of the year—but even still, I caught my breath when I saw the number in print. "Never mind,

Helen," said Iris, sweeping me away from the desk. "You are my guest this weekend."

"It's too generous, Iris," I said. "We should split expenses."

"We'll discuss it later," she said, which I understood to mean that the discussion was closed. I would have to find a way to repay her kindness, perhaps with a Christmas gift. I intended to visit the famed Khan el-Khalili market while I was here; perhaps I'd find a souvenir for her there. "Oh look, it's Fern and Allan!"

She ran over to a man and woman descending the main staircase. "Engaged!" I heard her exclaim with pleasure. "How wonderful. Come and meet Helen. We must have a toast."

Iris commandeered a table on the crowded terrace and ordered a bottle of champagne. In short order, the table had grown from four to seven, the pop of the cork acting as a kind of summoning bell for British archeologists in the vicinity. I couldn't keep track of the names, but I recognized the sites of their employment: el-Amarna, Karnak, Deir el-Bahri. Two of them—the pair that Iris had greeted in the lobby—had plans to marry in February and were visiting Shepheard's to make the preliminary arrangements. These appeared to fascinate Iris, who was full of questions about the wedding service, clothes, and menu.

The man seated next to me was one I recognized, vaguely, from my time in Rome. He had been a student at the British Academy, I recalled, a friend of one of the English girls who had lived in the same pensione as I did. To the extent that our studies permitted it, the international academic community mixed with each other, especially during the spring lecture season. After winding up their excavations, it was customary for many archeologists to visit Rome, and the schools—German, Swiss, French, British, American, and, of course, Italian—to take turns hosting them for public talks. We were all desperate to hear firsthand what the season's efforts had pulled from the earth in Egypt, Greece, and Mesopotamia.

"Are you staying at the hotel?" I asked.

"Good god, no," he said. "Nice for those who can afford it. No, Pip and I are bunking at a hostel a few blocks from here. This place is for treasure hunters: sportsmen in search of crocodile hides, invalids seeking wholesome air, bored rich people looking for diversion, and ladies wanting husbands."

How had he categorized me? I wondered. I changed the subject. "I believe I recognize you from the lecture circuit in Rome last spring. Where are you excavating?"

"Oxyrhynchus," he said. "With Grenfell and Hunt. And you?"

"Calliopolis," I said. "With Olsen."

"Olsen!" he said. "Were you at his speech last spring at the German Institute?"

I laughed and told him that I had been. It had been a memorable event, with Emmett slinging insults at the French and British teams who had excavated Calliopolis in past seasons. "Is he as disagreeable as he seems?" he asked.

"Not in the least," I said. "He is very respectful." I felt disloyal speaking about Emmett behind his back, even in positive terms. "And how is your experience at Oxyrhynchus? I thought they'd dug up everything they could on their first pass, six years ago. I hope you are finding it worthwhile."

"You know I can't say," he said, but I could tell from the set of his mouth that it had been a disappointment to him so far. "Are you an artist, like Iris?"

"I'm a papyrologist," I said. "Hence my interest in your site."

"Ah," he said, wagging his finger. "I've got it now. You're Percy Wilson's student. There was a rumor circulating in Rome that Olsen had found a scroll, and that he asked Wilson to translate it. Is it true?"

The discovery of the Menander scroll would remain secret until Olsen published on it, likely the following spring. Professor Wilson and I would receive a generous acknowledgment, I was sure. That, along with the essay Professor Wilson and I had submitted short weeks ago about our restoration methods, would secure my career in Egyptology. I did not need to trade confidences. "You know I can't say," I told him, parroting him and earning a sharp look.

"I see," he said. "I shall keep an eye out, then. It sounds as though you've drawn a lucky hand, Miss Gardiner."

"Beware, everyone," said Iris, in an urgent tone. "Guard your tongues. She comes."

"Who comes?" I asked the man next to me.

He turned to look over his shoulder and sighed. "Hortensia Musgrave," he said. "The author of *Miss Musgrave's Advice for the Lady Traveler* books. She is a legendary gossip. Tell her nothing." He rose from his seat, as did the other gentlemen at the table. "Miss Musgrave," he said, executing a small bow. "Roger Adderson. How nice to see you again. Would you like to sit down?"

"I would, thank you, Mr. Adderson." She took his chair, and Roger went to arrange for another small table to be joined to ours, so that he and Miss Musgrave's companion, a young woman carrying a large carpetbag, could sit. Miss Musgrave was a lady in her later years, with gray hair gathered at the nape of her neck, and an enormous bust which seemed to precede her like the prow of a ship. Her skirt and jacket were tailored in a modest navy-blue stripe, but her hat was topped with conspicuous ostrich feathers, which swayed as she walked. She held out a hand to her companion. "My glasses, please."

The young woman extracted a pair of wire-rimmed spectacles from the carpetbag and handed them over. Miss Musgrave's gaze landed on each of us in turn, coolly appraising.

"You are the American girl at Calliopolis this season," she said to me. "Miss Gardiner, am I correct?"

"You are," I told her. "Helen Gardiner. It is a pleasure to meet you."

"You will, of course, know of my books," she said. "Julia!" The girl opened the carpetbag and produced a copy of *Miss Musgrave's Advice for the Lady Traveler in Egypt*, handing it to her employer. "I will sign it for you," said Miss Musgrave, accepting a pen from Julia and writing her name with a flourish. "You will no doubt find it useful, although my publisher is clamoring for an update."

"Thank you," I said, catching Iris's eye and trying not to laugh.

"Miss Baker was the papyrologist at Calliopolis last season," Miss Musgrave continued. "I understand that she fell ill. Poor thing. I hope she is recovering?"

"I cannot say," I told her. "I have not met her."

"Mr. Olsen will be keeping you busy," she said, conspiratorially. "I hear he has found a substantial cache of papyrus."

"Is that so?" I said. "How interesting."

She tilted her head, considering her next move. "I should like to visit Calliopolis," she said, finally. "But sadly, it is not open to tourists except by personal invitation, and Mr. Olsen is one of the least sociable excavators in the Nile Valley. I would like you to put in a word for me."

"I would be delighted," I said. I could predict the words I would receive from Emmett in return, but Miss Musgrave didn't require that information.

"Excellent," she said. She turned her head to scan the terrace, and I saw her eyes light up with malicious intelligence. "Is that Mr. Carter? I'm astonished that he would show his face here."

Howard Carter had been the rising star of the Egyptian Antiquities Service, a favorite of Mr. Maspero, who had named him chief inspector after several stunning successes in the Valley of the Kings. But his fortunes had soured earlier in the autumn when he was called to a break-in at Saqqara. The intruders were French tourists, made violent by drink and arrogance, and they attacked the Egyptian monument sentries who were Mr. Carter's employees. Mr. Carter instructed his men to defend themselves. Far from humbled, the French complained to their consulate, which contacted Mr. Maspero and insisted on an apology. Mr. Carter had refused to provide one, and he was now out of a job. It was a cautionary tale, I thought, about the consequences of siding with local people against the Europeans. However reprehensible their behavior, the French controlled excavation in Egypt.

"Why do you say so?" I asked. "He was badly used, in my opinion. I would have done the same."

Miss Musgrave laughed. It was a tinny sound, utterly without joy. "I can imagine that you would," she said. "You have a great deal to learn, I see."

Iris sprang to my defense. "Miss Gardiner is a newcomer, true, but there are few minds to match hers in Egyptology, I assure you."

She had drawn Miss Musgrave's fire and now had to endure it. "And where is Mr. Dunn, Miss Wentworth? I thought I saw him arrive with you. Julia noticed him right away. She finds him quite a striking figure." Julia made a small noise of protest, but Miss Musgrave waved her off. "There is no shame in it. He is a fine-looking man. Perhaps you feel the same, Miss Wentworth? You needn't worry. I keep Julia very busy indeed. I receive reams of correspondence from my readers, as you can imagine. No, Julia is no danger to you."

Iris looked furious, and Julia's face was bright red. She looked to be near tears. Miss Musgrave raised a glass of champagne and sipped it, triumphant. "So, Miss Gardiner. What does a mind as fine as yours plan to do in Cairo?"

"I intend to see the museum," I told her. "I thought I might go tomorrow."

"But that is exactly what we are doing!" she said, clapping her hands. "Mr. Maspero himself is providing me with a tour of the facilities in Tahrir Square. I'm preparing a new edition of the guidebook with up-to-date floor plans." She smiled, but it did not reach her eyes. "You will join us. You cannot possibly refuse."

FOURTEEN

SACRAMENTO, 2019

"You're not bad with a crowbar," Maddie tells Gareth. He's a Midwestern farm boy, she's learned, handy with tools and cheerful in the execution of physical tasks. When she asked him to have someone move the remaining crates to her office, he volunteered for the job himself. There's still a farm, he tells her (corn and soybeans, Iowa), and his oldest brother plans to take it over when his father retires.

"Farming wasn't for you?" Maddie asks.

"God, no," he says. "I miss the farm sometimes, mostly the open sky, but not the life. It's punishing, and it never lets up. School was such a luxury by comparison."

It occurs to Maddie that Gareth has a better attitude than most people she's met in university communities. Revise that: than most people she's met. He has the personality of an early summer day: sunny, open, fresh, and full of possibility. He has none of the changeability of May or the lassitude of August about him.

Gareth stands and brushes the cobwebs from his pants. "Okay, then. I'm off to the lab. I have a meeting before the big show. I'll see you in an hour or so?"

"You bet." The papyrus is coming out of the vault today, to be subjected to whatever Brett and his team have devised for it.

Maddie has time to unpack one more crate, which she drags across the floor to the desk. She curses as she feels a splinter prick her thumb and grits her teeth as she lifts the lid that Gareth has loosened for her. More books. It seems that Reverend Banks bequeathed his library and the contents of his desk to Resurrection College, assuming they would be as fascinating to scholars as they were to him. Or perhaps trying to bring decades of paperwork into a semblance of order was more than he could face.

She reminds herself that she had no expectations of the archive until she found the letter about Helen. If it is the only treasure, it will be worth the annoyance. She continues cataloging the titles, one by one. Before returning them to the crates, she pages through each, checking for hidden letters like a detective in a Christie novel, but there are none.

As she works, she thinks about Clifford Cogswell's letter to Reverend Banks. It outrages her, this barter between men: Helen's dreams were nothing to them. At the same time, she feels Helen's loss with renewed poignancy; Helen had people who cared about her, worried about her safety, grieved her death and built a memorial to her—the very library in which Maddie now finds herself.

When Maddie arrives at the lab, she sees Brett in his glassed-in office, along with Gareth and two men she doesn't know. Brett catches her eye, waves, and beckons her over. "Maddie," he says as she opens the door, "I want to introduce you to Simon Cogswell and Michael Grey." She shakes their hands, noting the Cogswell surname. "Simon is a great champion of our research. And Michael is an antiquities expert. They couldn't wait to see the scroll, so we've given them special dispensation to be here. Gentlemen, follow me and I'll get you signed in. Gareth, why don't you give the box to the team, and they'll start setting up the scan."

Gareth looks uncharacteristically tense and unhappy as he surrenders the red lacquered box. Maddie stands with him in the control room of the scanning area as the activity ramps up around them. She wants to ask what's wrong, but it's a small space with too many people milling about. Two technicians take the box into the X-ray zone, open it, and gently lift out a container with a honeycomb pattern, placing it on a pedestal inside the X-ray machine.

Brett comes over to stand with them. "We fabricated the container specifically for your scroll from the photographs we took when it arrived," he says. "Rebecca is the only person who is authorized to touch it outside the container. It's still inside the linen bag."

"Do you want to stay in the control room while we do the scans?" Gareth asks her. "Fair warning, it can get claustrophobic in here."

Maddie can see his point. "Maybe Brett could explain the process to me, and I'll wait outside until you're done?"

Brett nods. "Let me show you the machine up close." The scanner is a large, white open cube, with a film projector on one side and a little stand in the middle. "This is a micro-CT scanner, which is short for micro-computed tomography. It's like a CT scan in a medical context, but the resolution is many times higher." He points to the projector. "That's the X-ray generator, and opposite, there's an X-ray detector. And in the middle, we have the scroll. The platform is called the rotation stage. It spins a fraction of a degree after every image is taken. Are you with me so far?"

"Just barely," says Maddie.

Brett smiles and continues. "The images are two-dimensional, but we take them in slices, all the way through the object. And once we have all the slices, we can use a computer program to reconstruct a three-dimensional model."

"But you want it in two dimensions, so you can read it."

"We do. But the first set of scans aren't two-dimensional like a flat page. Have you ever sliced a leek open?" She has. "That's what the initial two-dimensional scans are like, basically. To get to a two-dimensional object you can read, you need to run the three-dimensional model through a computer program that digitally unrolls it."

"Brett is being modest, as usual," says Gareth. "He's famous for this technique. He wrote a computer program that can take the 3D model and turn it into a flat document."

Brett waves off the compliment. He's only a technician, he says. He needs a scholar like Rebecca to give his contribution meaning. "As much as I wish I could, I can't read the documents. I can only make them readable."

A graduate student comes over to tell Brett that the setup is complete. "Wonderful," he says. "Maddie, let me take you down the hall to the lounge. It will be more comfortable for you to wait there."

"I'll take her," says Gareth. "You've got your hands full. Ready?" They exit the lab, and he leads the way to a bright room with soft seating and an espresso machine overlooking a leafy quad.

"Is there something you want to tell me?" she asks. "You seem upset with Brett. What's going on?"

"It's Michael Grey," he says, his brow creased with worry. "Brett has no business letting him get this close to an artifact under the library's care. I don't trust him. Simon Cogswell is bad enough."

"Didn't Brett say that Michael was an antiquities expert? Maybe Brett wanted his expertise for some reason."

"He's an antiquities *dealer*," says Gareth. "Not the same thing at all. Although he is very knowledgeable. I'll give him that."

"And what's your beef with Simon?"

"Let's sit for a minute," he says, pointing to a sofa by the window.

Simon, he explains, is Clifford's grandson, the current CEO of the Cogswell Chocolate Company, and, through his foundation, the main funder of Brett's lab. A warning sizzles in Maddie's belly. It dawns on her, belatedly, that Brett is beholden to others beyond the university for his livelihood. "That sounds like a complicated relationship," she says.

"Donors are always complicated," Gareth says, matter-of-factly. "But universities can't survive without them, and if you want to rise in the ranks, you have to make donor relations part of your skill set. I don't blame Brett for trying to keep Simon happy by giving him exclusive access. But he's a collector, and he's brought his agent with him. That's taking donor relations too far, in my opinion." He shakes his head. "Brett gives everyone the benefit of the doubt. It's a nice quality, but not when the stakes are this high. Anyway. I wanted you to know who the players are. You deserve to be kept in the loop." He touches her arm. "I have to get back, but I have my phone with me. Text me if you need anything."

Maddie sets up her computer and opens the search engine. There are several pages of articles about Michael Grey, who appears to be the dealer of choice for wealthy Americans who aren't fussy about provenance and want artifacts from the Middle East. Occasionally, his clients have been asked to return cultural treasures intercepted by anti-smuggling agencies—a box of ancient cuneiform tablets from Iraq entering the US labeled as "tile samples," as one example—but so far, Michael Grey has been clever—and lucky—enough to avoid prosecution.

The door to the lounge opens and admits the very subject of her research, along with his Cogswell client. Maddie shuts her laptop with some force. "Top secret?" asks Michael Grey, and she laughs nervously.

"You startled me," she says. "I must be jumpy about the results of the scan." She goes over to the espresso maker and prepares herself an Americano. Caffeine is the last thing she needs right now, but it gives her a task.

She feels a presence at her shoulder. "Would you mind making a second one?" Michael asks. "I'm hopeless with these gadgets."

Michael isn't the first man she's met who knows how to deploy learned helplessness. Still, she makes him coffee. She's curious about him. "Would you like to join me?" she asks.

He thanks her and takes the chair opposite her. His expression is appraising, as if he is assessing her worth. He says, "I wonder if you realize just how significant this find could be."

It would be easy to take offense. At another time, she might. But today, she wants to borrow his expertise. "Tell me," she says.

"A new artifact hasn't surfaced from Calliopolis in decades. And after King Tut's tomb, it's probably the best-known excavation in the history of Egyptology, justifiably so. It has ancient temples, classical literature, Greco-Roman paintings, Christian artifacts. Extraordinary." He takes a sip of his coffee, then puts the cup down on the table between them.

"You will be under a great deal of pressure, and quickly, if Brett and Rebecca are correct in their suspicions."

She glances over to where Simon Cogswell sits on the other side of the room, apparently riveted by his phone. If he isn't eavesdropping on their conversation, she's sure that Michael will repeat it to him later. Already the circle of interested parties is larger than she can manage, and those are only the people she knows about. "What do you suggest?"

Michael reaches into the inner pocket of his jacket and pulls out a small silver case. He opens it and hands Maddie a business card. "You may find yourself in need of an expert. If you do, please call. Whatever you may have heard about me, you won't find anyone more knowledgeable when it comes to what artifacts from Calliopolis are worth, and who wants to own them."

She takes the card. "You mentioned Christian artifacts," she says. "I've been looking through the Banks archive here."

"The lost archive," he says. "Interesting."

"Not so far," she says, and he laughs. He's offered his expertise, and they have time on their hands, so Maddie asks him to tell her about Calliopolis's Christian history. Why had it captured the fascination of Banks and so many others over the years?

"Great question," says Michael. "If you've been in his archive, you probably already know that Alistair Banks believed Calliopolis to be the site of one of the earliest Christian communities." She nods. "While excavating there, he discovered a wall painting of a woman with a covered head. He believed that it marked the location of the first Christian church in Egypt, or even in history. A very holy site, if true."

"Is it?"

"Unlikely in the extreme," he says. Art historians, he explains, have considerable doubts as to the subject of the painting. "Banks's theory rests on the idea that the painting is an image of the Virgin Mary. But it's an atypical rendering for an altarpiece. Recent scholarship suggests that the painting isn't a religious work at all, but a portrait of someone who lived in the community. It's artistically very similar to some of the mummy portraits from the site. More to the point, Banks found very little else in his excavation—pottery shards and other relics of daily life, but nothing shedding light on the nature of the religious life of the community."

"And Mersis?" asks Maddie. "Where does all of that leave him?"

"Deprived of sainthood, alas," says Michael. "A source of great sadness for Reverend Banks. There are many, Simon included, who would be happy to champion an application even today, but the Vatican has made it clear that there isn't enough evidence yet."

"Yet?"

"You'd be amazed at what is sitting in private collections. Every year, things turn up that no one knew existed. In Egypt, theft seems to have been the rule rather than the exception. Everyone pocketed a piece or two—local diggers, tourists, archeologists, even museum directors were selling collections out the back door." Michael's eyes are cool. "It's easy to be high-minded about artifacts, but they are valuable commodities, and they get traded that way. Not only by individuals either. By governments. By museums. You think you'll never want my advice, and you aren't the first. But if you find yourself holding an object of great value, you'd do well to call, especially if there's a question of provenance. My motivations are a lot more straightforward than some others you may encounter."

Gareth comes into the room and stops when he sees Maddie talking to Michael. "He's worried I'm trying to corrupt you," says Michael.

"Aren't you?" she asks. And then to Gareth, "Are the scans done?"

"We're ready for you," he says.

In the lab, a small crowd of technicians and librarians gather in front of a large television screen mounted on the wall. Nearby, Brett sits at a computer. Rebecca stands just behind him with a hand on his shoulder. Maddie walks over to them, and watches Rebecca's hand fall away and glide into her pocket.

Brett's smile is bright. "We've had a good day," he says. "The data collection went as smoothly as it could have, and we were able to create the model very easily, with just a few tweaks. Look."

On his screen, Maddie can see an image of a scroll rotating in space, the exterior covered in symbols. Rebecca wears an expression of pure delight.

"What do you see?" Maddie asks her.

"Nothing I can read yet, but the script is uncial, which is what we'd expect to see for a literary scroll."

"And?" Maddie is sure Rebecca sees more than she's saying.

"And let's see it unrolled before I comment further." She looks almost playful.

The television screen lights up with the feed from Brett's computer.

"All right, everyone," says Brett. "Remember that this doesn't always work the first time. We may have to adjust the calculations as we go. Ready? Three, two, one . . ." The digital scroll begins to unroll to its full length.

"Oh, wow," says Rebecca, softly. One of the graduate students starts to cry.

Gareth whistles. "Will you look at that," he says. He moves closer to Brett and leans in, peering at his computer screen.

"Can you zoom in?" asks Rebecca. The camera pans in on a section of text. Maddie hears Rebecca catch her breath. "I'd like to start the translation right away," she says.

"What do you see?" Maddie asks.

"It's Eolic," Rebecca says. "I thought it might be. It's a rare dialect. Only a couple of surviving poets are known to have written in it. The most famous of whom was Sappho."

FIFTEEN

CAIRO, DECEMBER 1903

In the morning, I woke to a rose-colored dawn, the call to prayer echoing in the streets below me. It was an eerie sound, utterly foreign, entrancing. In her bed, Iris slept on, so I slid out from my own as quietly as I could and went to the window, where I watched the sun wash over the city as it climbed, light spilling downward from the spires of the minarets, and illuminating the date trees and gray-green palms in the hotel garden.

"What time are you meeting Miss Musgrave?" Iris's voice sounded fuzzy. I had excused myself after dinner, but she had stayed out into the small hours. I poured her a glass of water, which she accepted gratefully. None of her party would be joining the excursion to the museum.

"Eight o'clock," I told her. "We have been given a half hour's grace before the general public is allowed inside. Are you sure you don't want to come?"

"With that old witch? Hardly." Iris pulled the covers over her head. From beneath the bedclothes, her muffled voice asked me to send her kind regards to Mr. Maspero, and to tell him she would be by later in the day to view the items for sale in the museum's shop. I told her I would scout the offerings for her in advance.

"Angel," she said. I think she may have been asleep again before I left the room.

I didn't relish the prospect of Miss Musgrave's company, but she was offering a rare opportunity to see the collections with the museum's director. Mr. Maspero had his detractors, but they could only envy his astonishing range of talents. I was excited to meet him at last. Even without the lure of an introduction, it would have felt wrong to deny Julia Melton a few hours of relief; she seemed the sort of person who rarely asked for anything and expected nothing.

In our carriage, Miss Musgrave held forth on the landmarks of Cairo. She was at least a very informed guide, and when she drew a breath, I asked her about visiting the Khan el-Khalili market. "You must," she said. "But not under any circumstances without a chaperone. I could escort you in the morning, if you like."

"It pains me to say that I cannot," I told her, insincerely. "My schedule is not my own this week, and I may simply send a courier into the market for a few supplies. Perhaps you would be so kind as to write down the name of the shop you recommend for European medicines?" I hoped to replenish our pharmacy cupboard while I was in Cairo. Scrapes and infections were common on an excavation site, and we went through our supplies quickly.

"It is in my book," she said. "Julia will show you." And Julia pulled another copy of Miss Musgrave's guide from her omnipresent carpetbag and identified the relevant page. I wondered how many books she was required to haul around at any given time.

Our carriage pulled up in front of a spectacular edifice in salmon pink, decorated with white pillars, arches, and reliefs. "My goodness," I said. "How lovely. It is not what I expected."

"Far too showy, in my opinion. But what can you expect? Designed by the French, built by the Italians. Ah, here is our host now."

A compact gentleman with spectacles and a neat mustache and beard walked down the front steps to meet us. "Mademoiselle Musgrave, Mademoiselle Melton, what a pleasure to see you." He kissed each of their hands in turn.

"Mr. Maspero. May I present Miss Gardiner. She is helping Mr. Olsen at Calliopolis. A papyrologist."

Mr. Maspero tilted his head. "A papyrologist!" he said. "I will apologize in advance for the focus of our tour today. Miss Musgrave was quite specific in her requirements. The general tourist is not typically as interested in our papyri as he is in our monuments and our mummies. But we can arrange for another opportunity to view the collection."

"I'm honored to meet you," I said, honestly. "And to see the museum. I've heard that the design alone is worth the visit. Iris Wentworth is a friend and a colleague. She asked me to tell you that she intends to purchase some items from you." Iris had grown up in Oxford, where her father was a faculty member, but her parents had relocated to Canada in recent months. Professor Wentworth had taken a post as the first curator of a new museum in Toronto, and he was eager to make a few acquisitions.

"Very good," said Mr. Maspero. "I have some crocodile mummies from Tebtunis that might serve. I'll check our stock after the tour."

"Miss Gardiner was a last-minute addition to our party," said Miss Musgrave. "She is content to fall in with our agreed-upon schedule. If you do not mind, I should like to make a start on it."

"Quite right. My apologies," he said. "This way, please." He led us inside.

I caught my breath, and Mr. Maspero beamed at me. "It strikes me the same way," he said. "The first true museum on the African continent, and the first in the world dedicated to the study of the ancient Egyptians." We stood in a rotunda, natural light pouring though a high dome set all the way around with windows. Ahead of us stretched a long, vaulted hallway, double height, with stone monuments set at regular intervals between archways. The ceiling of the corridor was also made of glass, and the sunlight illuminated the profiles of the ancient pharaohs seated against the walls on massive granite thrones and the glossy sarcophagi spaced neatly along the floor. "If we had more time, I'd show you the basement," he said. "It is an engineering marvel—pillars, bearing walls, vaults. Built to support the heaviest objects on display anywhere in the world. And the library, and the conservation laboratory . . ."

"Mr. Maspero," said Miss Musgrave, with asperity. "We should move along. Our agenda is very full."

"Forgive me," he said. "Thank you for intervening before I started in on the ventilation system. It is a particular preoccupation of mine. Now, as we have fifty-one galleries on this floor, and fifty-five on the upper floor, and three hours, I'm afraid I've had to be extremely selective." He began to walk through the principal gallery, at a fast clip. "In this wing, we have the treasures of the Memphite Empire, many of which are already covered in your guidebook, Miss Musgrave. This is the period from 5000 BC until roughly 3100 BC, which produced, in my opinion, the finest examples of sculpture from the ancient Egyptians. The sculpture portraits here are of great religious significance and are meant to represent the dead individual in form and feature, and in the activities he enjoyed during his mortal life."

He stopped at a case and pointed. "The dwarf Khnumhotep. One of my personal favorites. You see how the body is rendered? It is ideal but not imaginary. The limbs are short. And the expression! The half smile, the glint of humor and intelligence. A remarkable piece." He moved us through several additional rooms before stopping at another portrait sculpture. "One of the most lifelike in the collection: Prince Rahotep and his wife, Nofret, dating from the end of the Third Dynasty. Look at the eyes." I did. It was uncanny: The eyeballs seemed to move and follow us. "There is an opaque quartz ball in the eye socket, with a quartz iris, and a metal pupil. Exquisite workmanship, from an artist who died before the pyramids were constructed."

We continued moving through the rooms at speed, thousands of years unfolding at a glance. The names of great cities flashed by, typed on white cards by the displays: Thinis, Tanis, Heliopolis, Bubastis, Hermopolis Parva, Elephantine. "I will make sure to come back at the end of my contract and spend more time," I said, as much to myself as to Mr. Maspero. It was unbearable to leave so many priceless works unexamined. "I could happily spend weeks with this collection."

"I have spent years," he said. "And I still find fresh pleasures every day." We crossed to the east wing and walked through the rooms dedicated to the Theban Empire, from the period 3100 BC to 1000 BC, pausing at a funeral stela from Abydos, and at a colossal statue in red granite from Karnak. In the central atrium, we paused before heading upstairs.

"I see empty pedestals," said Miss Musgrave.

"You are quite correct," said Mr. Maspero. "We will have obelisks and additional colossi here, but for now, they remain in situ. It is an undertaking to transport them, to say the least. The budget is another preoccupation of mine, even more tiresome than the ventilation." He guided us to the staircase. "The upper floor has all of the objects without excessive weight," he explained as we climbed. "The mummies and their coffins, which are extremely popular with tourists, but also household objects, jewelry, tomb furniture, and so on. I suspect you may not be as compelled by the mummies, Miss Gardiner, and I will not be at all offended if you wish to explore on your own. Rooms G, H, and I have all our papyri. They are mostly examples from the Book of the Dead, some of which are very fine."

He explained how I might find them, and I parted company with the group; Miss Musgrave was clearly put out, and Julia disappointed, but they would recover. As I walked, I stopped with pleasure at some of the cases holding small, everyday objects that wouldn't merit inclusion in Miss Musgrave's opus: the perfume boxes and children's games, the musical instruments, the sandals made from plaited rushes, the simple linen shirts that had somehow survived the ages.

The papyrus rooms were quiet; I had them to myself. Mr. Maspero was correct. The collection was exceptional and almost exclusively funereal in nature, and I wondered how many of the specimens had come from cartonnage. I smiled to myself, remembering my aunt's reaction when Reverend Banks had explained the term to her. Unlike the other items on Mr. Maspero's tour, papyrus was a treasure for the initiated, hiding in plain sight.

―――

We returned to the hotel for lunch, and I found Iris sitting on the terrace. She agreed to accompany me to the market, and I went to ask the concierge to arrange it. He was perturbed. "I cannot recommend visiting Khan el-Khalili without a guide," he said. "It is a dangerous place for ladies."

"Find us a guide then," I said. "Or I could do so myself, if you wish, by hailing one of the men out front." The concierge radiated distress, and I softened my tone. "I have lived independently for some years. Perhaps you might direct me toward a driver you trust?"

We went outside, and the concierge gestured to an Egyptian dressed in traditional clothing with a red felt cap. "This is Ali, Miss Gardiner, Miss Wentworth," he said. "Ali, our guests wish to visit the Grand Bazaar. You must accompany them at all times." I greeted Ali in Arabic, to both men's surprise; Ali seemed delighted, and praised my skill in the language. I gave the concierge a cheerful wave as we set off at a trot.

"We are quite capable of exploring the market on our own, you know," I told Ali as we drove.

"Of course, madam," he said. "I would not have thought otherwise."

We arrived at the market as the vendors were opening for the day. Ali brought the carriage to a halt outside an ancient stone arch carved with Oriental designs. I recognized it from my Baedeker Guide as the al-Ghuri gate, dating from the early sixteenth century and in an exceptional state of preservation. After a spirited debate as to the wisdom of unchaperoned exploration, Ali agreed to meet us at the same gate in two hours' time. But meanwhile, the winding medieval streets and archways beckoned.

At the entrance to the souk, we passed carpet merchants and silversmiths, and a sword maker, sparks flying as he sharpened a fearsome blade on a whetstone. A water merchant pulled buckets from a well and filled huge earthenware jugs, which young women then placed on top of their heads and carried away, their hips swaying under layers of draped skirts. A woman in a headscarf crouched before a millstone, her face lined with the labor of decades, her golden bracelets clinking as she crushed her grain. Next door, several boys shoveled flat rounds of dough in and out of a clay oven on a wooden paddle, filling the street with the fragrance of warm bread. A veiled lady riding a donkey disturbed a flock of pigeons, which took flight, surrounding her in a cloud of wings, so that only her jeweled slippers were visible. There were sellers of copper, of saddles, of slippers, of lanterns, all of them calling and waving at our approach, and adopting expressions of extravagant disappointment as we passed by. At one point, I saw a man who looked suspiciously like Ali dart behind a pillar as I turned my head.

"We are being followed," I told Iris.

"You can hardly blame him," she said. "His livelihood depends on the concierge at the hotel. He has his instructions."

"Did you know he would shadow us?"

"Of course," said Iris. "The concierge wasn't wrong, you know. It can be dangerous here. It's good to have some protection against pickpockets. Ali will call out if they try anything with us."

Before long, we arrived in a different part of the market. The streets were quieter there, and wider, with storefronts rather than stalls. I'd seen engravings of Old Cairo, but they had failed to capture the intricacy of the window lattices, the metalwork, or the mosaic tiles on the buildings. The houses were high and tall, the upper floors projecting outward. The effect was one of ornate building blocks on the verge of toppling into the street.

"Oh, look!" said Iris, pointing to a window display of brightly colored jewelry boxes. "Aren't they charming?" We entered the shop and discovered that the boxes were made to order, with secret compartments and hieroglyphic messages painted to the buyer's specifications. I ordered two of them, one for me and one for Iris, as a Christmas gift and to thank her for inviting me as her guest. I had our boxes personalized with our hieroglyphic names, adding to my own a favorite spell from the Book of the Dead, the Spell to Repel Reptiles and Snakes: "Get back! Crawl away! Get away from me, for you shall be decapitated with a knife!" The wording had always amused me. The seller assured me that the boxes would arrive at Beni Suef within the month.

We continued wandering, and soon arrived in the quarter reserved for serious buyers of antiques and antiquities. I recognized the names of famous dealers like Albert Eid & Co. and the Khawam Brothers. It was a known risk to buy in these shops if you planned to remove your purchases from the country; more than one enthusiastic collector had been separated from their acquisitions at the border. It was recommended that collectors buy directly from Mr. Maspero's sale room at the museum, where you could be sure that the objects had been verified as genuine, had been excavated legally, and had been cleared by the government for export. But I had seen those finds firsthand this morning, and they were mediocre at best, Mr. Maspero having deemed them unworthy of public display.

I peered into a window for a closer look at an alabaster statue and stopped short. There was a man inside the shop that I recognized. I watched him place a box on the counter and open it for inspection by the dealer. I did not want him to see me. I spun around and took Iris's arm, pulling her away. "We should experience a real Egyptian café," I said. "Can you smell that coffee?"

Iris inhaled deeply and turned in the direction of the scent, as I had wanted her to do. I waved, and Ali dashed to our side. Within minutes we were seated in an alleyway outside the El-Fishawy Café, surrounded by men puffing on water pipes who stared at us openly. The dark Turkish brew was stronger than the Italian espresso I had come to love as a student in Rome, but still wonderful.

"Did you have fun last night?" I asked Iris.

"Great fun," she said. "We went to the Sphinx Bar and stayed out until three in the morning. James met up with us, and he fit right in with the group. I'm sorry you missed it."

"Next time," I said. I did not say that I had seen James just now, through the window of the antiquities shop. I did not say that he had been carrying an excavation box.

SIXTEEN

SACRAMENTO, 2019

Several days after the big reveal, Brett's team continues to process the scans, a time-consuming and impenetrable activity that thrills Brett and his initiates but no one else. Brett has announced that the ink is carbon, which means he can use an infrared filter. He is jubilant. "We should be able to see some text from the underside of the first layer of the scroll," he tells Maddie.

Maddie envies Brett's energy and focus. After several days of earnest activity, she has sent a couple of chapter outlines to Pete for approval. She's heard nothing since his reply email: *Great! Will review.* So she waits, for Pete's comments and for Brett's lab tests, bouncing between hope, irritation, and anxiety. In the meantime, she reads Julia Melton Dunn's memoir, Pete's gift to her on her arrival in San Francisco. It's not revelatory, to say the least, but it gives Maddie some insight into the gossip circulating in the Egyptology community following Helen's death.

> Miss Musgrave was distressed to learn that I would be leaving her employment, and this perhaps explains her behavior, while not excusing it. She advised me to return James's ring, as Miss Wentworth had done.

She had heard rumors, she told me, which she declined to share for fear of reprisal. She would only say that there were those at the highest levels of authority who were not satisfied with the investigation into the deaths at Calliopolis. She felt strongly that I should not form a connection to someone who had been at the center of the tragic events.

I replied that whatever cloud had settled over Calliopolis under Mr. Drake and Mr. Olsen had surely passed with the former's death and the latter's departure from the site. It is no secret that Mr. Olsen had a weakness for drink, that he and Mr. Drake quarreled excessively, and that the excavation lacked the decorum and discipline necessary for safe and effective operation. Under the circumstances, it is hardly surprising that the concession had been removed from American hands and awarded to the British, who wisely appointed James as their lead excavator, a display of confidence that should quiet even those most inclined to suspicion.

Suffice it to say that my friendship with Miss Musgrave withered thereafter. I observed latterly that she did not hesitate to promote the so-called Curse of Calliopolis in her subsequent guide to Egypt, and I concluded that whatever rumors she had referenced in our conversation had been as fantastical as the ones she published for profit.

No wonder she wrote a memoir, thinks Maddie. Obviously, the stink of foul deeds had lingered around James even as he advanced in his career. His wife's desperation to paint him as a man of unimpeachable moral fiber oozed from the pages of her book. It didn't make for scintillating reading.

Gareth knocked on her office door. "Tacos?" he asks.

"How did you know?"

"That you'd want tacos? Who doesn't?"

They walk a few blocks to a food truck, parked near a landscaped plaza. They sit and eat under a generous oak, and Maddie relaxes as the midday heat melts the air-conditioning from her body.

"How did you get into archeological history?" asks Gareth.

"Archeology's the family business," she says. "Iris Wentworth—the woman I wrote about for my dissertation—was the first of three generations of female archeologists in my family. She trained her daughter, Alma, who in turn trained her son, my father. My mother was one of my grandmother Alma's graduate students; that's how my parents met. They all excavated at K'abel, in Mérida, Mexico." An image of her mother arises, sitting in shadow at the foot of the Pyramid of the Jade Queen, her long hair—dark but with wings of silver at her temples—clipped in an untidy bun.

"But you didn't become a field archeologist. You weren't tempted to continue the tradition?"

"When I was a kid, I thought I would. K'abel was my family home. I couldn't imagine another life for a long time." She tells him about the site, one of the great cities of the Mayan empire, a once-thriving city of ten thousand people that dominated the region for five hundred years before fading, abruptly and mysteriously, in the mid-ninth century. She tells him about the temples and pyramids, the sculptures and colonnades, the ball courts and the funerary monuments. She tells him about the hacienda where her family lives. A stately home on a prosperous sisal plantation during the colonial period, it's now divided up: The main floor is shared between her family's residence and the K'abel Museum, while the upper floors are broken into apartments for graduate students and visiting archeologists.

Maddie has learned more about K'abel in her brief time at the Alcott Library. After Drake's death, Nora turned her attention to New World archeology and, over time, K'abel became her singular focus. She was K'abel's major funder for the first half-century of excavations there. Nora's records are meticulous, and there are copious documents in storage relating to the site, starting with the purchase agreement for Hacienda K'abel in 1909.

The agreement covers both the house and the monuments on the property, most of them buried and overgrown at the time.

Most of the records are enclosed in letters from Nora's property manager, Claude Butler, who tracked all expenditures relating to the site and oversaw operations at K'abel in Nora's absence. The letter foisting Claude on Iris is an amusing insight into Iris's administrative skills, or at least Nora's opinion of them. (*"I am sending you a personal secretary, Claude Butler. I have trained him myself to the highest standards. You have met him, and I know that you will welcome him. I will continue to pay all of his expenses; you need only accept his help. He will free you from the tedium of bookkeeping and oversight of workers, so that you may concentrate on those activities which best employ your considerable skills."*)

"That sounds like a romantic way to grow up," says Gareth.

"I loved it as a young kid," Maddie tells him. "It was a whole different story when I hit adolescence. I wanted to be in Toronto with my friends. I hated that I had to leave at Christmas every year and do my studies by correspondence during the winter term. My mother was pushing my father to change their routine so that I could do middle school and high school without moving around, but he was—is—extremely stubborn and absorbed in his work."

There were always graduate students at K'abel, she tells him. To her, they were objects of adoration: smart, young, beautiful. She followed them around, eavesdropping on their conversations, only to discover that they complained, bitterly, about her: how she distracted them, how her mother prevailed on them to babysit. It was a humiliation unlike any Maddie had experienced before.

"I thought they might miss me if I disappeared for a while," she tells Gareth. "So one day, late in the afternoon when everyone was tired and distracted, I ran away, into the jungle." Even now, she can remember the satisfying tang of revenge as the jungle closed around her, the green light trickling through the dense thickets of branches and leaves, how quickly the sounds of the excavation site were replaced with the immediacy of rustling and crackling, trilling and cawing. She remembers the sun dropping like a stone after she realized she was lost. Her back against a tree, calling for help and hearing only the scuffle of invisible creatures.

"How long were you out there?" asks Gareth. His eyes are kind. "You must have been terrified."

"A few hours," she says. "They acted fast, and I knew enough to stay in one place. I was covered in bugbites and scratches, but that was all. The bigger consequence was that my mother put her foot down, and the two of us moved back to Toronto. She went to K'abel in the summer, and I went to camp in Algonquin Park."

"Your dad didn't join you in Toronto?"

"Rarely," she says. "He came a few times a year for a visit. I realized over time that their marriage was difficult. I think the separation agreed with them. My mom and I settled into life in Toronto pretty quickly. I was happy, and I think she was too. She taught at the university and wrote a few books, and I went to school and did teenage things. I didn't spend any significant time at K'abel again until I went down to do research for my PhD."

"Are you and your mom still close?" asks Gareth.

The excavation lacked the decorum and discipline necessary for safe and effective operation. A line from Julia Melton Dunn's memoir rises in Maddie's mind unbidden, bringing with it darker thoughts of K'abel. Maddie swallows, her throat suddenly dry. "Yeah," she says. She checks the time on her phone. "Alistair Banks is calling my name. Are you ready to go?"

Truthfully, there isn't any urgency. She's been going through Alistair Banks's crates slowly, drawing out the task, resisting the inevitability of another dead end, and dead time. Gareth has cracked the lids on the remaining four crates, and she chooses one at random and sets the lid aside, expecting to see the requisite neat rows of religious texts. Instead, she sees a metal box.

She texts a quick note to Gareth and then extracts the box, placing it on her desk. The lid has been scratched, as if to remove a mark; she can see some flecks of red paint that have escaped the knife. She fiddles with the clasp, which squeaks but gives way, and then peers inside. Tiny scraps of papyrus flutter at the disturbance of air, and she closes the lid hurriedly. The scratches, she now notices, are not only on the lid but also on the front edge of the box, above the clasp. She's seen photographs of the storage boxes from Calliopolis, with catalog numbers painted in these exact spots. *Don't get carried away*, she thinks.

Gareth walks in. "The library got a lot more interesting when you showed up," he says with a grin. He opens his satchel and brings out a pair of cloth gloves and a pencil case. He extracts a pair of tweezers from the case, puts on the gloves, and opens the box.

"Is it what I think it is?" she asks.

"It's definitely a box of papyrus fragments," he says. He leans in further. "Hang on. Do you see that?" He points. "There's a piece of linen poking up right there." He takes the tweezers and moves several fragments aside, revealing a stained scrap of linen, then sits back on his heels.

"Is that what I think it is?" asks Maddie. She has seen ancient linen before, concealed in her own jewelry box. She wills herself to be calm. What is the likelihood of two such discoveries in a lifetime? Vanishingly small, she knows.

"If you're thinking there's a scroll underneath all of these scraps, I'm right there with you," he says. He looks at her, shaking his head slightly. "This is a lot of excitement for a country boy, Maddie. Let's get this out of the library and over to the lab, pronto. Can you tell Brett we're coming?"

"On it," she says, tapping out a text. "And I'm letting Pete know as well. He loves a bit of drama."

Gareth raises an eyebrow. "You said it, not me."

It's only a ten-minute walk to the lab, but Gareth drives, piloting his ancient Honda Civic with Maddie in the passenger seat, clutching the box. "Try not to get us killed," she says.

"That," he says, tearing around a corner, "is exactly my objective here." He breathes a sigh of relief as he pulls up in front of the lab and sees two security guards waiting on the curb beside Brett.

Brett grips Gareth's shoulder and gives Maddie a warm smile. "You bring me the best presents," he tells her. "Let's get you inside." He catches Maddie eyeing the security guards. "It's overly cautious of me, I know, but why take a risk when we have these gentlemen available to help?"

They enter the building. One guard walks ahead of the group, the other behind. No one offers to take the box, which is just as well. Maddie isn't ready to let it go.

"It's a scroll or a collection of rolled documents," Gareth tells Brett. "I didn't remove it from the bag. If it's like the other one, it's extremely friable."

"Did you tell Rebecca we were coming?" Maddie asks Brett.

Brett shakes his head. "I only interrupt her when necessary. She's immersed in the translation of the first scroll. But we'll let her know now that you're here." He taps a staccato pattern on his phone; Maddie hears the *whoosh* as his message flies off toward Rebecca.

"Any idea how the translation is going?" asks Gareth.

Brett laughs. "Oh, I know better than to ask. But they were smiling earlier, which was a big improvement over yesterday. I had dinner with Rebecca, but she refused to talk about it. She says she doesn't want to jinx it."

Minutes later, Rebecca strides in, exasperated. "I told you we needed a couple more hours," she says to Brett. "What's so urgent?"

Maddie holds up the box. "We found a missing box of fragments from the Calliopolis excavation, and quite possibly a scroll as well, in the Banks archive."

Rebecca's face registers bewilderment. "The Banks archive? Why on earth would there be a scroll in there?"

"No idea," says Gareth. "It's been sitting in the basement of the library since 1940, and likely in Banks's lawyer's office—in the same crate—for another ten years before that. I doubt there's anyone alive who can tell you how it got there."

Rebecca turns to Brett. "Let's test the ink. We'll know more once we do. And we may as well catalog as we go. Gareth, can you source some acid-free boxes and paper?"

"On it," he says.

"Is there anything I can do to help?" Maddie asks.

"Actually, yes," says Rebecca. "I'd appreciate it very much." If the scroll is buried under a pile of fragments, she explains, they'll have to remove each fragment, photograph it, and store it securely. "And we need to do it quickly, because I don't know what kind of ink we're dealing with. Iron gall is sensitive to light. We'll need as much help as we can get, even if it's just cutting up the paper to layer between the fragments. You don't need any expertise, just discretion. I don't want any leaks." She looks at Brett now. "Michael Grey isn't still lurking around, is he?"

"He's gone," Brett says, with a touch of asperity. "I told Simon that this part of the process would bore them to tears. Michael didn't want to go, but he understood that he wasn't welcome without Simon. I promised you that I'd get rid of them, and I did."

A glance passes between them, and Rebecca seems to soften. "Thank you," she says. "Okay, everyone, let's get to work."

Maddie is gratified to fall into Rebecca's circle of trust, although she understands that Rebecca is casting it widely in the circumstances. Brett's lab techs and grad students form an assembly line, along with Gareth and Maddie. Following Rebecca's instructions, they move through the top layer of the excavation box, discovering to their relief that most of the fragments are larger than expected. It takes a couple of hours to expose the linen bag, which Rebecca then removes to a neighboring table for closer examination. Another hour passes, and Maddie's shoulders twitch in protest.

Rebecca's phone breaks the silence. "Yes?" She listens and then says, "I'll be there in a minute." She comes over to the table where Maddie is sorting and storing the papyrus.

Brett smiles at her. "What's the news?"

"It's good," she says. "Very good. My students have finished checking my translation on the final stanza of Helen's scroll." She turns to Maddie, her smile radiant. "You brought us a Sappho, Maddie. I'd stake my career on it."

SEVENTEEN

CALLIOPOLIS, JANUARY 1904

Mr. Drake and Miss Alcott returned to the site in mid-January. They had left us three weeks earlier, traveling up the Nile to spend Christmas with friends at the Winter Palace Hotel and to meet with Mr. Drake's preferred dealers in Luxor. Mr. Drake had made no secret of his boredom with the excavation activities during their stay; there were no more prearranged caches of jewelry, only the daily search for increasingly damaged papyrus fragments as we cleared several properties adjacent to the scriptorium. We were all glad to see them depart.

When they returned, Reverend Banks was with them. He emerged from their carriage into the blazing sun, in a full set of ecclesiastical robes, a collar, and the same flat-topped black hat he had been wearing the last time I had seen him, at lunch with Aunt Margaret in Rome. Propriety made no concession to climate, it seemed. "Miss Gardiner!" he cried. "Who would have imagined that we would reunite here?"

He caught me up on his activities in Rome, where he had been granted access to the Vatican Library. He had been there at the behest of the Archdiocese of New York, collecting evidence in support of beatification of Mersis of Calliopolis, an early Christian leader from the late second century. "An immense honor," he told me, "since I am not myself of the Catholic persuasion." He had not expected to find himself fundraising for the project, but said, modestly, that he had proven himself adequate to the task. Since our last meeting, he had secured enough support for excavations in Calliopolis, Nitria, and the Scetis deserts and had spent two months living in a cave as Mersis himself had done. It had been, he told me, the most meaningful spiritual endeavor of his life. "I believe we are very close to understanding Mersis's journey," he said. "A journey which began right here." He pressed a hand to his chest. "God is with us."

"Without a doubt," I said. "Calliopolis is heaven on earth for a papyrologist. It is good that you are here." I told him about my work in broad terms; I had learned my lesson when it came to speaking out of turn. I still shuddered inwardly when I remembered Emmett's face, twisted with rage, after I revealed the Sappho discovery to Mr. Drake without his permission. I had thought he might strike me. "*You will know your place*," he had said to me. "*I can make you, or I can ruin you.*" I had tried to keep a safe distance since then, even while I was more motivated than ever to show him my worth.

Today, after the official greeting of our benefactors, I was returning to the village house to catch up on my recordkeeping. Iris and I were responsible for logging all the finds in the storeroom in Olsen's excavation diary, and in my enthusiasm for restoration, I had fallen behind in cataloging the papyri. Although he seemed to have settled down, I did not want to give Emmett a reason to let me go. One of Mr. Drake's carriages was heading back to the steamer, and Miss Alcott offered to have it deliver me home. I accepted gratefully; the tufted velvet seats with silk fringes offered significantly more comfort than my usual donkey ride.

As I drove out of the site, I saw Miss Alcott standing with Emmett some distance from the others. Her posture was animated; his was frozen. I saw him bow stiffly and stalk away, and I wondered what she had said to him. It was my observation that these visits altered everyone's behavior: Olsen drank more and was prone to tantrums; James, who treated me as an equal colleague when we were alone, became remote and excessively polite; Iris took more care with her appearance and looked for opportunities to cultivate favor with Miss Alcott. A break from these social complexities was welcome.

I settled in at my desk and opened the record book that I'd brought with me from the site. It was mostly empty; we had started with a fresh book on January 1st. So far, it contained a simple running tally of boxes of papyrus fragments, the total number of which now exceeded one hundred. I began recording detailed features of the Sappho fragments I'd identified earlier in the month.

I still hadn't handed the Sappho over; I wanted to make sure that the translation was impeccable before losing custody, and to conserve the fragments so that they would be safe in less careful hands than my own. I had ordered thick sheets of glass and mounted the papyrus between them. Tomorrow, I would give the treasure to Mr. Drake and Miss Alcott, but for tonight, it was mine. I copied my translation into the record book for posterity. I hoped to return to Rome for the summer and prepare a scholarly article on the poem for publication.

Iris returned in the evening, and we had supper, a simple vegetable stew with flatbread and some canned peaches for dessert. "You were smart to leave, Helen," she said. "Emmett is in an absolute fury. He was well into a bottle by midafternoon, sulking in his tent. Honestly, the behavior! Men are like children when they don't get their own way."

I was not surprised, though grateful not to be the object of his ire this time. We had reached the end of a papyrus vein, and a decision had to be made about where we would focus our energies next. Emmett hoped to concentrate our efforts on another possible scriptorium site, but he anticipated strong resistance from Mr. Drake, who was obviously weary of fragments. "Mr. Drake didn't agree with him?"

"Not only did he not agree, he insisted on moving the focus of the excavation to the cemetery. He said he wasn't going to fund any more digging near the main square. He said that he wanted Emmett to stop wasting his time and focus on finding objects with 'value visible to the eye.' Emmett said that Mr. Drake didn't understand the concept of value, and then Mr. Drake said that he would hand the reins to James if Emmett wouldn't take direction."

"Oh dear."

"Meanwhile, the Reverend commandeered Rubi for the afternoon and sent him off to recruit another twenty men to dig on the west side of the town. He said he had a vision of Mersis compelling him to excavate there. So now there are going to be two active excavations, neither of which Emmett wants to open right now." I had not known the Reverend to speak of visions, and it worried me. I hoped he was well. He would not be the first man to have lost himself in the desert. I vowed to myself that I would check on him the next morning.

"But surely the cemetery offers some prospect of success?" I said. Greek and Roman cemeteries had proved fruitful on several recent digs, notably Hawara, and not only for the mummies themselves. Burial rites in the Ptolemaic period had included spectacular portraits, scrolls, and jewelry. I could well understand why Mr. Drake was keen to explore there.

"It does, of course," said Iris. "But Emmett knows that he'll never get the attention back on the scriptorium once we go there. The potential finds are flashier, certainly, but he thinks the intellectual value of the scriptorium excavation is far superior. He wants to be the man who proves beyond a doubt that Calliopolis is the literary capital of legend. He wants to write the definitive monograph on the subject. I gather he feels it will be incomplete without further study."

Although he had been cooler toward me since my misstep with the Sappho revelation, I still admired that Emmett was no mere treasure hunter. Like me, he wanted to understand the past. I shared his frustration that there were so few of us, even out here, who loved knowledge beyond all other prizes. "Is that what he was angry about earlier this morning? I saw him arguing with Miss Alcott."

I felt Iris tense. "I cannot say."

"Iris," I said. "Is there something I should know? I am trying to follow your example. I do not wish to cause upset, but it would be easier on the whole if I knew where the tender spots were and could avoid them altogether."

"It is not my secret to tell," said Iris. "I can only say that your predecessor got too close to Emmett, and it was to her detriment. Alice went to Miss Alcott for advice, and Miss Alcott helped her as best she could. If I had to guess, I would say that the argument this morning had to do with Alice's situation, but I do not know for sure. I'm worried about Alice myself. I haven't heard from her in months."

I could see that Iris would not say more on the subject, but it did not take a wild imagination to fill in the parts of the story that she had left out. We rose from the table, leaving Khalid to clean up, and went into the storeroom, where we both had our desks. "What do you think of my day's labors?" I asked, holding the freshly mounted Sappho poem for her inspection. She hadn't seen the fragments since Khalid and I had cleaned them; I had wanted the pleasure of seeing her awe at their transformation.

Iris did not disappoint. "Oh, Helen," she said. "You are brilliant. You really are. I can hardly believe what I'm seeing. This could have been written a decade ago." She turned the frame over. "I've never seen it done this way, with the glass on both sides. You get so much more light through the page." She smiled at me. "It will be hard for you to let her go."

I smiled back. "I'll see her again. Mr. Drake has been talking about building his own museum, according to James. I'm sure my Sappho will have pride of place. And in the meantime, we haven't exhausted the possibility that there's more of her to find."

We were out at the site early the next day, and it was already humming. From a distance, we could see clouds of dust rising from two unfamiliar locations; Mr. Drake and Reverend Banks must have set the crews to digging at first light. We found Emmett in the mess tent, lingering over eggs and coffee. He handed me an enameled tin mug, and we sat together at the table while Iris went to join the group at the cemetery.

"I have something to show you," I told him. "You will want to give it to Mr. Drake. I expect it will please him."

I handed him the parcel I'd brought and watched him unwrap it. A broad smile creased his tired face.

"Extraordinary," he said. "I have never encountered another with your talent for restoration, Helen. And I owe you an apology. I've been a bear. I'm not the man you met in Rome, I know."

"I expect he's still in there somewhere," I said.

He shrugged. "He was overcome with jealousy, plain and simple. This poem will be famous, you know." I nodded. I did. It was only a few lines, but it was Sappho's voice, clear and true.

"We all share in the discovery," I said. "It's your dig, yours and Mr. Drake's."

He shook his head. "It's Drake's dig. If you had any doubt before, look around you. But this?" He skimmed a fingertip over the frame on the table. "This discovery belongs to you. Without you, it would still be in a box in anonymous pieces. And now it is a treasure."

"Thank you," I said, my cheeks warm with his praise. For all his faults, I respected him, and his recognition meant a great deal to me. "What will you do now?"

"Oh, I'll stop licking my wounds and go over to the cemetery," he said. "Why don't you join me? I was going to spend all of next season out there, so it hardly lies in my mouth to say it isn't a promising location." He winked. "We can't let James get too big for his boots or he'll be unmanageable when Drake leaves. Shall we?" He pushed the bench back from the table and stood.

"Can you wait for a minute or two?" I asked. "I want to hand the Sappho off to Miss Alcott."

"She's at the cemetery as well," he said. "She's pitched her silk tent there for the day. Drake wants her close to the excitement."

I felt a great weight lift knowing that Emmett and I were once again friends. I had missed being able to talk to him; he was the only other person at Calliopolis who shared my passion for papyrus. It had been painful to feel the rupture between us. Now, as we walked, I felt almost giddy. "I envy you your pants," I told him.

"I beg your pardon?"

"Your pants," I said, shaking my skirt for emphasis. I had shortened it as much as dignity would allow, but it was still cumbersome, especially when it came to climbing ladders and scrambling up and down sandbanks. "I was thinking of having some made for myself. Do you think the men would be horrified?"

He laughed. "I hardly think it matters. You'll draw some attention, but I have confidence in your ability to ignore it. The good Reverend may be scandalized, but don't let that stop you."

"Thank you," I said.

"You are an unusual woman, Helen Gardiner," he said.

"It has been said," I told him.

We were at the edge of the cemetery when we were distracted by shouting coming from the opposite direction. We turned, and saw a figure in black stumbling across the sand. "It is the Reverend," I said, startled. "I hope there has not been an accident."

"James!" shouted Emmett.

James's head popped up. "Boss."

"Get the first aid kit. There's a problem with Banks." Emmett and I dug our feet into the sand, launching ourselves in Banks's direction. There was no running in the desert. There was only vastly increased effort for moderate increases in speed. Short legs and skirts were a huge disadvantage, and soon Emmett and James were both well ahead of me.

I could hear the Reverend calling to them. "Come quickly! You must see!" Having delivered his message, he turned and hurried back the way he had come. Mr. Drake pounded past on horseback.

"Helen!" I stopped and waited for Iris. "Do you know what it is?" I shook my head. "Well," she said, "I have my sketch pad. I hope they've found something. We're coming up empty in the cemetery. There's water damage. Everything is completely decomposed. Nothing but bones and rotten wood. My mother would literally swoon if she knew what I was up to."

We arrived at the edge of the new pit, and looked down at a striking tableau. The local men were continuing to dig, clearing a larger area around Reverend Banks, who was kneeling on the ground, his eyes closed and his hands clasped in front of him. James and Emmett stood on either side, gazing at an image on the wall before them.

"I guess I'm needed after all," said Iris, pulling out her sketchbook and settling herself on the edge of the drop. "I'll get a closer view when it empties out a bit." From our vantage point, it appeared to be a painting of a figure with a circle of light around its head, clasping a book.

"I'm going down," I said, and waved to the workers to bring me the ladder. On the ground, I stood beside Emmett and considered the painting. It was a female figure with white hair, visible wrinkles on her forehead, and a large nose, her head framed by a glowing orb. She was not beautiful, but she had an expression of great serenity. The book in her hands was ornate, studded with gems.

"Do you see?" said Reverend Banks, rising to stand beside me. "It is the Virgin herself. We are on holy ground." He brushed tears from his cheeks. "This is Mersis's own church, my friends, the earliest Christian church ever constructed. Here is the miracle I have been searching for my whole life." He opened his arms and bowed his head. "Thanks be to God."

EIGHTEEN

SACRAMENTO, 2019

"Alistair Banks, you dark horse," says Pete. As soon as he got Maddie's text, he says, he drove straight to the lab in Sacramento, and now he leans over the table where they are preserving fragments from the excavation box, bristling with anticipation. "What do we think it is?"

"Too early to say," says Rebecca. "Brett needs to work his magic."

"And the other scroll, the one Maddie brought from Toronto—you think it's a Sappho? Are you sure?"

"I'm sure," says Rebecca.

"Holy shit," says Pete, his eyes bright. "This is going to be huge."

Rebecca seems about to say something in reply, but she hesitates and then turns instead to Brett. "I need to get back to my students for an hour or so," she says. "Can you manage here without me?"

"Absolutely," says Brett. "It's all in hand. I need some time anyway, to take measurements for a container before we put it through the X-ray. Do you want to test the ink together when you're done?"

"Yes, please." Rebecca shoots a rebellious glance at Pete before standing on tiptoe and planting a kiss on Brett's cheek. In the moment of hushed astonishment that follows, she says, "Maddie, could I speak to you for a moment?"

Maddie follows Rebecca out of the lab and into the hallway. "I've sent you an email with a link and access code to Nora Alcott's diaries," Rebecca tells her. "I had them digitized, but they aren't publicly available. I thought you might know how to make use of them."

"Thank you," says Maddie. She pauses. "Can I ask why you're sharing it with me?"

Rebecca grimaces. "I understand why you'd ask. I've given you no reason to consider me an ally. I know I've been . . . frosty, let's say." Maddie waits, not disagreeing. "A friend suggested I might be projecting feelings onto you that were more appropriately directed elsewhere, and I decided they were right."

"I understand," says Maddie. "I have complicated feelings about my ex too."

Rebecca nods. "That's gracious of you. Thanks. Listen, Maddie, I need to run, but we'll talk again. I promise. And one more thing: Could you tell Gareth to keep Pete out of the Banks archive? We have no idea what else could be in there, and he shouldn't be rummaging around unsupervised."

"Sure," Maddie says. Part of her wants to ask Rebecca why she distrusts Pete, but she isn't sure she wants the answer. She senses that Rebecca's objection is more professional than personal, however messy their breakup may have been. Maddie elects not to return to the lab but makes her way to the lounge instead. She sits by a window and opens her email, clicking on the link that Rebecca has sent and entering Rebecca's personal identification and password. The screen fills with scanned pages of Nora Alcott's handwriting.

December 6, 1903

Calvin and I have arrived at Calliopolis at long last. It is good to be anchored, and to have ready entertainment for Calvin. He does love playing archeologist. We had Mr. Olsen for dinner on the steamer this evening, and his face was an absolute picture as Calvin outlined his plans for the visit. He drank an entire bottle of wine on his own. He reminds me of a bear I once saw at a zoo in London, the wildness still alive in it and waiting for the opportunity to show itself. I have told Calvin not to provoke him, and my suggestion was ill-received. Calvin says Mr. Olsen is brilliant—but I have heard far more men described this way than can lay claim, credibly, to the classification. Too often, in my observation, it is deployed to excuse those who should be too intelligent to behave as badly as they do. I must remember that suspicions are not proof, and Calvin must manage Mr. Olsen as he sees fit.

December 7, 1903

We rose early today and drove out to the excavation. I had a shock when I realized that Alice Baker hadn't returned this season as expected. It appears that she hasn't been in communication with Miss Wentworth, who was a particular friend of hers. The general feeling seems to be that Alice became ill at the end of last season, returned to England, and settled into life there without a backward glance. I fear that the reality is more sinister, but I won't expose her by probing further.

Calvin had a good day: He found a bracelet and some coins after no more than half an hour of digging. The items were obviously planted by Mr. Dunn, who has the easy smile of a young man bent on his own advancement. Is it possible that Calvin is unaware how many of us are managing him? In any event, it was a celebratory afternoon. Alice's position has been filled by Miss Gardiner, who is connected by marriage to the Cogswell fortune. She is independent-minded, which I admire, and obviously brilliant when it comes to the study of papyrus. She believes that she has identified a few lines of Sappho, which would be a huge coup, if true. Olsen has instructed her to complete the restoration as soon as possible; I had the distinct impression that he hadn't known about the Sappho before she told us about it. If I have the opportunity, I might offer her some guidance on the womanly art of preserving male pride.

December 20, 1903

Calvin is in a terrible temper. Mr. Olsen's stubbornness knows no bounds. He is quite obsessed with his scriptorium, to the detriment of the excavation as a whole. I believe that a change of scenery is in order.

I have persuaded Calvin to take a short trip to Luxor. There is usually a jolly crowd at the Winter Palace for Christmas, and Calvin is anxious to see what his dealer has set aside for him. I'll arrange for Howard Carter to dine with us while we are there; he is prickly and dislikes most everyone, but he is also observant and reliably full of useful information. Calvin has in mind that he might sponsor a dig in the Valley of the Kings next season.

We have invested too much time and money in the Calliopolis site to cancel our involvement now, although Calvin says he will do exactly that if Mr. Olsen will not follow his instructions. As for me, I'm increasingly concerned about Alice Baker's well-being—something else to investigate in Luxor.

December 27, 1903

I left Calvin with his dealer and took a calèche to the last address I had for Alice, a guesthouse used principally by French and German scholars. She had written to me from here to thank me for my generosity and to tell me that she had taken my advice and posed as a young widow whose husband had died on an excavation due to a mishap with some dynamite. As long as she avoided the British contingent, she was unlikely to be questioned closely; competing nations rarely share information about their excavations until the end of the season, and even then, they only share their successes. But the landlady informed me that Alice had not been there since November. Under questioning, she admitted that Alice had vanished, leaving all of her possessions behind, and when I insisted on seeing the items, she became sly and secretive, and told me that rent was owed. I shall go and see Dr. Simpson at the Thomas Cook Hospital tomorrow and see if he knows where she has gone.

December 28, 1903

I have had some very distressing news today from Dr. Simpson. He tells me that neither Alice nor the female child survived the birth. Alice arrived at the hospital with her labor well advanced and with considerable bleeding that could not be controlled. The child suffocated in the process. Dr. Simpson was kind, and we had a glass of brandy together which restored us both. He walked me out to the hospital cemetery where Alice and the child are buried, and I left him with a donation to provide for a headstone and the maintenance of a small garden. I am heartsick. I confess that I had come to believe that our plan would succeed. At my request, Dr. Simpson had made contact with a well-regarded adoption agency in Cairo, and if things had ended differently for Alice, she would have returned to Calliopolis at the start of the season with no one the wiser, while the baby would have commenced life with one of the

British or European families stationed in Egypt. Poor Alice! I cannot help but feel that I ought to have done better for her—but if she had returned to America with us, there would have been no way to keep her secret from Calvin, who would have insisted that none of this was my responsibility. I cannot help feeling that we have a duty to protect the women who work for us. They risk so much—their health, their respectability, their future marriageability—and it is all to our benefit. Or perhaps it is only that, at times like this, I can see how easily I might have shared Alice's fate.

January 14, 1904

We returned to Calliopolis today, having collected Reverend Banks from the train station in Beni Suef. He takes immense pleasure in his own rectitude, which makes him a dull dinner companion even without the interminable lectures on the topic of his ancient cleric.

Calvin met him at a dinner for the archbishop in New York and was persuaded to invite him to dig on our concession, provided that the Reverend would pay his own way and share his finds with us. Everyone seemed to think they had come out of the deal well; as Calvin said, one had to make choices about where to dig, and he and Olsen agreed that their focus would be on the pre-Christian city, but he wasn't going to turn his nose up if someone else wanted to do the work for him and give him a few souvenirs in the bargain. So it was all arranged, and now Mr. Olsen is stuck with the Reverend for the season. It is the least of what he deserves.

I had not planned to speak to him about Alice, given that she had never confirmed the identity of the man who had placed her in difficulty. But I was certain, and felt as though I might burst with outrage, and I pulled Mr. Olsen aside almost as soon as we arrived. He was furious, of course, and denied any knowledge of Alice's condition or his role in it. He even had the temerity to act as if I had insulted his honor! I must make sure to warn the two women here now about the perfidy of men in general, and of Mr. Olsen in particular. I should invite them to tea sooner rather than later.

January 30, 1904

Reverend Banks has discovered a painting in one of the buildings on the east side of the site, the portion inhabited during the early Christian period. He is quite agitated and convinced that it is a significant depiction of the Virgin Mary. I have asked Iris Wentworth about the painting privately. She is knowledgeable about religious portraiture, and although she would never contradict Reverend Banks publicly, she says that the painting is most unusual in its realism, and lacking many of the symbols that she would expect to see in an image of the Virgin. Calvin has very little interest in excavating there himself; as he says, any wealth had left the town by then, and he is no churchgoer. I think Reverend Banks is disappointed that his enthusiasm is not widely shared.

February 15, 1904

The last week has been among the most exciting of my life. I've barely slept, returning to the boat late at night, and leaving again at dawn. We have made a discovery for the ages. I will not say so to Calvin, or to Mr. Olsen, as I speak to him only when necessary, but it seems that Mr. Olsen may be brilliant after all. His calculations led to a cemetery site out by the ridgeline, where the rock-cut tombs from the ancient dynasties are located, and it is in a state of exceptional preservation. The treasure is not what we sought when we came here, but it is rich indeed.

Mummy portraits, in the dozens, as fresh as if they had been painted only a decade ago. And they are not idealized portraits, but show the full measure of each person's humanity. Calvin has been desperate to tear into the wrappings and extract the precious objects within, but we have been holding him off long enough to preserve the panels . . . we shall see how long it is possible to do so.

March 2, 1904

There has been a theft in the village house. Mercifully no one was injured; it is assumed that the crime occurred in broad daylight, while Helen and Iris were out at the excavation site. The poor women discovered several pieces of jewelry missing from the storeroom late in the evening, and spent a sleepless night wondering if the thief would return. They are on the boat now, while the men pack up the storeroom and arrange to ship the artifacts to Cairo. The investigators say that the culprit is the houseboy, although Helen and Iris say it cannot be so.

Calvin, meanwhile, shrugs and says that some theft is to be expected and we are fortunate to have lost only a few objects. It is quite out of character, and I will press him further when the atmosphere is less frantic; for now, we have armed guards around the boat at all hours, and two extra houseguests, and no time at all for private conversation.

March 11, 1904

It is unbearable to write these words, but I must set them down: Helen Gardiner is dead, murdered. There is much responsibility to be shared for this outrage, and there will be an answer for it. I cannot sleep. I walk on the decks late into the night, trying to exhaust myself. When I close my eyes, I see Helen being carried from the house, covered in a sheet.

April 5, 1904

Today, I buried Helen next to Alice in Luxor. It gives me some comfort, and the strength to do what lies ahead. I will write no more.

There is a knock on the lounge door, and Rebecca steps in. "I thought you might be in here," she says. "How are you doing with the diary?"

"Nora's a gold mine," says Maddie. "Thank you. The diary proves that Helen identified the first Sappho fragment, the one in the Drake Collection. It wasn't Olsen, even though he got the credit. I had a feeling. Are we sure there aren't any more journals somewhere? Did she really stop writing them in 1904?"

"It seems so," says Rebecca. "That's everything we have in the Alcott collection." Rebecca takes a seat across from Maddie. "Do you have a few minutes to talk?"

Maddie closes her laptop. "I think we both know I'm not a critical member of the team. My time is flexible." She hears a note of bitterness in her voice.

"I know I've made you feel that way," says Rebecca. "Again, I'm truly sorry. I can offer an explanation, if you'd like to hear it?"

Maddie isn't sure she wants to know, but curiosity wins out. She tells Rebecca to go ahead.

"I guess I should start by saying that Pete and I used to be married." Maddie nods. "It wasn't an easy relationship. Pete needs to win, and being in competition for the Olsen Chair finished us. He undermined me at every opportunity. Sour grapes aren't a good look for a woman, and so in public, I'm never anything but professional with Pete. Privately, though, I stay as far away from him as possible. There is literally no one on earth I trust less than Pete Bahar."

"And me by extension?" asks Maddie.

Rebecca smiles slightly. "Well, you aren't in the same category, obviously. But there is the matter of . . ." Rebecca pauses, uncomfortably.

"My father," says Maddie. "And the article about us."

"Well, yes," says Rebecca.

"I know what people say about me," Maddie tells her. "Some of it's true; most of it isn't."

Here is what is true: Sometime after her mother died, Maddie was approached by a reporter from *The Atlantic*, who was doing a story about health and safety risks in archeology. The article, "The Human Cost of Excavation," argued that modern excavations were too often out of compliance with regulations, particularly when it came to shoring up the walls of deep trenches. The journalist was looking at three separate cases on well-known sites, including Silvia's. When asked about the safeguards at K'abel, Maddie had said, "It shouldn't have happened. Everyone knows that the walls of a trench need to be secured beyond 1.5 meters. The lead excavator was cutting corners, and my mother paid the price." It is also true that the lead excavator was, and remains, David Sloan, Maddie's father, who was quoted in the same article as saying that Maddie had "lost all reason" and "turned a tragedy into a crime" when her mother died in a gruesome trench collapse. He said he felt sorry for his daughter, but her accusations were "full of sound and fury, signifying nothing." He expressed profound disappointment in Maddie's choices.

The article reverberated, circulating for months in an academic community which was short on scandal and long on malice. Maddie's currency on the job market evaporated, dispossessed of both her intellectual reputation and access to her research materials, her father having barred her from K'abel. Ben Cupul, who had grown up at K'abel—his father was a laborer on the site, and his mother sold souvenirs from a tent in the parking lot—and who was seen by both David and the Mexican government as the incumbent recipient of the excavation permit, had a choice to make. Which was not, as it turned out, to ask Maddie to marry him, but to safeguard his position at K'abel by rushing to David's defense.

"I know your thesis supervisor," says Rebecca. "Carol Oblinsky. We sat on a committee together last year. I called her to ask about you."

"What did she say?"

"She told me she has a lot of respect for you and that you were scandalously mistreated. She felt that your thesis project was impressive. Even with the job market the way it is, she thought you would have been a strong candidate if it hadn't been for the bad publicity."

"Maddie Sloan threw her own father under the bus. Who wants a colleague like that?" Maddie summarizes.

Rebecca is quiet for a moment, and then says, "Carol told me there was an investigation after the article came out. Your dad was fined for maintaining unsafe working conditions."

"Yeah. Still, he's in denial. He believes I engineered the audit somehow. As if I have contacts in the Mexican government." Maddie brushes away a tear. "I know he was devastated when my mom died. I'm sure he blamed himself. But that article sent him into orbit."

Rebecca looks hesitant. "Ben Cupul is a colleague. I like him. He's a good scholar. I thought you should know that he's never said a negative word about you to me."

"I'm glad." The Ben Maddie knew would have protected her. But she doesn't know him anymore. She's lost confidence in her memories of him.

Rebecca glances at her phone. "Brett's starting the scan. We tested the ink on the Banks scroll before I came in here. It's carbon, and it seems to be quite stable. It won't be long now." She pauses, and then says, "I hope you'll accept a piece of advice from me, Maddie: Be careful around Pete. I don't know what he's promised you, but he will do what's best for him, every time. That's how he's wired. Keep your research for yourself. You don't have to share it with him. And pay attention to what he's contributing. His name isn't enough."

Maddie thinks Pete's name is worth quite a lot to someone in her position. At the same time, she finds herself very touched by Rebecca's concern. She says so.

Rebecca holds her gaze intently. "What you've done, bringing us these scrolls . . . it's going to change people's lives. Mine, Brett's, Pete's, yours. Don't sell yourself short." She stands. "Brett should be finished with the scan by now. Let's go and see what it says."

NINETEEN

CALLIOPOLIS, 1904

With the Reverend's discovery and the open conflict between Emmett and Mr. Drake, the mood at the site was strained. So were our resources. The workforce was now split over three separate excavations.

On the east side of the site, in an area which we called the Chapel, Reverend Banks continued his feverish search for evidence of a Christian settlement. So far he'd found a few pottery shards and a reed mat, but little else; he was expanding the digging radius, urging the men—none of whom shared his religion or his zeal—to have faith, and praying regularly before the painting of the Virgin. On the west side, at the cemetery, James—with Mr. Drake's encouragement—had excavated a quarter of the area and had met with some early success, harvesting several lovely pieces of jewelry, including a beaded necklace of carnelian, emeralds, and onyx, with a central cabochon garnet; a gold diadem with a pattern of flowers and leaves; a pair of ruby and pearl earrings; and a gold ring set with a carnelian, an image of clasped hands carved into the stone. Emmett himself occupied the central portion of the site, the scriptorium, but little excavation was occurring there.

After a ferocious argument about Drake's strategy for the cemetery, Emmett was now refusing to assist him until he "saw sense." Emmett claimed to be catching up on writing, but on those occasions when we encountered him in the mess tent, he was unkempt and stank of liquor.

I spoke to Iris about it, and she said to leave him alone. "He'll snap out of it," she said. "It's best to ignore him when he gets like this."

I was spending most of my time at my lab in the village house, overseeing restoration and doing translations. Most of the fragments were proving to be commercial in nature—interesting, certainly, but no match for a literary scroll. I found myself restless in the hunt for another treasure; I began making notes for an article I hoped to publish about the Sappho fragment. Every few days, I would travel to the dig site to make a report to Emmett and examine the active excavation for evidence of *afsh*. I was worried that Emmett's inattention might lead to the destruction of a promising vein at the cemetery, as unlikely as it was.

On that day, Rubi was supervising the men, who were digging at a slower pace than usual. It had been several days since the team there had uncovered a grave. Rubi waved, and I called out, wishing him a good morning. He pointed to the large canvas tent that Mr. Drake had acquired and outfitted with furniture from the ship, indicating that I would find James there. Mr. Drake was staying in the tent most nights, his staff bringing fresh food from the ship and cooking lavish meals twice daily. Iris sometimes joined them, as Miss Alcott liked her company.

Loud voices emanated from the tent: James and Mr. Drake. "It is unconscionable," Mr. Drake sputtered. "It cannot continue. I am depending on you to ensure that I receive what I am owed. I shouldn't need to tell you that your future with me hinges on it."

I called out and lifted the flap. Mr. Drake's face was red; James looked haunted. "Not now, Helen," James said. There was a map of the site spread out on the table in front of them.

"My apologies," I said, retreating. I wondered what it was that Mr. Drake felt he was owed. Emmett's labor, presumably. I could not blame him for his fury, if so. He was an unpleasant man, and a greedy one, but not unreasonable in his expectations of his lead excavator. I felt sorry for James, though. Emmett would do what he wanted, when he wanted; James could no more force his compliance than Mr. Drake could.

Did I have any sway over Emmett? I was not invested in the financial outcomes of the season. I felt that Emmett and I trusted each other to care for the site itself, not merely for the objects we might extract from it. It was not my place to intervene—I was sure this was what Iris would say—but I felt what I can only describe as a sense of duty to Calliopolis, to ensure that it was treated with respect.

I made a pot of coffee and took it over to Emmett's tent, calling out for him. He emerged, wearing pajamas. "What is it?"

"Are you unwell?" I asked him.

"Not in the least," he said, taking the coffee. "Thank you."

"Do you think perhaps that you should come out to the cemetery?" I saw no point in beating around the bush. "Mr. Drake is quite angry."

Emmett laughed. "You are an extraordinarily unsubtle woman, Helen. No, I am not worried. When the history of this site is written, it won't be about the Christians, and it won't be about the jewelry. It will be about the literature. The papyri. And as long as they're digging in the water-damaged part of the site, it's a waste of my time." It was true that the coffins themselves, and any papyrus they might have contained, had long ago disintegrated.

"Are you not concerned that he might fire you?"

"He needs me. I told him I'll come back when he's ready to dig on higher ground. There's an area on the north side of the cemetery, near the ridge, where there might still be some papyrus. He's a stubborn old goat, and James is only too happy to pacify him. Meanwhile, I'm getting a start on my book."

"Are you? It seems to me that you are mostly drinking," I said.

"Thank you for the coffee, Helen," he said, and let the flap fall. I could do nothing, I supposed, if he would not help himself, but I was sorry to see him like this. It always annoyed me when grown men behaved like children, but never more so than when the man in question was gifted, capable of greatness.

In the carriage that evening, I asked Miss Alcott if we should be concerned about Emmett's relationship with Mr. Drake. "Heavens, no," she said. "I think they enjoy arguing with each other. Neither can abide being told what to do. But they need each other, make no mistake. Calvin will realize that he needs Mr. Olsen's guidance, and Mr. Olsen will stop sulking. And they'll both get on with it. If I had to guess, I'd say it will happen soon, perhaps as early as tomorrow. You should come in the morning and see for yourself. In the meantime, progress is being made." She winked at us. "I'm getting at least one new piece of jewelry out of it."

She was right. The next morning, it was as if a storm had passed. When we arrived, Emmett was out at the cemetery, freshly shaved and washed, and he and Mr. Drake were huddled together over a map of the site. "Right," he said, seeing us. "We're ready to move to the next section of the cemetery. We're going to shift to the ridge, where the rock-cut tombs from the earlier city of Kiste are. We'll have drier conditions, and I'm guessing that the original Ptolemaic burial ground was there. No one would have put a cemetery this close to the river when Calliopolis was at its height. This cemetery was obviously created after the river receded and the town entered into a decline."

Emmett summoned Rubi and issued his instructions. Rubi nodded, then strode over to the pit and began shouting to the men, who immediately climbed up to ground level and gathered around him. As a group, they began walking toward the ridge, all fifty or so, their robes flapping in the wind. Watching them, I felt the simultaneous strangeness and rightness of my life, and the impossibility of ever returning to what Aunt Margaret had imagined for me. Olsen and Mr. Drake mounted horses, and set off after them, while the servants were left to collapse the tent and move it and its contents a hundred yards to the northwest. I did not understand their words, but they shook their heads and rolled their eyes, and there was no mystery as to what they felt.

"You see?" said Miss Alcott, quietly, coming to stand beside me. "Mr. Olsen needed time to rethink. And Calvin needed to assert his authority for a while. But Calvin went to see him last night, with my encouragement, and they apologized in the way that proud men do, and now they're fine." She patted my arm. "If you want to stay in this business, my dear, you'll need to figure out how they think."

"They seem complicated," I told her.

"Not at all," she said, shaking her head. "Quite the opposite, and thank goodness. One has to stay a step ahead."

We watched Emmett and Rubi in discussion by the ridge, pointing at the distinct knolls and humps of the landscape to determine the starting position for the new area of excavation. Rubi's advice was generally determinative; he was understood to "read" the desert better than anyone else in the five villages within a day's walk from Calliopolis. Once the location was identified, Calvin Drake received a full report, which he pretended to understand so that he could give his approval.

"Thank heavens," said Miss Alcott, who had watched the entire proceeding unfold. "Now we can set up our tent and get out of the sun. Tea?"

I stayed for the afternoon, at a desk in Miss Alcott's tent. There was an air of celebration that had been absent for weeks, and I didn't want to miss out on the excitement. I had brought the draft of my Sappho paper with me, thinking I might discuss it with Emmett, but he needed no distraction—he was striding about and issuing orders, dust billowing around him, the air alive with the scraping and clanging of shovels.

The men joined us late in the afternoon, dusty and excited, and we toasted each other with warm champagne. Supper that evening was a fine affair, with all the men in high spirits; and even James, no longer basking in the glow of Drake's attention, smiled and laughed with the rest. I hoped that we would look back on the evening with delight, and not with the bitterness of dashed hopes.

A frantic energy was palpable from a mile away as we drove in the next morning. There were thick dust clouds over the fresh pit, and the buzz of men's voices. "Well, well," said Miss Alcott. "That's the spirit." She clapped her hands. "What fun." We parked by the tent and clambered out.

"You're late!" shouted Emmett. "Quickly! All hands on deck!"

"What is it?" I asked, coming up to stand beside him. James was in the pit, I saw, directing the diggers. "How on earth did you get so far down?"

"We kept going after supper," he said. "Lit the torches and had the men remove another six feet of dirt. Why waste good daylight on that? Now, down you go, Iris. We have paintings to preserve. And as for you, Helen, I've been waiting for you to open the coffins. I've practically had to restrain Drake and James."

"Paintings? Coffins?"

"Go down and see for yourself," he said.

"What are you doing up here if the action is down there?" I asked him.

"Mapping," he said, showing me the excavation diary in his hand. "I want to be able to see the layout of the graves before we pull the coffins out. We won't find all of them if we don't see the pattern in how they are organized. But I'll come down now so we can begin extraction, starting in this corner." He pointed to his map. "You and Iris are assigned to preservation. I had the mess tent moved over here at sunrise this morning. Consider it your laboratory, yours and Iris's. It's about to be full of mummies."

"Ptolemaic period?"

"Helen," he said, "I wouldn't want to spoil the surprise. Down you go."

I flew down the ladder. On the ground, I could see that there were five rectangular holes. I walked to the corner that Emmett had specified, restraining myself from looking into the other trenches as I passed them. James met me, his face red with exertion. "You've never seen anything like this," he said. "Wait." He moved behind me and put his hands over my eyes. "Take three steps forward. I won't let you fall." I did what he said. "Ready?"

Nothing, I thought, could match the anticipation, but I waited while he counted down from three, and removed his hands. I opened my eyes.

TWENTY

SACRAMENTO, 2019

"We need a distraction," Gareth tells her. They are waiting, again, for Rebecca's translation, this time of the Banks scroll. "We're not needed in the lab, and we're both stir-crazy. I've been meaning to go to the railroad museum since I moved here. What do you say to some sightseeing?"

Maddie brightens, as she tends to do around Gareth. She's been wanting to visit the Old Town but had intended to sneak away one day on her own. She senses that her academic colleagues have more high-minded tastes, but she should have guessed that Gareth wasn't in that category. "Count me in," she says.

Gareth drives them to the historic district, where they fall, willingly, into each and every tourist trap. They climb aboard an antique railway carriage, visit a one-room schoolhouse, and take a photo outside the Pony Express depot. Maddie has almost forgotten that this kind of uncomplicated fun exists.

"Maybe what you've forgotten is that you're entitled to it," says Gareth. "Most adults don't play enough."

It's true that she was never encouraged to play as a child. That changed somewhat when she and her mother moved north, but at K'abel, climbing and running were dangerous, both for her and for the monuments her parents were trying to protect. She remembers being praised for maturity and scolded for childishness. Her sobriety has continued into adulthood. She says, "I probably worry too much about being taken seriously."

"I get that," he says. "I had a massive attack of imposter syndrome when I went away to college. But when midterms rolled around, I figured out that I knew how to work as well as anyone. After that, I felt more comfortable going my own way."

She asks him how he ended up studying early books. "It was serendipity," he tells her. "I got a work-study placement at the main library on campus as part of my funding package. I was supposed to be doing a science degree so that I could go to veterinary school, but I liked the library so much that I switched to information studies after my freshman year. Most IS students lean into the technological side of things—that's where the jobs are. Not me. Paper all the way, the older, the better." The smell of fried chicken wafts out of a restaurant, and Gareth stops short. "Please say you're hungry."

Before long, they are clinking bottles of cold beer in a leatherette booth over a barbecue platter and bowl of hand-cut fries. "I feel excellent about this decision," Maddie says, licking her fingers. She hesitates, then says, "Can I ask your opinion about something?"

"You bet."

"If the scroll is what we think it is, what happens next?"

Gareth seems to reflect on his answer for a second before he speaks. "Well, you'll receive a lot of attention quickly. You'll want to have thought about your options ahead of time."

"Tell me more."

Gareth signals to the waitstaff for another beer. "Would you like another as well?" She says she would. Once the orders are in, he sits back from the food. "I take a political position on artifacts," he says. "I think they should return to the country of origin where possible. Not everyone agrees with me."

"What if the country of origin doesn't know the artifact exists?"

"It's every bit as important to return it in that case," he says. "Maybe even more so." Looting, he tells her, strips objects of their context and diminishes them in the process, but it also breaks the continuity of a people's cultural history. "Sometimes, the books I'm assessing aren't that valuable, monetarily. They aren't strictly worth the effort we put in to return them. But the symbolic value is massive. In the case of a scroll, you're dealing with an object that is extremely precious in both senses."

Maddie thinks about Helen, Iris, her parents, Michael Grey. "Who owns the scroll, in your opinion?" she asks.

"I don't know," he says. "I think it might be the wrong question. What if it's about where it belongs, not who owns it?" The UNESCO 1970 Convention, he explains, was supposed to prevent illegal trafficking of artifacts from that date forward and allow for repatriation and restitution of cultural property stolen in the past. But it became a shield, used by colonizing nations to hold on to cultural items illegally exported prior to 1970. "Artifacts ground identity," he says. "An object behind glass in a Western museum has an educative function, sure, but isn't it more valuable as a repository for cultural memory in its country of origin?"

Maddie doesn't disagree with him, not exactly. Debates on the ethics of archeological investigation are hardly new to her. If she were in charge of the British Museum, the Elgin Marbles would be on a plane to Athens. But surely there's room for some nuance, some balance? Not every glass case in an American museum should be emptied. "Take the Banks scroll, for example," she says. "Isn't it the property of the Cogswell Library? Alistair Banks had the authority to remove the scroll from Egypt, under the country's own rules at the time. And Resurrection College received it as a bequest made in a legal will."

"I agree, the Banks scroll is an easier argument to make, with the caveat that the rules were made by the French, in a sharing agreement with other colonial powers. Helen's scroll is more complicated, though, don't you think?"

Maddie feels herself flush. "As far as I or anyone knows, Helen hid the scroll in her jewelry box to keep it safe when she realized how rare it was. There's no evidence she intended to steal it. She was murdered. Then it came into Iris's hands without her knowledge, and she brought it to North America by accident. You're making me feel like I'm complicit in something ugly." Her mother, also, which is a stickier problem. She realizes that she's connected the scroll to Silvia in an intimate way, weaving it into her memories of their years together in Toronto. She pictures herself sitting on her mother's bed, watching Silvia put on her jewelry for a night out. She feels irrationally defensive.

Gareth takes a breath. "I'm sorry," he says. "I'm not maligning your intentions. Of course I'm not." He presses his fingers against his temples. "I've had one beer too many, I think. It's only . . . I wouldn't want to see you pulled along into a mindset that says artifacts exist to enrich the finder. My own belief is that no one should own these objects. They're part of the history of the countries that produced them."

"Pulled along by whom?" Her voice is crisp, guarded.

"Pete Bahar, for one."

"He's my friend," she says, although even as she says it, she wonders if it is true.

"I'm not sure he has friends," says Gareth, bluntly.

"People around here don't seem to like Pete much," Maddie says. She's irritated. Pete has his flaws like everyone else, but he's been good to her. "Is that because of Rebecca?"

"I can only speak for myself. I don't like Pete because he's part of the problem. He sees objects as a form of currency and he consults for people who feel the same way. Do you know how many priceless artifacts are sitting in black-market warehouses, destined for private collections through deals brokered by people like Michael Grey?"

"Obviously not."

"Exactly. No one does. But it's a vast number, and it increases exponentially whenever there's political unrest. If you compare satellite images of Egypt from 2011 to 2013, during the Arab Spring, you see a five hundred percent increase in looting pits at major sites. Those finds get smuggled out of the country by organized crime and sold to the highest bidder."

"I'll say it again: That's not what happened with my scroll."

"And I'll say it again: It's not your scroll."

They stare at each other. "I think it's time to call it a night," says Maddie.

Gareth asks for the bill, waving her off as she tries to split it. "I spoiled a perfectly nice day," he says. "It's the least I can do."

She wants to reassure him, but she stays silent. Gareth has been the one uncomplicated relationship in her professional world lately. She's relied on him to be steady and kind and easy to read. She resents the strain he's introduced; she will have to be watchful with him now. She will have to keep things to herself.

They share an Uber. Rummaging through her purse, she realizes she's left her keys in a drawer in her office, so Gareth insists on riding back to campus with her. She doesn't put up much of an argument, but she feels unsettled, and estranged.

As they turn onto Library Drive, she feels Gareth tense beside her. "The lights are out in the library," he says. He pulls out his phone. "I need to call security."

As she glances up, she sees a flicker of illumination behind one window. "Do you see that? Someone's up there with a flashlight," she says. "What part of the building is it?"

He looks grim. "The offices."

Gareth is on the phone, opening the door before the car fully stops. He strides toward the building, disappearing through the entrance as she transacts with the driver. Stepping into the dark herself, she smells the college gardens, a mixture of hyacinth and rosemary and a peppery fragrance she can't identify. She's never noticed the scent during the day; it's as though she's never been here before. A shiver moves through her, and she hurries to catch up with Gareth.

In the lobby, a security guard named Clayton is talking to Gareth. He's an older man, with an air of exasperation, as if he can't believe the nonsense people get up to. Gareth tells her that they are waiting for the after-hours maintenance crew to come and check the electrical panel. They've learned that there's no widespread system outage on campus; only the library is affected. The lights have been out for fifteen minutes.

Clayton cautions them against going further into the building. He's seen some things in his time on this job. It could be a drug addict searching for something to sell. These folks are unpredictable, even violent, if you startle them. It's not worth the risk. Gareth thanks Clayton for his good advice and takes down his mobile number, promising to call in with a report from upstairs. He absolves Clayton of responsibility. "I'm not trying to confront them, whoever they are," he says. "But I'm hoping they'll stop what they're doing if they realize there are other people in the building. I can limit the damage, at least."

"Don't we need a flashlight of our own?" Maddie asks.

"I have one on my key ring," he says, pushing open the door to the stairwell. He grins, and she sees her friend again. "Be prepared. Boy Scouts training sticks with you. But you should stay down here. Clayton's right. It's risky and probably stupid, and I don't want to drag you into it."

Maddie shakes her head. "I'm coming with you."

They climb, guided by a tiny beam of light, the concrete amplifying their steps. Maddie is conscious of the sound of her breath, embarrassed at how ragged it sounds after minimal exertion. Three flights up, Gareth stops at a fire door. "Okay, here's the plan," he whispers. "I'm going to open the door and call out. If the person is friendly, they'll answer. If they aren't, we don't want to surprise them."

He pushes the door, hard, and the clang reverberates in the dark. "Hello?" he calls. "Who's there?" There's a crash, then silence, then the sound of running feet. A few seconds later, they hear a heavy metal door banging. Gareth exhales. "That's the stairwell at the other end of the floor," he says.

He dials Clayton's number, reaching him in the basement where he's supervising the maintenance team. A moment later, the office hallway is bathed in fluorescence. Maddie can see Gareth's face now, etched with concern. The power outage isn't an accident. Someone has accessed the utility room and switched the lights off.

"They must have had a reason," he says. "Let's walk around the floor and see if we can figure out where they were and what they wanted."

But Maddie, who has started down the hallway ahead of him, already knows. "They were in my office," she says. The wood is splintered around the locking mechanism, the door ajar. The crowbar she's been using to open the crates sits discarded in the middle of the floor, surrounded by lids. Maddie rubs her arms. The office isn't really her space, but the invasion feels personal nonetheless.

"What's missing?" Gareth asks.

She shakes her head. "I don't know. I hadn't even opened those three yet." She points to three crates that have been moved to the middle of the office floor. They're empty: The volumes have been removed and lie scattered around, some flung across the room and others splayed open, pale pages exposed. She hopes the intruder has been as frustrated with Alistair Banks's library of religious biographies as she has.

"Do you think Clayton's right?" she asks. "That it was a random stranger?"

Gareth surveys the broken door, the splintered crates, his expression unforgiving. "Do you?"

TWENTY-ONE

CALLIOPOLIS, 1904

I was staring at a face: a man's face, triangular, with a long, elegant nose, a thin upper lip and a plump lower lip, a short dark beard and mustache. His dark hair was wavy and adorned with a golden wreath. His eyes were large, brown, framed by bushy brows and thick lashes, his expression strikingly naturalistic, as if someone had hailed him and captured his likeness as he turned.

"I have never seen anything like it," I said. The face was painted on a wooden panel, secured over the mummified face beneath. The mummy itself lay cradled in a coffin, the lid of which was propped against the wall of the pit. The coffin was simple; the artistry had been reserved for what was concealed within.

"No one has," said Iris, joining us. "The painting technique is very advanced. We don't see this style of portraiture again until the Renaissance. This is a major find, Emmett."

"It is." He lowered his voice. "I told you that the story of Calliopolis would be its papyrus, Helen, but these portraits will be strong competition. We could spend the rest of the season recovering and preserving them. But we won't be given that kind of time."

I glanced up to the edge of the pit and saw Mr. Drake pacing and glowering. I understood the problem immediately. The mummy's wrappings were amazingly well-preserved, and there were signs even beyond the quality of the portrait that pointed to a person of wealth and status. The mummy was bound in layers of linen covered in plaster, which had been painted with images of Egyptian gods to ease the man's passage into the afterlife: falcons and a winged goddess with a sun disk above her head, her skin burnished with gold—Isis or Nut, I thought—and Osiris, too, wearing a gilded crown and flanked by cobras. The pigments—even the red—were still bright.

"It's a lead paint," said Iris. "Plant dyes don't stand the test of time, not on this scale anyway. It would have been expensive. Imported, probably from Spain."

"And if they went to this much trouble on the outside . . ." Emmett didn't need to complete his thought. There would be treasures beneath the bandages, amulets certainly, and in all probability precious personal ornaments.

"Let's get to business," Mr. Drake shouted. "All season, I've been waiting for you to show me results. Now you make me wait again. I am not a patient man, Olsen!"

"What should we do?" Iris asked. "We need to preserve the wrappings."

Emmett looked at her with something like pity. "We will do what we can," he said. "But if I were you, I'd focus on the portraits. If Drake had his way, we would have cracked every coffin in the cemetery like an egg, and had the job done before breakfast. He will not be stopped."

Iris's eyes were wild. "We have to do something."

"Listen to me," he said. "You must be calm. What we are going to do is move the coffins one by one, out of the ground and into the tent up there, and you ladies are going to come up with a method of preserving the paintings as quickly as possible. By quickly, I mean today, in the next few hours. Do you understand? You won't have a second opportunity."

"We'll do this together," I told her. "Come on, Iris. There's no time to waste."

We raced up the ladder and into the tent, where we saw, with relief, that Olsen had given us a long table and several buckets of water. Iris paced and spoke aloud, reminding me of Professor Wilson. "The portrait we saw is encaustic," she said. "The Greeks and Romans had a tradition of panel painting on hardwoods like lime or fig or cypress. They used mineral pigments mixed with beeswax—this one is Roman, I think; the style suggests it. Although likely a man of Greek descent, the communities mixed with each other—did you see the name written under his feet?" I had not. "Herakleides, son of Thermos. Yes, Greco-Egyptian. Sometimes they used tempera, but not here; tempera dries too quickly to get that level of detail. Encaustic is nice and hard; it won't flake, but it will hold the dirt and I'll need to clean it before anything else . . . oh, Helen." The flood of words stopped; she looked aghast. "I hope I'm equal to this."

"There is no one better," I told her. "Not anywhere in Egypt, not on any excavation. Trust me."

She gripped my hand as the first group of men arrived, carrying the mummy we'd already seen. "Iris," I said. "What do you need to do the job? I'll tell Emmett."

"Bread," she said. She was recovering from the shock, I saw with some relief. "As many loaves of fresh, soft bread as I can get."

"Bread? Will you tell me why?" I wondered if Iris was thinking clearly. I couldn't imagine how bread might assist us in our task, unless it was to fill our bellies and fortify ourselves.

"You'll see soon enough," she said. "I have a plan. Whether or not it will work, only time will tell. Also, I need paraffin and a burner to melt it. And clean strips of cotton."

"Like in a field hospital," I said.

"A field hospital for paintings," she said. "Yes, exactly."

I relayed Iris's instructions to Emmett, who was overseeing the arrival of the second and third coffins, which he placed in a queue outside the tent like the patients at our village clinic. As with the first, they had been painted very simply on the outside, and most of the decoration was worn away. Emmett took a piece of chalk and labeled the top and bottom of each coffin so that they could be reunited, and then he took a crowbar and began to pry the lid off one. James took hold of one end, and Emmett the other, and they lifted the lid and moved it aside. Another face gazed up at us, this time a young woman, with the same elongated nose and neck, large dark eyes, and wavy hair as we had seen on our first mummy. I wondered if they had been siblings. In her portrait, she was draped in luxurious golden fabric clasped with a large brooch, and rubies hung from her ears. Her hair was gathered in a complicated style of braids and tight curls, held with a pearl-studded comb.

"As if it was painted yesterday," said Mr. Drake, coming to stand with us. "I'll bet that brooch is there, and the earrings too."

"We're not going to ruin the paintings finding out, as we agreed," said Emmett, sternly. "James, help me with the next one?"

The third coffin also held a woman, her straight hair parted in the center without ornamentation. She had high cheekbones, a pert chin, a simple white robe. Large pearls hung from her ears. She stared directly out from the painting, her expression serious, even somber. There were letters painted over her right shoulder, and as I leaned in for a closer look, I caught my breath.

"What does it say?" asked Emmett.

"It's her name," I said. "It says 'Ermione Grammatike.'"

"Hermione the Teacher? A woman with a profession? It can't be, Helen. There's no precedent for it from the Greco-Roman period."

"Perhaps, perhaps not," I said. "The term can also be translated as 'literary lady.' It may simply refer to her level of education. Either way, she was a woman ahead of her time—female literacy was highly unusual."

"And reserved for the very wealthy," said Emmett.

"As you say," I told him.

"Right, then," said Emmett. "Let's see what Hermione took with her to the afterlife."

He and James reached into the coffin and lifted Hermione's mummy out. As they did, I caught sight of what appeared to be a pillow, where the mummy's head had been. "One moment." I ran back into the tent to grab my satchel, and, giving Iris a quick wave, came back out to kneel beside the coffin, pulling on my gloves.

"What is it?" asked Emmett, as I lifted it out.

"It feels like papyrus," I said. "Most likely it's an excerpt from the Book of the Dead; that would be typical for this type of burial. I'll tell you as soon as I can."

"Focus on the paintings for now," said Emmett. "I need your steady hands there." He leaned closer and murmured in my ear, "Is Iris up to it?"

"Yes," I told him. "She is. I have no doubt." I did, a little. I knew Iris's skill with watercolor paints and charcoal pencils, but restoration was a craft of its own, and I had seen many examples of butchery by otherwise talented artists. But he would not hear a whisper of doubt from me. Although I did not regard Emmett as one of them, there were many in archeology eagerly awaiting evidence of women's failure in the field. I would not fuel their campaign.

We watched the men carry Hermione into the tent. I heard an exclamation from Iris, and winced.

"Don't open any others just yet," I said. "Pull them out of the ground and stack them here if you must, but you're going to give Iris a nervous condition if you pile them in front of her, and fair enough. Anyone tasked with this restoration would feel the same."

"I can only hold him off for so long," Emmett said, inclining his head toward Drake, who had stalked over to the edge of the pit, where he smoked and surveyed the activity below with a proprietary air.

"Do what you can," I said, and went into the tent. I stored the linen bag from Hermione's coffin in an empty tin box to transport it back to the village house, and then I came to stand beside Iris. I could feel the weight of what we had been asked to do. I could only imagine how it pressed on my friend.

"I come bearing cotton strips, and bread, as requested," said Miss Alcott, entering the tent. She carried several folded bedsheets, a pair of scissors, and a basket of loaves. "Put me to work, ladies."

"Oh, thank god," said Iris. And then, catching herself, "Excuse me, Miss Alcott. I'm most grateful."

"Oh, heavens, call me Nora," she said. "Both of you. We are going into battle together! Tell me the plan."

Iris had us begin by warming the water—the kettle had moved with the mess tent, and we put Rubi to work making a fire for us, far enough away that it posed no risk to the dry coffin wood piling up at our door. Then we cut strips of cloth, and ripped the bread apart with our hands, forming them into soft balls.

Herakleides, son of Thermos, lay on the table before us. "The moment of truth," said Iris. She took a ball of bread and rolled it, carefully, over the surface of the portrait. Slowly, the dirt began to transfer to the bread, brightening the painting and exposing the richness of the colors.

"How on earth did you know to do that?" I asked.

"It's an old trick, from de Mayerne's manuscript." Seeing our blank expressions, she continued, "A royal physician in the seventeenth century. The king's paintings were blackening, so de Mayerne experimented with various solutions to lighten them. He's considered one of the fathers of art conservation. I wouldn't risk most of his methods, but bread seemed like a safe choice. It's very gentle, as you see."

Iris repeated the delicate process several times until she reached a point where the bread came away from the painting clean. "Now for the water," she said, and asked us to soak a handful of cotton strips for her. Ever so gently, she wet a corner of the portrait, blotting it immediately.

"What's taking so long?" Iris jumped as Mr. Drake roared into the tent.

"Calvin, dearest," said Nora, stepping between him and Iris, "we cannot rush genius."

"Can we not?" he asked. "I think we must."

"Drake!" Emmett burst in, breathing hard. I sensed that Mr. Drake had bolted, and Emmett had chased him down. "They have unearthed another group. Surely you do not want to miss it."

Mr. Drake scowled. "You are well aware of what I want." His eyes fell on Nora's shears. "Let us come to an agreement now, or I will cut them open myself, starting with this one right here."

"I have a proposal," said Nora.

"I'm all ears," said Mr. Drake.

"Mr. Olsen." She turned to Emmett. "Could I ask you to examine the mummies in the queue? Not all of them, surely, have decorations of this significance. In those cases, it seems to me, we could, without too much wringing of hands, dispense with the wrappings. Yes?" Emmett acknowledged that it was so. "Helen and I will come outside and remove the portraits from those mummies, and then you can proceed with your investigation."

"You have two hours," said Mr. Drake. "After which time, they are all fair game."

Nora kissed him on the cheek. "You are charity itself."

Emmett and Mr. Drake exited, and Nora squared her shoulders. "This will be painful," she said, "but it will be over quickly." She took her scissors and made a swift cut through the shroud where it met the top edge of the wooden panel. With a series of decisive strokes, she cleared several layers of stiff fabric away from the portrait and lifted it free. "There," she said with satisfaction. "Rescued."

"Not quite yet," said Iris, resigned, it seemed, to the desecration of the wrappings. "The paintings are vulnerable without a protective layer on them. Mr. Drake is right about one thing: I must move more quickly."

"We watched you clean Herakleides," I said. "I think Nora and I can take over the bread-rolling, at least, and likely the washing as well, if you want to heat the paraffin."

"But before we do," said Nora, brandishing her shears, "we'll try to save what we can of the plaster painting. Helen, can you help hold him steady?"

"Yes," I said. "But let's start with a more precise tool." I extracted a leather pocket roll from my satchel and selected a blade. I extended the handle to Nora. "Be careful," I told her. "It's extremely sharp."

"Perhaps you should do the honors," she said.

I made a careful slice across the base of the mummy, below the painted gold toe caps, and then continued the cut up the right side. The incision was shallow, no more than half an inch. "I'm not optimistic," I said. "If there is resin inside, we'll have to apply too much pressure, and the plaster will crack."

"What if we slice it into smaller pieces?" asked Nora. "The more surface area we remove at a time, the more likely it is to break, I think. We can puzzle it back together in the end, like your papyrus."

I saw that she was right. "You keep at it," she said. "I'll check on the men and bring the portraits in."

Within the hour, I had excised each painted image from the mummy's torso and reassembled them in a coffin on the floor. Meanwhile, a whole community of faces was laid out on the table, advancing through the cleaning process; several were ready for a coat of paraffin. Iris stood in front of one of the lesser portraits, holding a paintbrush. "I wish we had more time," she said. "What if the paraffin is too hot? I don't want to go down in history as the artist who ruined the only surviving examples of ancient panel painting. I'll be banned from the National Gallery. What if varnish is the better choice?"

"Iris," said Nora. "We don't have varnish. There is a great risk in moving the paintings without first protecting them, as I understand it." She put her hand on Iris's shoulder. "This is not the finest painting of the group, and we cannot know what will happen until we experiment. It's time to begin."

Iris dipped a wide brush into the hot liquid. "Wish me luck." With strong, sure strokes, she covered the first painting and stepped back. "I can't look. Is it melting the painting?"

Nora moved in for a better view. "No, my dear." Her smile was radiant. "We've done something today that no man in archeology has ever done. So, ladies, tell me: How does it feel to make history?"

TWENTY-TWO

SACRAMENTO, 2019

Maddie sits up in bed. It's early, before seven, and the sun is still rising. She hasn't slept much, unsettled by the events of the previous night. And by her argument with Gareth about the scroll. She hopes they are still friends. They parted ways after finding the empty crates; Clayton arrived and then there were reports to fill out and people to call, and no reason for Maddie to stay.

Now Maddie props herself up in bed and opens her laptop. In the quiet hours, far from the activity of the lab, she's painfully aware that she needs to define her role here. Rebecca will have the glory of the translation, Brett the success of another text rescued from illegibility, Pete the economic benefit of increased demand for his expertise on Calliopolis and more attention for his (their?) book. But Maddie will remain in the shadows until and unless she finds a story to tell—her own story.

She has been reflecting on Rebecca's warning about Pete. And Gareth's. She believes they are being unfair to him. And yet. If she's objective about it, he's footed the costs for a plane ticket, a couple of nights in an Airbnb, and a small stipend. She's provided the proof he required to identify the objects in the TAM collection, uncovered a previously unknown Sappho scroll, and located another mysterious document while conducting research on Pete's behalf. Meanwhile, Brett has paid for her accommodation and per diem expenses in Sacramento, without any suggestion that Maddie owes him in return. Perhaps the scales are more balanced than she thinks.

It came to her the other night that the Calliopolis excavation is a classic closed-door mystery. It's a book she'd like to write, maybe with Iris as the amateur detective. She opens a file and starts writing questions: What did Nora know about Helen's death? What action did she take to make someone answer for it, as she promised to do in her diary? Were the deaths of Alice Baker, Calvin Drake, and Emmett Olsen somehow connected to Helen's? Why did Iris break off her engagement to James and leave Egypt? What did the scroll in Helen's jewelry box have to do with any of it?

She types the word *Suspects* in bold, feeling both a thrill and a strong sense of embarrassment, as if caught playing a game for children. But there is no one else here, no one to please and no one to disappoint except herself. And if she does, it would hardly be the first time. She's living proof that failure can't kill you, even when you wish it would.

Emmett Olsen, she writes. A complicated man, a drinker, under significant pressure to perform or lose his funding. Nora Alcott believed he'd impregnated Alice Baker. Had he seduced Helen as well, and killed her when she wouldn't go away quietly, as Alice had done? Or had he killed her to take credit for the discovery of the Sappho poem?

Calvin Drake. Had he been involved with Helen? Had he killed her to protect his reputation? Or perhaps the crime had been about money, rather than sex. Drake was required to account for his discoveries and divide them with the Egyptian Antiquities Service. But he was known for skirting the regulations. Had Helen been hiding the scroll from Drake himself? Had he suspected she was concealing artifacts?

Nora Alcott. Nora had liked Helen, according to her diary; the tone was protective, almost maternal. And what motive could she have had? Unless, of course, Drake had turned his acquisitive eye toward Helen. Nora and Drake were not married, but Nora was insulated from scandal by Drake's massive wealth; without it, she would be an outcast, utterly disgraced. Perhaps her diary had been a cover, one that she'd found impossible to maintain; that would explain why she'd stopped keeping it.

Alistair Banks. His funding from the Cogswells depended on his ability to convince Helen to return to the United States. Killing her wouldn't have fixed that problem, though. And after the discovery of the painting, which preceded Helen's death, other prospective funders would have been thick on the ground.

James Dunn. He was a cipher. British, not American. Well positioned to take over the excavation after Olsen's departure. The spurned fiancé of Iris, ultimately accepted by Julia Melton. One of the few to have left Calliopolis unscathed—was that by fortune or design? Had he conspired with the British to seize the concession from the Americans in return for the top job? Two murders seemed like a high price to pay for a promotion, and based on his later career, James Dunn wasn't a psychopath.

Iris Wentworth. Maddie is duty-bound to consider Iris's culpability in Helen's murder. But she rejects it quickly. Iris had no motive and no opportunity, having been at a wedding in Cairo at the time of the murder.

Maddie sighs and closes the file. She isn't a detective, that much is clear. She crawls back into bed and pulls the covers over her head.

When she arrives at the office, she finds Pete waiting at her door with a takeaway cup of coffee. A day ago, she knows, she would have felt a burst of pleasure. Now she wonders what he wants. She blames Gareth for getting in her head.

"I heard about the drama last night," he says. "How are you?"

"I can't stop thinking about what might have been taken," she says. She pushes the door open and waves him in. "I wish I'd made more of an effort to catalog what was in the crates. It seemed like busywork, and I kept pushing it to the side." She surveys the office, which is still a mess. She'd been too distracted to tidy up last night. It looks like the inside of her brain feels.

"Have you been to the lab today? I'm dying to know what's happening, but I don't want to get in the way."

"Still lots of excitement," he says. "We're trying to keep Rebecca's identification quiet for now. Her students know it's a Sappho, of course, but they're under strict instructions to tell no one until Rebecca gives the go-ahead. Rebecca isn't usually forthcoming with me, but I have the sense that she's confident that the attribution won't be challenged." He gives her a frank look. "Do you have any idea how big this is?"

Irritation blooms in Maddie's chest. Sappho isn't her area of expertise, granted, but she's not without common sense. The poem is a discovery so dazzling that even she will be illuminated by its sparkle. "I have an idea," she says.

She thinks briefly of Helen. She resolves to speak to Rebecca about the coming announcement of the find. She wants Helen to receive what is owed to her—and to Alice, Nora, and Iris too. These women—their interlocking fates—are the reason she is now on the doorstep of career success. They are as much a part of the history of Calliopolis as Emmett Olsen or Calvin Drake. Maddie won't be yet another person who denies them their legacy.

Pete leans across the desk, and she pushes her chair back in response, claiming her space, marking a boundary. She wants to trust Pete, but she also wants to have enough distance to see him clearly. A furrow appears between his eyebrows. He says, "It will be worth a great deal of money."

"So you've said," says Maddie. "But maybe it shouldn't be sold at all? Maybe it belongs in a museum?"

"Museums have money," says Pete. "The point I'm making is that you and your family will need professional advice about all of this." Maddie's head snaps around to look at him. Up until now, he hasn't mentioned her family. She wonders why he is doing it now. "You should talk to Michael Grey. He's the best in the business. He's discreet, which is key. You don't want the government elbowing their way in before you figure out what you want to do." *Spoken like Calvin Drake*, Maddie thinks, with a twinge of distaste.

"You might want to trust Maddie to make her own decisions. I do." Gareth stands in the doorway. His stance is casual, hands in his pockets, but his shoulders are tense. His cool gaze doesn't waver as Pete rises, his jaw clenched.

"Okay," says Maddie, sliding between them. "Pete, I have an appointment with Gareth now. I'll talk to you about this later."

Pete gives her a curt farewell and edges past Gareth. She wonders what else Pete might have said if Gareth hadn't interrupted them.

"Hello," Gareth greets her. "How are you today?"

"Good," she says. "I'm good. Were you here late?"

"Late enough." He considers her, a question in his face. "A break-in at the library, barely any sleep, and you'd think I'd be ready to drop. Must be the adrenaline." He maneuvers a shelving cart into the room. "If you're up for it, I thought we could go through all the books and finish the initial catalog. Once we're done, I can wheel Alistair Banks's library out of your life for good."

"Now that," she says, "would be divine."

They collect all the volumes from the floor and stack them neatly by the desk. They break down the tasks, Maddie electing to read the title, author, and date of publication aloud, while Gareth records the information on her spreadsheet.

"Here's a page-turner," she tells him. "*The Heavenly Sisters; or Biographical Sketches of the Lives of Thirty Eminently Pious Females: Designed for the Use of Females in General, and Particularly Recommended for the Use of Ladies' Schools,* by the Reverend T. Sharp, 1822." Maddie wonders if Banks taught the book at Barnard, maybe for a class where Helen Gardiner was a student. In her mind, she imagines Helen rolling her eyes. She's doing exactly what a historian shouldn't, inventing an anachronistic personality for her subject. It's an impulse that Maddie's disobedient brain finds almost irresistible.

"Sure to fly off the shelves," Gareth agrees. "Next?"

"Next we have a Bible. Large, leather-bound, not one for carrying around with you. Maybe a family heirloom?" She opens the russet leather cover to check the flyleaf for identifying information but sees immediately that the book's interior is damaged. The pages have been cut away to create a rectangular hollow at the book's core. Nestled within it is a smaller volume with a soft calfskin cover.

"Gareth," she says, and he comes around the desk to stand beside her.

"There are some gloves in my office," he says. "Be right back."

While he's gone, she tries to guess what's in the concealed book. A record of Banks's excavation at Calliopolis? A diary of his experiences there? She hopes that whatever Banks has written down will contain some clues that will help direct what she thinks of as her investigation.

The mystery, though, only deepens when she sees Olsen's handwriting spilling over the page.

"It's the missing excavation diary," she says to Gareth. "Why on earth did Alistair Banks have it?"

TWENTY-THREE

CALLIOPOLIS, 1904

For days, we had been cleaning and removing mummy portraits from their hosts, and we now had a collection of thirty paintings of the residents of Calliopolis which Iris had dated to the first century BC. They were a prosperous group, it seemed, although their status in life did not protect them from the indignities of Mr. Drake's recent attentions. Once Iris, Nora, and I completed preserving the paintings, and detached them from their hosts, Emmett, James, and Drake moved quickly to unwrap them, removing any objects found in the linens. They then returned the denuded mummies to their original coffins, using the bandages as packing material. The mummies, even in this state, were not without value, and Drake anticipated being able to sell them to various American museums, unless he created a mummy display of his own. He seemed to favor the idea of a touring show, but he hadn't ruled out a permanent collection in California.

The local men were agitated, Rubi reported. They felt that the mummies were not being accorded the proper respect, and they were threatening a work stoppage. Drake scoffed at this. "Ridiculous superstition," he said. "If a man refuses to carry out an order, he gets his pay docked. If he does it again, he's fired. That's all there is to it. I used to go to parties in London where we unwrapped mummies. It was all the rage. Frankly, the only curse was that it was boring to watch. This, on the other hand . . ." He cut down the breastbone of the mummy on the table in front of him and peeled the layers back one by one. "Significantly more entertaining." He reached down and plucked a brooch from the body. "That's a beauty."

I had thought that Mr. Drake's rapacious energy might diminish once the season's success was assured, but it was not to be. He cared only for the next find. He behaved, in my view, with brazen callousness toward the workers, as if they were machines designed to move earth, rather than men with minds of their own. The balance and organization of the crew, its hive-like complexity, meant nothing to him; he thought, wrongly, that anyone could be replaced on a whim. Emmett knew that Rubi's men represented the most skilled workforce north of Luxor, with generations of experience in their blood. He negotiated with Rubi, providing *bakshīsh* to reward the local men for the cemetery treasure, while ensuring that they stayed well away from the area where we were unwrapping the dead. Mr. Drake would have been enraged by these concessions, had he known about them, but he did not. It was easy, after all, to distract him.

"Emerald," said Emmett, holding out a brooch for Mr. Drake's inspection. "And malachite, I think, although we'll have to confirm it. I have an expert coming up from Luxor later this week to evaluate the gems."

"Good, good," said Drake. "I'd like to know what I'm dealing with before I tangle with that idiot Frenchman from the antiquities service."

Emmett was recording all of the objects in his excavation diary, but it was a cursory accounting. Iris and I would need to clean each piece and catalog it in the record book, and even with Nora's assistance, we were falling behind as the men kept pulling new coffins out of the ground. In the evenings, after a long day of painting restoration, we would return home and start our second shift of the day. Iris would sketch items, and

I would write detailed entries beside her drawings. And she would do some preliminary restoration, mostly removing dirt with a fine brush or a damp cloth, while I wrapped the portrait panels and prepared them for transport, at least as far as Cairo, and likely across the Atlantic.

I took my time with them, though. Soon enough, these faces—twenty centuries gone, but hauntingly familiar—would belong to the world. But for now, they were our companions, watching over us in our village house. It was odd, how we became accustomed to them, and to the mummies and the coffins, most of which were stacked against the wall of the storeroom. I say accustomed, but at least for me, it was more complicated: I felt protective, and responsible, having altered their eternal arrangements.

"I can see the men's point," I said to Iris over supper. "The mummies look so plaintive, lying there exposed. And after having seen what they looked like in life, it's hard to be completely scientific in one's outlook." They had been strangely beautiful as well, their smooth faces inscrutable, untroubled. I don't know what I had expected, but it hadn't been the faint scent of juniper, green beeswax, and myrrh, or the crowns of braided hair.

Iris sniffed. "It's true about the mummy parties, you know. They were wildly popular. My parents attended one when I was a young child. I was terrified that the mummy's ghost would follow them home." She shook her head. "They used to grind the remains up after stripping them and make them into paint. It looked like mud if you ask me, but it was terribly expensive stuff. 'Mummy brown,' they called it."

I shuddered. "How vile," I said.

"As you say. The point is, you aren't the first to lose your scientific objectivity in the presence of a mummy, and you won't be the last."

"Not many have had the pleasure of living with them." I pointed to the door of the storeroom. "And safekeeping their treasures."

"Not while breathing, no."

"Seriously, Iris, should we have more security than we do?" Security in the village consisted of a pack of roaming dogs that surrounded strangers and barked at them for food, alerting everyone else in hearing distance to the arrival.

"We should, and Mr. Drake's arranged for it already. He hired some police constables from Beni Suef to come out at nightfall. They started patrolling last night, but you were preoccupied with your scroll."

It was true. In between all the other tasks, I had managed to squeeze in a few hours of precious time with the papyrus that had served as Hermione's pillow through the ages. It was stained—with what, I didn't like to think—but it was legible. There were a few wormholes, but not many, which was exceptionally lucky, and it hadn't been crushed. It was dry, but not more so than other scrolls I had seen in Professor Wilson's laboratory, and I felt myself up to the task of unrolling it. I had mixed a papyrus juice solution and was using my finest-quality blotting paper to rehydrate the page, inch by inch, with Khalid's assistance.

"We must move very slowly," I had told Khalid. Fragments presented one type of problem, but scrolls were much more complicated. It was terrifyingly easy to turn a scroll into a pile of disorganized fragments in the attempt to unroll it. Each morning, we unrolled the scrolls with tweezers, just a few inches, and then we would spray the next few inches of exposed papyrus with our hydrating solution and cover them with damp blotting paper. We'd secure the flat section with weights and begin the cleaning process for the sections that were dry.

"What is it, Miss Helen?" he asked. "Can you read it? Is it the Book of the Dead?"

"It is not," I told him. "It is something far more intriguing." I had known as soon as the first line was exposed that Hermione had not made a traditional choice for her journey beyond the realm of the living. This was not a book of incantations or hymns to the gods. Nor was it a record of her life and lineage.

It was poetry.

"I should get back to it," I told Iris now.

We cleared the table and washed up, and then Iris unlocked the storeroom, and we lit the lanterns in our work area. The sun set early at that time of the year—not much past five o'clock. The long shadows in the storeroom added to the otherworldly quality of our mummified friends, and I had caught Iris suppressing a shiver more than once. I didn't mention it, though, as I knew that her sensitivity—so necessary to her work as an artist—was also a source of embarrassment to her. I was already immersed in my papyrus when I heard her whisper my name. I looked over to see her bent rigidly, her hand resting on the record book, her eyes wide with alarm.

"What is it?" I asked. "Are you unwell?"

"A page is missing," she said. "It has been ripped out. Someone has been in here."

I stood up and went to her. "That's not possible, Iris. You and Emmett have the only keys."

She showed me the book, the ragged edge of a missing page clearly evident. "It's the sketch and description of the emerald and malachite brooch from a few days ago. Do you remember?"

I did. She had done a beautiful job with the restoration, and with the accompanying drawing. She was flipping pages now, frantically. "Oh, dear god, here's another one missing. And another." She stared at me, panicked. "Do you think they stole the jewelry?"

"I think there is every chance of it." I sat Iris down and poured her a glass of the brandy that I kept for emergencies. She was extremely pale. "I will check while you sit here and recover yourself. What were the catalog numbers?"

Iris consulted the book. "These were all larger pieces, so I gave them each a full page for the sketch and description. I had a separate cataloging system for the personal items from the mummies." I nodded. I knew this, as I had helped her box them in reused cigar and biscuit containers, and stack them on the wooden shelves that Khalid and his father had built for us. But it seemed to help her to talk through the process step-by-step, and I saw no reason to hasten the discovery of missing objects, which seemed all but certain. "So the missing pages are for box numbers 12 ... 38 ... and 145."

"Right," I said. "Let's get it over with, shall we?" I squeezed her shoulder. "This is not your fault, Iris. Or mine. It is the fault only of whoever made the decision to take what did not belong to him." I picked up a lantern and carried it with me to the open shelving. It had occurred to me before today that we were housing too many valuables here, but the pace of the excavation had outstripped our capacity to manage it, and the more precious the finds, the more reluctant Emmett and Drake were to reveal our success to anyone beyond our immediate circle.

Transporting the treasures out of the village meant either having Mr. Drake sail to Cairo, or trusting a courier, both of which he was unwilling to do. And so here we were, two single women guarding a trove that was likely to rank in Egyptology's most significant discoveries, with secrecy as our primary protection. It did no good to dwell on it. What was done was done. I traced my fingers over the box numbers in the watery light, noting each absence with a touch. "I am sorry, Iris," I said. "The boxes are gone as well. Only those three, though, from what I can see."

"The emerald brooch, the ruby and pearl earrings, and the carnelian and garnet necklace," she said. Of course, she knew. These objects were as familiar to her as the papyri were to me. It was a dreadful loss. And yet, she seemed stronger now, more resolute. "Should we send word to Emmett?"

I shook my head. It was too dangerous for either of us to travel out to the site on our own. We might have sent Khalid, but he had departed early today, leaving our supper for us. This wasn't unusual; Khalid had responsibilities at home. We debated the merits of walking through the village to Rubi's house to ask for help, but Rubi himself had warned us not to leave the house at night. In the end we determined to sleep in shifts.

"I'll get my pistol," said Iris. "He could come back."

"You have a pistol?" I was astonished.

"Where I grew up, shooting goes along with riding," she said.

"A pistol here, though? In this house? I'm surprised you never mentioned it."

"My father always said that a gun was most useful when no one knew you had one," she said. "Mostly, I pretend I don't have it. I despise shooting, and most of the people who enjoy it. It is a horrible sport. But my father had a pistol made for me when I first came to Egypt. He said he would withhold his permission to travel unless I promised to pack it. It's quite a lovely piece, as these things go. Engraved, even."

"Go and get it then," I said. It was unsettling to know that we'd had a gun in the house all this time. My father had been very much opposed to them. "What if I shot you, or the nurse, or one of the maids, thinking it was an intruder?" he had said. "I would never be able to forgive myself." But I had to admit that I was grateful for Iris's pistol and her apparent skill with it. I was not accustomed to vulnerability, and it sat unpleasantly with me. When she returned, I set up a bed on the floor near the coffin cases, where it was darkest. "You sleep first," I said. "I'm going to stay up and study the papyrus for a while longer. I'll wake you up if I hear anything unusual."

Iris soon drifted off, and I sat up at my desk, unwilling to wake her and feeling as energized and alert as a night creature. I unrolled the final section of my papyrus and began to transcribe it.

Hours drifted past like clouds in a gusty sky, and when Iris stirred, I realized that the sun was rising. I leaned back in my chair. My neck and back were so stiff that I felt almost mummified myself. I closed my eyes and forced myself to concentrate on the great responsibility that I had to discharge.

Even without having begun my translation, I knew that the papyrus on my battered desk would be recorded as one of the greatest artifacts pulled from this extraordinary site. If our invader returned, he might well turn his attention to it, since he was no common thief. How could he be? The lock was unforced. The key had been copied, but by whom? Rubi? Emmett? James? Some combination thereof? The intruder knew our schedules, knew the house and the cataloging system, and had made efforts to conceal his crime. He likely knew exactly which artifacts he wanted, and how to dispose of them safely and profitably. We could not assume that he was satisfied with his initial strike.

So how could I protect it? My eye lighted on the jewelry box I'd bought in the Khan el-Kalili market, which I used to store my restoration supplies—my unused brushes, my extra tweezers—along with a single strand of pearls that had belonged to my mother. Moving quietly, so as not to disturb Iris, I opened the box and pressed the hidden release to access the compartment concealed in its base. I measured its dimensions, and those of the scroll, and made a decision.

The papyrus was still slightly damp in the area where I'd been working overnight, but it was pliable throughout. It was not a long scroll. There would be some damage, but nothing I couldn't repair easily once the danger had passed. I replaced the sheet of blotting paper underneath the papyrus, and placed a second sheet over top of it, and then, without further hesitation, I rerolled the scroll and placed it in its original linen bag, the one that had cushioned Hermione's head throughout the centuries. I could hear it crack, and saw several flakes fall from the edges, and I felt the desecration as a physical pain. But whereas I could repair it, I could not replace it, and I soldiered on, scarcely breathing until I had tucked the bag into the hidden drawer and activated the lock.

The village was coming to life, and I heard Khalid come in with fresh water. I unlocked the door and stepped out of the storeroom, surprising him. "We have had a theft," I said. "A very serious one. Send Rubi out to fetch Mr. Olsen from the site immediately."

His eyes widened. "Oh, Miss Helen. Are you both well? No one is hurt?"

"We are fine. Distressed, but unharmed. Thank you, Khalid," I said.

"I will come back as quickly as I can," he said. I watched him run down the road to where the animals were kept, and I returned to the storeroom.

Iris was sitting up, and her eyes filled with tears when I helped her to stand. "I can hardly bear it, Helen," she said. "What will they think of us? And when we've worked so hard to prove ourselves to them!"

"They will think that we could have done nothing to stop it," I said. "They do not have such a high opinion of our fighting skills, you may be sure. Which means that they will be grateful we were not here when it occurred."

"They will not trust us with the artifacts any longer," she said.

I thought of the papyrus, safe in my box, and I felt the rightness of my choice. "It will be a difficult day, without question," I said. "But we must greet it all the same."

She blotted her face and attempted a smile. "I'll put the kettle on," she said, reaching out and squeezing my hand. "We will await our sentence together."

TWENTY-FOUR

SACRAMENTO, 2019

The excavation diary lies on a stainless steel table in the lab, Gareth and Maddie on one side, and Brett and Rebecca on the other. Rebecca, wearing gloves, reaches first, brushing her fingers over the leather binding of the diary. She opens the cover, and reads the text on the flyleaf: *Calliopolis, Excavation Diary, January 1904–, volume 2 of __*. "Handwriting is so intimate, isn't it?" she says. "A whisper from the past. We've lost so much in the computer age."

"We've gained a few things as well," says Brett, without heat. Rebecca nods. She knows better than anyone what magic he's conjured with his machines.

"Is Pete on his way?" Rebecca asks Maddie. "We'll start without him if he isn't here soon."

"I texted him," says Maddie. "He's coming."

Pete arrives then, the metal doors clanging behind him, and joins them at the table. "If everyone agrees," says Rebecca, "I'd like to focus our attention today on any entries relating to the Sappho scroll. I think it would be useful to build a timeline of the scroll's history for provenance purposes."

"Agreed," Maddie says.

"Agreed," says Pete, although the scroll does not belong to him. Maddie feels a prickle of irritation and reminds herself that she would not be here without his support.

Rebecca doesn't look at Pete. "Maddie, I should tell you, I've compared the scroll to all the known Sappho fragments. There's a publication from 1971 by a German scholar that is considered definitive. I believe Helen's scroll may be a much more complete version of what is known as Fragment 58."

"That's a good thing, I take it?" says Maddie.

Rebecca smiles at her. "Oh, yes. If we are right, we have in our possession one of the longest and most complete poems by Sappho in existence. It's a marvel." She seems to steady herself against the lab table.

Brett covers one of her hands with his. "Which is why we are going to move slowly and cover all our bases."

"Exactly right," says Rebecca. "So. Let's have a look at this excavation diary, shall we?" She lifts the book and examines its binding. "It's in good condition. No cracking, although there are some loose pages here." She opens the diary to the center point, where it bulges around a sheaf of paper. "What's this? Not part of the book, that's for sure." Rebecca removes the document and separates the pages, laying each one on the table, scanning them as she does.

"That's Helen Gardiner's handwriting," says Maddie. "I recognize it from the excavation diary at the Drake Museum."

"These are her notes on the Sappho poem," Rebecca says. "Her Greek transcription, her English translation, and her drafts on both. I need a minute to concentrate."

They are all silent as Rebecca studies Helen's pages. When she speaks, she says, "Her translation is better than mine. Much more beautiful. Truly brilliant. Listen." She reads aloud:

> *You, children, be zealous for the beautiful gifts of the violetlapped*
> > *Muses*
> *and for the clear songloving lyre.*
> *But my skin once soft is now taken by old age,*
> *my hair turns white from black.*
> *And my heart is weighed down and my knees do not lift,*
> *that once were light to dance as fawns.*
> *I groan for this. But what can I do?*
> *A human being without old age is not a possibility.*

"It was meant to be recited, you know," she continues after a long pause. "You're the first people in nineteen centuries to hear it as it was intended. That's not something I'll forget." She clears her throat. "Helen's version of the poem isn't complete. There are a few more lines that she was working on when she died. I've done my own translation of them. I'll work with Helen's notes, and when we publish, she'll get the credit she deserves. The world should know who she is."

There is a knock on the lab door. Gareth goes to answer it and calls over his shoulder: "Maddie, there's a delivery for you."

"Oh, god," says Rebecca. "Maddie, I'm sorry, I was supposed to tell you this was coming, but I got distracted when you showed up with the excavation diary. The package is from your father, and Ben Cupul is going to be here later this afternoon to tell you the story behind it."

Maddie feels as though she's been slammed against a wall. She eases herself onto a stool and perches there, her chest tight and sore. "Ben is coming here?"

"Yes," says Rebecca. "As I understand it, your father has been doing a deep dive into the archive at K'abel since he learned that Helen's scroll was here."

"And how did he learn that?" asks Maddie. "He didn't hear it from me. My father and I don't really speak to each other, as all of you and most of the rest of the world knows."

Rebecca looks pained, but her gaze is steady. "I told him," she says. "After my preliminary examination of the scroll. I felt that I had an ethical responsibility to do so. I asked Ben Cupul to put us in touch. I should have spoken to you about it first, but I didn't know you well enough at the time to judge what you would do."

Maddie digests what Rebecca has said. She's angry and embarrassed to learn that she's been shunted aside, but knows, also, that Rebecca is right. The scroll is part of her family history. Her father has a voice in this story too. "No more lying," she says, firmly. "No more omissions, no more puppeteering."

"I promise," says Rebecca. "Thank you. I intend to earn your trust." She places a hand on the courier package. "Ben couldn't carry this on the plane from Mexico, so he sent it ahead and asked me to begin some testing on it while he's in transit. Are you comfortable with my doing that?"

"Sure," says Maddie. She watches as Rebecca splays open a pair of scissors and slices through the tape on the courier box. She bends the cardboard lid and extracts a large plastic ziplock bag, placing it on the metal table with a clank.

"I can see why he couldn't carry it on the plane," says Gareth.

The object in the bag is a knife, stiletto-thin and honed on both edges.

"It's a letter opener," says Rebecca. "It was in the archive at K'abel. David Sloan found it, along with some information suggesting that it was used to kill Helen Gardiner. He's asked Brett to do a DNA test."

Maddie feels slightly dizzy. "And you say that Ben is on his way to speak to me?"

"Maddie, are you okay?" Gareth puts a hand on her arm. "You look wobbly. Who's Ben?"

"Her ex-boyfriend," says Pete.

"He's a professor at Stanford," says Rebecca. "I'm writing a paper with him."

"He works with my father at K'abel," says Maddie. "We grew up together. And dated. And lived together for a couple of years before he broke up with me."

"Do you want to see him?" asks Gareth.

"I don't know," she says. She's grateful to Gareth. No one else seems to feel that she has a choice in this. "We didn't part on the best of terms."

Rebecca hands her a printout of an email. "He said to give you this if you were resistant to seeing him."

> Maddie, I know it's been awkward and that's my fault. I'm sorry for that. I'd like a chance to apologize in person if you are open to it. I'm coming for another reason, though, on behalf of your father. He has found information in the K'abel archive that he wants you to have. He wasn't sure if you would see him, so he asked me to use my connection to Rebecca to get it to you. With my best, Ben.

Maddie shows the email to Gareth. "It's not only Ben," she tells him. "My father and I . . ."

"Are in a public feud," says Pete.

"For god's sake, Pete," says Brett. "Maddie is obviously upset. You're being insensitive."

"When is he not?" asks Rebecca.

"Be quiet. All of you." Gareth sits down next to Maddie. "Can I help? Do you want me to go with you to meet Ben? You don't have to do it alone, you know."

"Thank you," she says. "I might take you up on that. I just need a few minutes to process everything." Her brain is teeming with questions; she starts with the one that feels easiest to ask. "How can we do

DNA testing when we don't have another sample of Helen's DNA for comparison?"

"Leave it to me," says Brett. "I have an idea."

"Okay," says Maddie.

"Maddie?" says Pete. "I need a word. In private, please."

"Okay," she says, again.

Pete suggests the lounge, and leads her down the hall, where he ejects a pair of graduate students and locks the door behind them. Maddie raises her eyebrows. "Why the secrecy?"

"The circle is getting larger, thanks to Rebecca," he says. "The more people who know about the scroll, the greater the risk of theft. We need a plan to protect it."

"You don't think the university vault is safe enough?"

"You tell me. Someone broke into your office a couple of days ago. Did the university's crack team of security experts fill you with confidence?"

"Clayton isn't in charge of the vault," she says, mildly. If Gareth, Brett, and Rebecca had faith in the library protocols, who was she to question them? "But for the sake of argument, what are you proposing?" Even as she says it, she has an inkling of where this conversation is going. She hopes she's wrong.

"You should arrange to sell it. Michael Grey wants the commission, and he's the best dealer out there. He'll store it and insure it, and you can breathe easy. Not to mention that he'll get an extraordinary deal for you."

"Michael Grey should hire you to do PR," she says. It's a joke until she sees his expression harden, become bullish. A silence sits between them. "I see," she says, slowly. "What's your cut?"

"Half of his fee," he says. "Why not? It doesn't affect the size of the windfall to you. Not to mention that you wouldn't know about the scroll at all unless I'd helped you discover it. Why begrudge me a share?" He stands and begins to pace. "There are benefits to getting the scroll out of sight, Maddie. Look at it this way: Helen Gardiner stole it from an excavation under the jurisdiction of the Egyptian Antiquities Service. Technically, you moved a looted artifact across an international border. If ICE hears about it, they'll confiscate the scroll and investigate you for trafficking."

"What are you talking about?" she says. "Nothing was trafficked. The scroll came as a part of a loan between museums. You set it up."

"Did you read the loan documents? No? I didn't think so. They mention the box, but not the scroll. TAM believes they loaned Iris's box—the one already in their collection—and the letter that was found inside it. They don't know about the scroll."

Maddie digs her nails into her thigh. She's trying to focus on what Pete is saying while continuing to breathe, but she's finding it hard to do both at the same time. "I saw the documents," she says. "You had me sign them. You told me what they said. And what about Claudia and Luisa? They must have read them. Didn't they notice there was a different box?"

"People see what they expect to see," says Pete. "As far as they know, you, Maddie Sloan, a trusted employee of TAM, packed the objects for loan and prepared the documents for signature. They'll be very disappointed to hear that you put their reputations at risk. But perhaps it won't come as a surprise, given your history. It will certainly be the end of your career, and that's the best-case scenario."

Since her mother's death, there have been times when Maddie has woken from a nightmare, feeling the earth closing over her head. Now the sensation scrabbles just at the edge of her consciousness. She wills herself to be calm. "You set me up," she says. "Did you break into my office as well?"

"Of course not," he says, as if offended.

"You mean you wouldn't take the risk yourself. But you know who did. You were involved."

He doesn't deny it, which is an answer.

There's a sharp knock at the door. "Leave it," Pete says, but Maddie ignores him. She wants out of this room and away from him. When she sees Gareth on the other side of the door, her body shudders with relief.

"Are you all right?" Gareth asks. "Why was the door locked?"

Behind her, Pete stands, his posture stiff and angry. "We're finished in here," he says, preparing to leave.

"We sure are," she says.

"Think about what I said, Maddie," says Pete. "I think you'll discover you don't have a choice."

"Maddie?" Gareth stands in front of her. "You look like you might fall over. Did something happen with Pete? Do you need to sit down? Do I need to call someone?"

"There's no one to call," she says. "I have no one."

"That's not true," he says, reaching for her hand. "You have me."

TWENTY-FIVE

CALLIOPOLIS, 1904

The first person to arrive at our door was Rubi. He looked unwell, as if he had aged overnight. Khalid, he told us, had conveyed the terrible news. Mr. Olsen and Mr. Drake had been informed, and we were instructed to move to the steamer at once.

"I'm sure Khalid can help us with the move," I said. "You must be busy today."

"Khalid is needed elsewhere," said Rubi. Mr. Olsen had asked him to oversee the move personally. He suggested that we pack our trunks so that we would have whatever we needed if we were not able to return quickly. He was, as usual, prescient. We were immediately welcomed as Miss Alcott's guests and offered every comfort except the ability to leave.

Meanwhile, Mr. Drake and several armed police officers returned to the village house to retrieve all the remaining valuables. The small items were stored in an onboard safe; larger objects were loaded into an empty bedroom and a guard set outside. Telegrams were dispatched: one to Mr. Maspero, directing him to come to Calliopolis immediately and travel back to Cairo with the artifacts under military protection or risk his share of the discovery; another to Mr. Mohassib, Mr. Drake's preferred Luxor dealer, presumably to evaluate whatever he didn't want Mr. Maspero to see.

Iris and I met with the investigating officer and gave statements with Emmett and Mr. Drake listening in. It did not seem that anyone held us responsible, which eased Iris's distress somewhat. When the interview was over, Nora bustled in and insisted that we retire to our cabins and rest, reminding everyone that we had missed a night of sleep under harrowing conditions. I thought to humor her by putting my feet up for an hour or so but surprised myself by waking in the afternoon. I emerged, groggy and sweaty, and climbed to the upper deck. I chose a chair with a view of the water. I preferred to watch the river birds and the local fisherman instead of the performance on the quayside, where armed officers were marching up and down in formation.

I closed my eyes, feeling the boat sway. Leaving the village house after a long and frightening night, I'd left all considerations of the theft behind with the men. Alone there on the deck, my mind could not help but return to them. Any villager, it was true, could have gained access to the house; Khalid was often out, running errands for us and for his own family. The sturdy lock on the storage room had seemed protection enough. And this was another pressing question: How had the door been opened? As far as I knew there were only two keys, one that hung in a ring on Emmett's belt, and one that had hung around my neck until this morning, when I'd surrendered it to Emmett in front of the police. It was possible that another key had been made at some point, or that Emmett himself had been involved. But surely not. Emmett was not in the archeology business for money. He was here for the same reasons I was: knowledge of the past, and a place earned in the history of our field.

I wondered what had fired Emmett's fascination with Egypt. I remembered vividly the spark that had ignited my own: a trip to the Brooklyn Academy of Music to hear Amelia Edwards speak. Had it been 1890?

I thought so. I had been around the age of twelve. Aunt Margaret was arguing with my father in the carriage over his decision to allow me to write the entrance exams for Brearley, a school based on the radical notion that young women should be educated to the same intellectual standards as men. My father was already hampering my marriage prospects, she felt. "No man wants an overeducated wife," she told him, a statement I took to heart, though not in the way she intended.

My father mostly ignored her and talked to me about Miss Edwards's Egyptian Exploration Fund, which had sponsored much of Flinders Petrie's work in the field. I asked him whether he had ever thought to make the journey to Egypt himself. He looked wistful. His own studies had taken him to Greece, he said. He had hoped to see the pyramids one day, but life had taken him in another direction. I knew that he meant my mother, and also me.

At the theater, we met my father's cousin, Clifford Cogswell, who made a very favorable impression on Aunt Margaret. I disliked him immediately, despite his occupation in chocolate making. Miss Edwards's book *A Thousand Miles Up the Nile* had pride of place on my bedside table, and I had been waiting weeks for this opportunity to see my heroine in the flesh, but Cousin Clifford said he hoped it would at least be entertaining. One couldn't have much in the way of expectations of a lady lecturer, he said, and quoted Samuel Johnson: "It's like a dog walking on its hind legs, isn't it? It's not done well, but you are surprised to find it done at all."

He was wrong. Amelia Edwards, though small in stature, had the presence of a giant. Even Aunt Margaret, whose opera glasses scanned the audience for fashion offenses like a searchlight, was startled into attention as she began to speak. Her topic was, unexpectedly, books, and she told the room that the Egyptians were the first people of the ancient world to write and read and own and love books, although they did so on papyrus rolls rather than bound paper.

In that moment I saw myself, not as a girl with unnatural interests, but as an independent thinker devoted to the written word, connected to the woman on the stage and to people as far back in history as the ancient world. What a strange and beautiful gift it was to know my own mind and heart, even as I sensed that I would have to relinquish a great deal to keep them whole.

"May I join you?" James Dunn interrupted my reverie.

"Certainly," I said. "But why aren't you out at the site?"

"There was no digging today," he said. "All the men were put to work building crates for transport, and Emmett and I were packing them. Maspero arrives at noon tomorrow, Mohassib at dinner tonight. In a couple of days, we'll have shipped all the finds to one destination or another." James signaled to one of the servants and ordered himself a gin and tonic.

"Are you not required to show all of the finds to Mr. Maspero before you show them to Mr. Mohassib?"

"You are not so innocent as that, Helen," he said. "We will follow the same rules that everyone else does. Maspero may not understand precisely what those rules are, but he will not push too hard. The antiquities service doesn't run without foreign money, and if people like Calvin Drake are expected to fund excavations, they require incentives. Signing over the best half of the bounty to the national museum is untenable."

Innocent? Hardly. I was wise enough to understand that my opinions held no sway here. So what if I believed that Mr. Maspero had a right to see what emerged from the sites under his jurisdiction? Mr. Drake could make his own rules, which was not a privilege that would ever be extended to me, or to Iris—not to mention one of the villagers. I had learned to keep my anger to myself: Honest expression was too high a price to pay to be thought irrational. I changed the subject, and asked how the investigation was proceeding.

"I'm sorry to be the bearer of bad tidings," he said. "But it seems you had a viper in your nest. Your houseboy has disappeared, and they found a statue hidden in his father's house."

"That is a filthy lie," I told him flatly. "A monstrous lie. Khalid is a bright, hardworking young man. He has been a great help to me in my work, and an excellent student. He respects what we do. He would never steal from us."

"You do not know him, Helen," said James. "You made a pet of him. That is your fault, not his."

I felt ill. Khalid was innocent, I was certain. But I suddenly feared that my efforts to teach him had made him vulnerable. I had set him apart, and now the authorities would view his exceptionality as an opportunity for crime. And what of his own people? A theft like this would tarnish the entire village. Would they protect Khalid if it meant that their livelihood was threatened? No. He would be sacrificed on the altar of greed, one way or the other.

"Don't fret," said James, seeing the expression on my face. "They will not find him if he does not want to be found. One boy swaddled in white cloth looks much like another." He waved his hand, dismissing the issue. "That is not what I came to speak to you about."

Fury bubbled up, and for a moment I imagined pushing James over the side of the boat, seeing his white linen splattered with mud and his hat floating, seeing the crocodiles shift lazily on the bank and glide into the water. "And what was that?" I said.

"I have it in mind to propose to Iris," he said. "I'd like you to put in a good word."

"I see," I said. I marveled that, for all his intelligence, James could be so thoughtless. If Iris wanted to marry a man completely indifferent to Khalid's fate, I would not stand in her way, but neither would I facilitate it.

James's drink arrived. "You don't want one?" I shook my head. I did not wish to drink with him as if we were friends. "To your health, then," he said. "I must say, Helen, you seem out of sorts. I don't doubt that it was a rough night. But you'll be quite safe to move back to the village once all the artifacts have shipped out. We will make sure that the word is spread through the local communities that we are no longer keeping objects of value there." He seemed disappointed by my lack of enthusiasm for these efforts. "Is that not a comfort? Certainly no one blames you or Iris for what happened."

"I should hope not. I don't require any incentive to be here beyond the work itself."

"A useful quality in an employee."

"I used to think you were the same. But perhaps I was mistaken." I had not intended to tell James what I knew, but anger made me reckless.

Beside me, I felt James straighten in his chair. "Oh?"

"I saw you in Cairo," I said. "At the market, in an antiquities shop. One not unlike Mr. Mohassib's, I'd wager."

"It is part of the job to know the dealers," he said, slowly, as if considering his words. "You know this."

"You had an excavation box with you."

"Did I? I don't remember."

Did he suppose that my principles made me ignorant? I had imagined that he and Emmett believed me to be an equal colleague, but perhaps that had never been true. Perhaps they considered us fools, good only for our narrow expertise and nothing more. "I think you do," I said. I'd sat up in a wooden chair all night, biting the inside of my cheek to stay awake, eyeing the pistol that I'd pushed to the far corner of the desk, while Iris dozed fitfully in the shadows: I would not forgive the man who had put me there.

His expression grew hard and unyielding. There was no embarrassment, no apology. "You think you know a great deal more than you do, Helen," he said. "Do you see the budgets for this whole enterprise? Do you understand what it costs to keep an excavation running? How to feed as many mouths as we do, and supply them with tools and medicines and shelter? And do you know what percentage of those costs is covered by Drake's contribution? No? I thought not." I opened my mouth to speak, but he held up a hand. "Do you know that the men are insisting on higher wages because of the unquiet spirits of the mummies? And do you know that Drake refuses to pay it because he thinks Rubi is stirring them up? And perhaps he is, but it must be paid, because we cannot create more time in the season. So where does the money come from?"

"I don't know," I said.

"Of course you don't know. You know about papyrus. You have a specialty, and that is useful. But it is not enough, nowhere near enough, to run an excavation, or to judge how Emmett chooses to do so."

"These objects belong in museums. They should not be handed over to dealers to be sold on the quiet, without any documentation. It's a grotesque abuse of the privilege we have in excavating these sites."

"Tell that to Calvin Drake," he said. "And if you think I'd take the jewelry that he's obsessed with behind his back, you're mad."

I understood, finally. "Mr. Drake had you take it," I said. "He asked you to take his favorite pieces so that they wouldn't be in the pool for division with Mr. Maspero." I wished that I had accepted his offer of a drink now. "How have you been rewarded for your loyalty?"

For a moment, he looked lost, and I felt that I had hit my mark. "Calvin Drake is not a man to cross," he said. "He is a man who takes what he wants."

"You are a coward," I said.

"Perhaps," he said. "Or perhaps I know that discretion is the better part of valor. There is a good reason why so few ladies are invited on excavations: They are too sheltered to understand the politics of what we do, to make the hard choices that must be made. Do you not understand what you owe me, all of you, for holding the balance between a bully and a drunk each and every day?"

"I will not tell her to accept you."

"I gathered as much," he said. "That's of no consequence. She'll marry me regardless. I can offer her the life she wants."

"You're very sure of yourself," I said, my voice as cold as I could make it. His comments about women had stung though. I was frightened for Iris, and for myself. How had we missed so much of what was happening around us?

"Why shouldn't I be? I can protect her."

"She can protect herself."

"Like Alice Baker could?" He stood. "I thought you naive, Miss Gardiner, but not foolish. My future wife cares about you and would be distressed to see you hurt. So please believe me when I say this: Calvin Drake is a dangerous man."

TWENTY-SIX

SACRAMENTO, 2019

Gareth's house suits him—it's bright and homey, and full of books. Maddie has taken up residence on his sofa while he makes arrangements, and tea.

She cannot stop apologizing, so Gareth has instituted a ban, which she violates as soon as Brett and Rebecca arrive. "I should have seen it coming," she says. "I've implicated all of you in an incredibly unpleasant situation. I'm mortified."

"It's not your fault that you took Pete at his word," says Brett. "Why wouldn't you? As far as you knew, his reputation was impeccable."

"That's about to end," says Rebecca. "Pete's always been unscrupulous, but this is a new low, even for him. The way he's treated you is outrageous, Maddie—unethical at the very least and bordering on extortionate. There are going to be consequences this time."

"I can't believe I was so naive," says Maddie.

Rebecca doesn't disagree, but her eyes are kind. "If it's any consolation," she says, "it's not personal. It's just the way he is."

Maddie begins to say something about cold comfort, but there's a knock at the door, and suddenly Ben is in the room, as familiar to Maddie as her own crushed heart. She hasn't seen him in six months. He is still recognizably her old love, but also not. He seems shinier somehow, polished. At ease in this company, no longer a student. His dark hair is longer, curling slightly at the collar of his expensive linen jacket. His skin, sallow in the Toronto winter, glows bronze and is peppered with fashionable stubble. He looks successful.

He introduces himself to Gareth and Brett, and she realizes that he's nervous. "Maddie," he says. "Rebecca filled me in on everything that's happening. I hope that's okay."

"It's fine," she says. Oddly, it's true. She doesn't need to try to make Ben love her anymore. She doesn't need to be perfect for him.

"Before we begin, I wonder if we could speak in private?"

She considers this. The private conversations she's been having lately have left her wary. But she's hesitant to air their old business in front of Gareth and the others. "Yes," she says. "Let's go out to the front porch."

Outside, Maddie sinks into a rattan armchair. "What do you want to tell me?" she asks.

He sits and seems to gather himself. "First of all, I want to apologize," he says. "I handled our breakup badly. I carry a lot of regret about it."

"It's okay," she says, her voice thick and scratchy.

"It isn't," he says. "Before anything else, we were friends. Best friends. I feel . . . I feel that I shouldn't have let us become more than that. It was always going to be so complicated between us, because of my relationship with your parents, and with K'abel."

"So we were a mistake? Is that what you're saying?" She brushes away tears. What Ben is saying is more than difficult, almost intolerable, but not wrong.

Ben sighs. "The stakes were so high for us. I think it was too much pressure to put on a relationship. That doesn't mean I didn't love you, or that I don't love you. It means that I think we are family members, and I didn't figure that out until we started living together. It didn't feel right to me, but I couldn't put my finger on why until I left."

She can see it now, how intertwined every part of their lives had become. How that might have felt stifling to Ben, even if it didn't to her. "I think I understand," she says. "I'm going to need some time."

"Of course," he says. "I only want to say that I miss you and I very much want to rebuild a friendship with you. You matter to me."

They sit in silence for a minute or so, tactfully ignoring each other's tears. She thinks about Ben's relationship to K'abel itself. How he has said from the beginning—from the time when they played there as children—that he felt his ancestors on the land, from the original Mayan residents of the great city to the plantation workers to the laborers on Iris's excavation. She knows what it would mean to him to become the first lead excavator of Indigenous descent; what it would mean for his community.

Ben clears his throat. "This next part is even more delicate," he says. "It's about your dad."

"He loves you," she says. "I know that. You are a son to him, and he is a father to you."

"You think he chose me over you."

"Yes. Of course I do."

"You're wrong, Maddie. That's not it. Not at all. You are his child. I'm not. You weren't there when Silvia died. He wasn't himself, not for months. That interview—when the reporter called—he was in a rage. He already blamed himself for Silvia's death. He couldn't bear hearing that you blamed him as well. He regretted his comments almost immediately, but it was too late. The damage was done."

"It certainly was," says Maddie.

"He wants to redeem himself. He's not an ideal parent, I know. But he's trying. Since he heard about the scroll, he's been buried in the K'abel archive, trying to find material that might help you."

"Did he find anything? Aside from a knife?"

"He did. It's one of the reasons I'm here. I've brought it to you. But first, we need to deal with the Pete Bahar problem."

"My dad knows about that, too, does he?" Rebecca has been thorough in her report, Maddie notes. She wants to summon up some righteous anger, but all she feels now is tired. Did Pete ever intend to write a book with her? Has it all been an elaborate con?

"He does. He's furious."

"I'm sure he is." Maddie puts her hands over her eyes. "I've been a complete idiot."

"He's furious with Pete," says Ben. "Not with you. He's arranged a meeting with the group here."

"It's my mess," says Maddie. "I should clean it up."

Ben shakes his head. "Maddie, for once in your life, could you try to believe that no one does it alone? Not me, not your dad, not anyone sitting inside this house. Why should you be the exception? Why would you want to be?"

They decide to do the meeting in the lab. Brett sets up a camera to record it, and Gareth arranges for a security guard, just in case. Maddie doesn't think it will be necessary, but Gareth insists that people have been known to behave strangely in the presence of precious objects. "You might call it a curse," he says, wryly.

"Okay," says Ben. "Let's get David on the call before the others arrive. Are you ready, Maddie?"

She nods. Ben taps on the keyboard, and suddenly her father is there, his face filling the screen. He's aged, she realizes. He's thinner, his cheeks narrower than she remembers them. His hair, always dark, has silvered, and the stubble on his chin is white. "Hello, Mads," he says. There is no one else alive, she realizes with a shock, who calls her by this childhood name.

"Hi, Dad," she replies. "I . . . it's been a long time."

"Yes," he says. "I'm so sorry for that. There is so much I want to tell you. Could I call you once we are finished here today?" He's sitting in his office at K'abel, in the part of the hacienda that was their family home. She can see the bookshelf behind him, covered in messy stacks of books and articles, and a leather chair in the corner where she used to sit and read mystery novels while he worked. There's a window just outside the frame with a view of the Pyramid of the Jade Queen, and she remembers how she used to watch her mother excavating from there. How Silvia would catch her sometimes and laugh and wave.

Maddie feels overwhelmed by a desire to step through the screen and into that room. She cut herself off from K'abel, after her mother died. It is only now, seeing her father's face etched with loss, that she can feel the truth of what Ben has said: She is not alone—not in her pain, not in her struggle. She has a history, and K'abel is part of it. "I'd like that," she says.

Michael Grey and Pete arrive together. Pete takes in the recording equipment, the security guard, and the on-screen presence of Maddie's father with an unruffled gaze.

"This seems unnecessarily theatrical," he says, "for a conversation between friends."

"We aren't friends," Maddie says. "Friends don't threaten each other."

"Don't be ridiculous," says Pete. "I did no such thing."

"You'll be able to tell that to your dean when you receive a copy of David and Maddie Sloan's complaint," says Rebecca. "As you are entitled to do according to the provisions of your faculty agreement. A complaint that is bolstered by letters from Brett, Gareth, and me."

Pete sits down. Michael remains standing. He's taking a read of the room, and he doesn't seem to like what he sees. "So we're all on the same page," says David, "the scroll is registered with the Canadian government, and administrative errors in the inter-museum loan documents have been fixed, with the assistance of Luisa Ortega. The Sloan family has retained Professor Field and Professor Cooper to identify the scroll and confirm its provenance to the best of their abilities. It is our intention to donate it to a public institution, and we anticipate hiring an agent to help us find the right home for it, although that person will not be Mr. Grey."

Michael stands. His ethics may be questionable, Maddie notes, but his manners are impeccable. "I appreciate your time," he says, and he walks out the door with barely a glance at Pete.

Pete's face is hard. He turns to Rebecca. "You must be thrilled."

"I am not," she says. "Far from it."

Pete turns to Maddie. "You would be nowhere without me," he says. "I saved you, and this is how you repay me? You ungrateful little bitch."

Maddie feels her friends moving around her, and she holds up a hand. "Do you know what's sad?" she says. "I would have shared all my research with you, and the scroll, without a second thought. I would have been glad to do it. But you manipulated me, and endangered me, and tried to steal from me. That's on you. I owe you nothing."

"Time to leave," says Brett, nodding to the security guard, who escorts Pete out of the lab.

Gareth puts an arm around Maddie's shoulders. "Are you okay?" he asks.

She nods, takes a breath, and turns to the group. "That takes care of one piece of business. Who's up next?"

"I am," says Brett. He opens a drawer and extracts the letter opener, still housed in its plastic bag. "I've run some tests and can now confirm that this is the knife that killed Helen Gardiner," he says.

"How?" asks Maddie.

"We tested a familial DNA sample: Simon Cogswell's. He was excited to cooperate, especially once we filled him in on Pete's plan with Michael Grey to profit from the scroll. He seemed to want to distance himself from the whole affair, understandably. His great-grandmother, Margaret Cogswell, was Helen's maternal aunt."

"Where did you find it?" Maddie asks her father, who has been watching from Ben's laptop screen with an impatient expression.

"In a minute," says David. He explains to the group that he's been doing his own excavation of sorts, in the archive at K'abel. "When Ben told me that you'd found the excavation diary in the Alistair Banks archive, it suddenly occurred to me that secrets can take years, decades even, to come out. I hadn't checked our archive because I knew it hadn't existed prior to 1915, when Nora Alcott sent Claude Butler to sort out the records. But I remembered that my own mother had been interested in the oral histories of the site, and I wondered if Iris had passed down any stories that might be relevant to you."

"Who was Claude Butler?" asks Ben.

"He was Nora Alcott's personal secretary," says David. Nora had been the principal funder of the excavation for at least a decade at that point, he explained, and over that period, the number of staff had increased steadily, along with the budget. It had begun to attract the attention of local authorities. After her experience in Egypt, Nora wanted to ensure that her management of the site was unimpeachable and that someone on the ground was tending to the necessary relationships with government officials. "She sent Claude to manage the business side, and he remained at K'abel for over forty years."

"I saw a letter from Nora to Iris about him," says Maddie. "Nora didn't think much of Iris's bookkeeping skills."

"She was an artist," says David. "An extraordinarily talented woman in many ways. But no one is good at everything. I know I'm not."

Maddie nods, accepting this rare admission.

David continues: "What I found in the archive was that my mother, Alma, embarked on a project in the early 1970s to preserve the history of the excavation itself—like you, Maddie, she had an interest in how sites are interpreted by the people who work on them. Recording technology had become accessible to laypeople by then, and she got herself a little cassette recorder and microphone. I remember her using it. Her mother had died in the late 1960s, and she knew it wouldn't be long before the memories of those early days were lost for good. She started collecting oral histories of the people who worked at K'abel, some—like Claude Butler—for decades. I've been listening to them and converting them to digital files."

"Enough suspense," says Maddie. "Dad, what did you find?"

"I'm going to let your grandmother tell you," says David. "Ben, play them the recording."

TWENTY-SEVEN

CALLIOPOLIS, 1904

Two days later, we finally returned to the village house to find it full of sand, patterned with the imprints of male boots. The storeroom looked desolate with all the treasures removed: shelves of cardboard boxes containing jewelry and delicate objects; most of the stone statuary; the painted coffins stacked one on top of the other; the paraffin-coated portraits tilted against every available wall. Only a few lonely boxes of fragments now remained, all of which had been deemed low priority; the men had run out of wood for shipping crates and left a few behind for the last transport. The room seemed huge, and our desks relatively tiny, like the ones used for children's lessons. Standing there, it seemed to me that our scholarly contributions had been insubstantial, and I felt a deep sadness.

We were determined to sleep in our house, despite Nora's protestations. It had been rare for both of us to have such privacy, and we relished it. We compromised by agreeing to return to the boat for tea so that she could try once more to persuade us. In the meantime, we tried to reclaim our workspace in the hours available to us. The next day we were due to return to our normal schedule on the excavation, and both of us worried that we had lost our status as colleagues now that we had been damsels in distress. From now on, we had been told, finds would be stored on the boat as soon as we cleaned and documented them. Mr. Drake was planning to remain in Calliopolis for the balance of the season, at which point Mr. Maspero would return a second time to divide the spoils, following which the site would be closed again until October.

But now there was much to be done, and no time to waste in wallowing. We did not speak of Khalid. It was too much to bear. Iris took off her hat and hung it on a hook. She had a smock that she used when she was painting, and she put it on over her dress. Seized with a strange energy, she began sweeping. I retreated to the storeroom, dusting my books, lining them up on the now empty shelves, and washing down my papyrus table. Iris came in with the broom and took a layer of grit off the floor and then returned with a mop and bucket. Gradually my mood brightened as the room was restored to order, and I sat down at my desk to continue with my translation.

There was a knock at the door, and Iris went to answer it. "Reverend Banks is here to see you," she called.

"Show him in," I called back. The Reverend entered, and I greeted him. "Do we have any tea?" I asked Iris.

Her face was grim. "It appears to have vanished along with the sugar and a few other items from the pantry in our absence. I'll have to send . . . Rubi into town for replacements." I saw her bite her lip and knew that she was thinking of Khalid. There was still no sign of him, and Rubi refused to discuss his whereabouts. Iris turned to the Reverend. "I'm very sorry that we can't offer you refreshment," she said. "I'm afraid we are in no state for guests. We've only just arrived ourselves and have found the house in disarray."

"Please don't trouble yourself," he said. "I'm on my way to town, as a matter of fact, and would be happy to acquire whatever you need.

Would you like to make a list? I can pass by again this evening with your shopping."

"How very kind of you," she said, and went to check the cupboards, leaving me alone with him.

He was carrying a tin excavation box, and he set it down on my desk. "I am hoping that you might examine this for me. We found it in the church. I have been continuing my work there and in the surrounding buildings. You may not be aware of my progress, as I know you have been much occupied with the discovery of the cemetery." His look was disapproving, although whether it was directed at the disinterment of bodies that had lain peacefully in the ground for centuries, or at the corresponding decline of interest in his own excavation, I could not say.

"I regret that I have not been kept apprised of your work," I told him. "As you say, Miss Wentworth and I have been pressed into service as conservators. But perhaps you could tell me what you've brought?"

"I'm hoping that you'll be able to tell me," he said. "It is a wooden box containing a scroll. The wood is very deteriorated, but the papyrus seems in better condition. I could not risk touching it myself, although the anticipation is quite distracting." He told me that box had been in a square depression in a corner of the room, covered with the remains of a fitted board and a rush mat. "Whoever left the house in the end must have forgotten it was there," he said. "It was concealed too well! But their loss is our good fortune. I hope that you will be able to turn your attention to it right away."

I thought of my own scroll, still hidden, and my transcription. The translation was extremely difficult. I had appreciated time away from the excavation, which had allowed me to use precious daylight hours on it, and I sensed that I was close to understanding the poet's mind. But I was moving with patience and precision. The ancient writer deserved no less from me.

At the same time, I had no wish to signal to the Reverend, or to anyone else, that I had found a scroll worthy of attention. The lessons of the Sappho poem had not been lost on me, although they were not the lessons that Emmett had hoped I would learn. Nora and Iris had urged me to become strategic; but why should the end of a woman's strategy be to win the favor of men? Could I not imagine one that had my own distinct objectives in view? The scroll would not be missed for now, and if Emmett asked what I had found under Hermione's head, I could simply say that it appeared to be an excerpt from the Book of the Dead, although a poor copy and much deteriorated. I had little experience of lying, but I was beginning to understand that a certain flexibility with the truth was a useful tool, like a set of lead weights that could hold a surface steady while you kept your focus where it needed to be. I told the Reverend that I would fit his project in as quickly as I could, but that I would at least make a preliminary assessment over the next several days.

Iris returned with a folded sheet of paper. "Thank you again, Reverend," she said, handing it to him.

"I imagine the villagers helped themselves to your supplies? When the cat's away, as they say. I should be off before the day gets away from me." He inclined his head in a small bow. "Miss Gardiner, Miss Wentworth. I'll let myself out."

We heard the door close. "He brought you a piece of papyrus?" Iris asked.

"Apparently so." I put on my gloves and opened the tin box. "He found it in the church."

"Poor man. I hope you're able to give him what he wants." She sighed. "It is generous of him to do our errands for us. I wish he were less . . ."

"Grating?"

Iris laughed. "It's terrible, but unfortunately true. I hear his voice and I want to run in the opposite direction. 'If you have never seen a portrait of the Virgin in this style, Miss Wentworth, that is simply more evidence of the miracle that occurred in this desert town. A religious landmark and an artistic one, may God be praised!'"

I laughed. "You don't think it's an altar painting?"

"I don't know what it is. It's certainly interesting, from the standpoint of portraiture, in the same way that the mummy paintings are. It's a major discovery and deserving of study. But evidence of the first Christian church? I think the Reverend sees what he came here to find. And I'd mind that less if he would stop trying to get me to agree with him."

"Ah, well," I said. "We are all caught up in our own stories about this place. If I find my version more captivating than the Reverend's, that is not his fault."

Nora's carriage came to gather us, as promised, and we returned to the boat for tea. We had an invitation to stay overnight if the house was not suitable for habitation after being trampled through by a police regiment, but Iris had wrestled it into reasonable condition by then, and my own standards were not as high as hers. We resolved to stuff ourselves enough at tea that we might fall into bed as soon as darkness fell and go without the trouble of supper.

I had been in Nora's sitting room recently, but it still startled, coming in from the village: the wall of leather-bound books, the Persian carpet in a pattern of red flowers and blue vines, the elegant writing desk, the chesterfield with a curved back framed in carved roses, and several soft chairs that made me want to tuck my feet under me like a bird in a nest, as I had done in childhood. All these items had been shipped from Nora's study in America and would return with her at the end of the season, an astonishing expense.

I could understand the desire to be surrounded by familiar things; I had left many precious books in Professor Wilson's care, and others remained in Boston with Aunt Margaret, along with a few pieces of furniture from my family home in New York that had belonged to my mother. We had agreed that she would ship them to me when I was settled; I understood that I would not be so, in her eyes, until I was in my home country and married. I knew that I was less attached to material objects than most other people I had met, but I still had a vague sense that those few items I cherished kept me bound to people and places far away and never fully occupying the ground where I stood.

Before sitting down, I asked if I might have a private word with Nora. She agreed and invited Iris to help herself to anything on the bookshelf while she waited. We stepped into Nora's private office, and she closed the door. "What is troubling you?" she asked.

"It is a conversation with Mr. Dunn," I said. "I do not know what to do."

"Start at the beginning," she said.

I did. I held nothing back. "I do not know what he believes happened to Alice Baker, or what role Mr. Drake might have had," I said. "He only hinted at it. I hope I do not distress or offend you. I felt you should know what he was saying about your . . . about Mr. Drake. I thought you would know what to do about Iris."

She nodded, seriously. "How to tell her about Mr. Dunn's character?"

"Yes," I said. "I'm afraid of alienating her if I speak."

"Iris likes Mr. Dunn."

"I think so," I said.

"You think he is unworthy of her?"

"Is that not obvious?"

"I don't disagree with you," she said. "I'm simply ascertaining the facts." She thought for a moment, then said, "Will you trust me to ensure that Iris does not marry James Dunn? I do not think I can prevent the engagement, which I understand to be imminent, but I believe I can avert the wedding if I have some time. There is more I need to understand about what is unfolding here between James and Calvin. Once I do, I will speak to Iris myself. Can you leave that responsibility in my hands?"

I said that I could, and we returned to the sitting room. We sat around a low table laden with cakes and sandwiches. If Iris was curious about the substance of our private discussion, she was too polite to ask. Nora poured the tea, her wrist gleaming where a golden snake chased its tail. She caught my gaze. "It is as secure on my arm as in the safe while I'm on the boat," she said. "When we return home, it will be under lock and key, or on display. Someday, perhaps, I'll sell it. But for this short time, I'll wear it as it was meant to be worn."

"You would sell it?" said Iris. "Why, when you love it, and you don't . . ." she trailed off.

"I don't need to?" Nora smiled. "I am older than either of you by more years than I would admit to. It is true, I love the bracelet, but I love my freedom more. And freedom, for a woman, is a rare thing, a dangerous thing. We are taught to seek security in marriage, although I have not had occasion to test that theory myself. So if a time came when I had to trade my bracelet or anything else for independence, I would not hesitate."

"Please excuse me," Iris said. "I should not have implied . . ."

Nora's expression was gentle. "I know what people say about me," she said. "Here is what is true. I came to stay with Calvin and Martha, his wife, as a companion. Martha is my cousin—the eldest daughter of my father's sister. She wrote to my father asking for one of us to go to her. Our family was a good one, but my father's business had fallen on hard times. Martha was extending us a kindness. I arrived at their home when I was sixteen. Martha wasn't well when I arrived, but her health declined over the next several years and has continued to do so. She required nursing care more than a companion." She paused. "Over time, I became a companion to Calvin instead."

Iris gazed into her teacup, looking as if she wished to vanish. But I looked straight into Nora's eyes. I had no inclination to judge her. "It is unconventional to be a female archeologist," I said. "I do not worry much about the disapproval of others."

Her eyes sparkled. "That is good," she said. "Never forget that the world will try to persuade you to choose the smallest possible life. The only thing worth having is freedom, and the world will fight against you having it, at every turn. If you desire approval, you will have to abstain from adventure. That is the choice we women must make: to bind ourselves to convention or to leap into the void and trust that we can fly."

TWENTY-EIGHT

SACRAMENTO, 2019

> ALMA WENTWORTH: It is March 26, 1965. I'm Alma Wentworth, the lead excavator at K'abel, and I am recording interviews with some of the people who have lived and worked on our archeological site since my mother broke ground in 1908. Today I am very lucky to be speaking with Claude Butler, K'abel's chief administrator for over forty years.
>
> CLAUDE BUTLER: You're making me sound far more important than I am, dear girl.
>
> ALMA: You are very important, Papa Claude. Not only to me, but to K'abel. I shudder to think what would have happened if you hadn't come along. Mama wasn't much of a bookkeeper.
>
> CLAUDE: She was a genius. I was proud to help her. I miss her every day.
>
> ALMA: Oh, dear. Both of us crying already! This isn't going to plan. Let's stop and try again. (*Tape paused.*)
>
> ALMA: You came to K'abel permanently in 1915, correct?
>
> CLAUDE: An auspicious year. I had been working alongside Nora Alcott for several years by that point, managing the accounts for her various excavations, including K'abel, and helping her set up the museum.

She and your mother were great friends, as you know. We used to spend a month here at Christmas. Miss Nora liked to say that she wanted to check on her investments, but really it was because Iris was the dearest friend she had in her life, aside from me.

ALMA: She must have been sad to let you go.

CLAUDE: She was. But she knew that I was happier here than anywhere else. She felt she owed it to me. K'abel reminded me of the place where I was born.

ALMA: Where was that?

CLAUDE: A small village in the Nile Valley. We called it Kiste.

ALMA: You were born in Egypt? I had no idea. Why did you never tell me?

CLAUDE: Miss Nora wanted my origins to remain a secret while she was alive. I understood her reasons. I agreed with them. I taught myself not to think about the village, my grandfather, my mother. But when you brought this little machine here and told me you wanted to hear my stories—to record them!—I thought perhaps it was time to remember. I am seventy-five years old. Who knows how long I have left?

ALMA: You'll live forever, Papa Claude!

CLAUDE: Unlikely, my dear. Now then, here's something else you don't know about me. My name at birth was Khalid Nassim.

ALMA: Khalid Nassim?

CLAUDE: That's right. I carried that name until I was fifteen, which is the age I was when I left my village for the last time.

ALMA: Why did you leave your village?

CLAUDE: That is a very long story and to tell it properly, I need to go back a bit.

ALMA: Take your time.

CLAUDE: Thank you, my dear. As a child, I grew up in my grandfather's household. His name was Rubi Nassim, and he was the headman of our village. He was also the overseer at Calliopolis, the excavation nearby. That meant he controlled which men got jobs at the work site. He was very clever, especially at managing people.

ALMA: Like you!

CLAUDE: I learned from watching him.

ALMA: Were you close?

CLAUDE: Oh, yes. I worshipped him. He was like a god to me. I did not know my own father; I was given to understand that he was a violent man, and that it would be best if he didn't know about me. My mother had returned to her parents' home in our village when she was pregnant with me. I went everywhere with him. After my lessons, I would visit him at his job, learning what it took to oversee an excavation.

ALMA: Is that how you met my mother and Nora?

CLAUDE: Yes. Iris and Miss Nora spent two seasons at Calliopolis, 1903 and 1904.

ALMA: I know Helen Gardiner and Calvin Drake died in 1904. Mama would never talk about it. I must have asked her a thousand times, but even after I became an archeologist, she refused. She said it upset her to think about it.

CLAUDE: She was protecting me.

ALMA: From what?

CLAUDE: From discovery. The police in Egypt thought I was responsible for Miss Helen's murder. I was working as a butler for your mother and Miss Helen when she died.

ALMA: That's ridiculous. You could never hurt anyone!

CLAUDE: Perhaps if someone threatened you, I could. Or your mother. But you are right: I had nothing to do with it. Miss Helen was enormously kind to me. She made me her laboratory assistant and taught me how to restore papyrus. I would never have hurt her, never. As for the people in my village, none of them would have hurt a foreigner. My grandfather would have expelled them from the community immediately. There were other villages nearby, full of men who wanted to compete for the work, but the foreigners liked my grandfather. He was honest and very hardworking.

ALMA: Why on earth would they blame you for Helen's death?

CLAUDE: Well, the police were controlled by the British then. They would not arrest a foreigner if they could find an Egyptian to blame; that is how it was. And I was already in hiding when she died, because I was a suspect in a robbery.

ALMA: What robbery?

CLAUDE: Miss Helen and Iris lived in a house in the village. It had a secure storeroom, like we have in the hacienda here. Artifacts from the dig were stored there before they were transported to Cairo for assessment at the museum. Two weeks before Miss Helen was killed, some jewelry was stolen while everyone was out at the site during the workday.

ALMA: Why were *you* in hiding? You had nothing to do with it. (*Small pause.*) Did you?

CLAUDE: No, it was Mr. Dunn who took the jewelry. My grandfather had eyes everywhere in the village, and he knew about it right away. One of my cousins watched the house when it was empty, because my grandfather knew that the foreigners almost always stole from their own excavations, and he didn't like to be surprised. But this time was different. No one had told your mother and Miss Helen, you see. And they kept excellent records. So when they discovered that there had been a theft, they sounded the alarm. My grandfather went to the house in my place the next morning and saw what transpired. When he returned home, I saw that he was frightened. He wanted to hide me away until the trouble passed. He had a brother who worked in Beni Suef, a town nearby, and I stayed inside his house until my grandfather returned for me.

ALMA: Were you scared?

CLAUDE: Mostly I was bored. I knew my grandfather was worried, but I had confidence that he would fix it. Also, I knew I hadn't stolen anything, so they wouldn't find any evidence. I was young, and I didn't yet know how it was—the world, I mean.

ALMA: Did he come back for you?

CLAUDE: He did. He came late one night. I was asleep. He explained that Miss Helen had been killed and that the police thought she'd caught me stealing. That they believed I'd returned for more, since I'd been successful the first time. He said the police had come into the village and found a statue in our home that had been taken from the storeroom. He said I couldn't return to the village yet or I'd be arrested and executed. He was weeping. That is how I knew he was telling the truth. I had never seen him cry.

ALMA: Would you like a break?

CLAUDE: No. It is only . . . I haven't thought of this in so many years. It was . . . a terrible time. Terrible. Perhaps some tea would be nice.

(*Tape paused.*)

ALMA: Are you sure you want to continue?

CLAUDE: I'm sure.

ALMA: Where did your grandfather take you?

CLAUDE: He took me to Miss Nora's boat. She met us there in her parlor. She explained that she was sailing for Luxor at first light, and I was to come with her. She showed me to a small room in the staff quarters which was to be mine for the journey. She said I would have to stay inside until we reached Luxor, that no one was to know I was aboard except her lady's maid, who would bring my meals. She stepped out of the cabin then and left me alone with my grandfather. He sat down on the cot, as if all his strength had left him. I knew then that we would be separated, and I started to shake. My grandfather pulled me into his arms and stroked my hair. He said that I would be safe with Miss Nora. I had to trust her and him. He kissed me on the forehead and then he stood up and walked out, and I heard a key turn in the lock. I never saw him again.

ALMA: (*Blows her nose.*) That is just awful. I feel so sad for you.

CLAUDE: It was very sad indeed. (*Tape paused.*)

ALMA: What happened when you got to Luxor?

CLAUDE: Miss Nora came to get me after dark. She told me that the staff had been given an evening off. She had hired a carriage, and we drove to Luxor Hospital. On the way, she told me I would need a new name for now, a European name. She had chosen one for me: Claude Butler. She said that it would be easy for me to remember because Claude sounded like Khalid; if I made a mistake and used my old name, it could be smoothed over.

ALMA: And Butler because it was the job you'd had.

CLAUDE: Yes, that was her thinking. At Luxor Hospital, she introduced me to her friend Dr. Simpson by my new name. I stayed with him in his lodgings for a couple of weeks. Miss Nora came and went; she was staying at the Winter Palace and had social engagements to attend. I remember that she attended a small funeral for Miss Helen in the cemetery at the hospital. I didn't mind being there. Dr. Simpson was a good man, and I was able to be outside again. I worked in the garden and the kitchen, which took my mind off my troubles. I assumed that my grandfather had arranged for a job for me at the hospital and that

I would hear from him eventually when circumstances changed at home.

ALMA: But that wasn't the plan.

CLAUDE: I don't know. The plan may have changed when Mr. Drake was killed. I was told very little at the time.

ALMA: How did you hear about Mr. Drake's death?

CLAUDE: Dr. Simpson told me. It was in the newspaper. When Miss Nora returned a day later, she was in mourning clothes. She explained that Mr. Drake had been shot at the encampment during an attack from a group of desert raiders. She had to return to Calliopolis to collect Mr. Drake's body and close the excavation for the season. She told me that my grandfather wanted me to travel to America with her. That he felt it would be a wonderful opportunity for me. She had arranged for me to travel to Alexandria by train later in the month, where I would meet her, and we would sail for New York.

ALMA: And you agreed?

CLAUDE: It wasn't posed as a question. But I believed that it was what my grandfather wanted, and so I never considered doing otherwise.

ALMA: Were you afraid that you would be arrested?

CLAUDE: I wasn't. The threat never felt real to me. You have to understand, I wasn't present for any of the events that made headlines. I was at my great-uncle's house, and on the riverboat, and at the hospital, and on a train, and then on a ship to America. I was homesick, but not frightened.

ALMA: You were brave.

CLAUDE: I was adventuresome. I was never alone either. Miss Nora made sure that I had a responsible person with me whenever she couldn't be there. She had a member of the riverboat staff accompany me on the sleeper train to Alexandria and assigned Mr. Drake's personal secretary to bunk with me on the ocean crossing.

ALMA: Did you go through Ellis Island?

CLAUDE: No. I was never sure how she managed to get me into the United States. She must have paid for false identity papers, and perhaps she bribed an official or two. Miss Nora had her ways of getting done what needed to be done. She was an extremely practical woman.

ALMA: You worked for her for a long time.

CLAUDE: Yes. Many years. When I first came to America, I didn't work at all. I was surprised, but Miss Nora insisted that I focus on my education. I had tutors who caught me up to American pupils of my age. And when the time came, she insisted that I attend university at Berkeley. In retrospect, I'm sure she had to persuade the university to admit me; I stood out on campus. It had always been my dream to become an archeologist, and I did take some courses in that department, but I took a degree in accounting in the end.

ALMA: Are you getting tired?

CLAUDE: Somewhat.

ALMA: Do you want to stop for today?

CLAUDE: Not yet. I want to show you something. Could you hand me that box?

ALMA: Here you go.

CLAUDE: Thank you, dear. Miss Nora's lawyer sent it to me after she died. She had left instructions in her will. There was a letter with it. (*Paper rustles.*)

ALMA: Do you want me to read it?

CLAUDE: Please.

ALMA: "Dear Claude, You have been my faithful friend since you were a boy. I have tried to repay your loyalty in all the ways I could, but I know I could not replace the family you lost when I brought you with me to America. There are chapters of your own story that I have never told you. It seemed the wisest course, both for you and for me. However, if you are reading this, I am gone, and no longer at risk of any earthly judgment. Inside this box, you will find the rest of your story. You do not have to open it. You may choose to continue as you have done. Either way, it will be your choice and yours alone, as it should be. With great affection, Eleanor (Nora) Alcott."

ALMA: Why didn't you open it before now?

CLAUDE: I was afraid it would change how I felt about Miss Nora.

ALMA: And now?

CLAUDE: It doesn't matter what's in the box. Miss Nora wasn't perfect, but I know she did the best she could for me. I'm an old man now. I want to understand my life.

ALMA: All right, then. Let's open the box, shall we? Oh. My.

CLAUDE: Alma. Is that a knife?

TWENTY-NINE

CALLIOPOLIS, 1904

I could not stop thinking about Nora's exhortation to leap into the void. It buzzed in my ears as I labored over the final lines of my translation, for our fears had been realized: Iris and I were no longer equal fellows on the excavation. The change was subtle, but we felt it keenly. No longer were we invited into the pits, or kept close to the action in case our expertise was needed. Instead, we were left to attend to our scholarly projects in the mess tent, and items were delivered to us for cleaning or documentation, sometimes only at the end of a shift. The site was not as busy now, it was true, and if there were suddenly another cache discovered, we would be pressed into service. But the cemetery where the mummy portraits had been found was mostly clear now, and what was left would not be part of archeological lore. There were objects to be removed, and cataloged, and eventually studied, but they would not make anyone more famous, or wealthier, than they already were.

A malaise had settled over the dig with six weeks left in the season, a sense that the story of the year had been written. Even with the thefts, it had been exceptional by any measure. No new pits would be dug now. There was danger in opening up an area when there was no time to finish what you had started; you could be sure that the local men would empty it of anything valuable during the summer months. Meanwhile, the pickmen lazed in the shade, waiting to be summoned; they would not lift a trowel, for that was a job reserved for the trowelmen. They were not resented for it, at least not by their fellow workers; you were a pickman, a trowelman, or an overseer, as your father and grandfather had been before you and your children would be afterward. Did Khalid imagine a life beyond the one dictated for him by his grandfather? Would he have stolen for it? I would not believe it.

Emmett alone seemed content in this time; he was now free to return to his beloved scriptorium with a few men and continue his excavation of the surrounding buildings. James was with Drake at the ridgeline cemetery—we had begun to call it Hermione's cemetery by then—and it appeared not to be a plum assignment, judging from his sour countenance. Or perhaps that expression was reserved for me alone; we had barely exchanged two words since our set-to on the boat.

If my pride was injured by being pushed aside, I did not mind having more time to think and to dream. In truth, I was only tinkering with the translation now. I knew exactly what it was: another Sappho, longer this time, and offering a rare view into the aging poet's mind. It was truly beautiful, and I thought of how much my father would have loved to read it. I hoped one day to share it with Professor Wilson.

I felt a powerful resistance to the idea of sharing her with the men on the site: Drake, who thought only of his own enrichment, and nothing of his duty to share knowledge of the past; James, who collaborated shamefully with whomever paid his wages; and even Emmett, whose weaknesses too easily overcame the better nature I was sure he possessed. The scroll, tucked underneath Hermione's head, would have been destroyed without my intervention; Drake would have crushed it trying to get to his jewels, an overgrown child with neither prudence nor discipline. I had saved her, and now I wondered if she might do the same for me.

In the evening, while Iris packed for her trip to Cairo—she was returning to celebrate her friends' wedding—I tended to Reverend Banks's papyrus. It had turned out to be not one, but two documents: one seemingly literary, the other a personal letter. I would finish the transcription tonight and spend my day off on the translation. As much as I enjoyed Iris's company, I was anticipating with pleasure the prospect of long hours alone in the house. Solitude was precious on a dig, and even harder to find than treasure.

"Are you sure you don't want to come? Fern said you'd be very welcome." Iris was in the doorway.

"Please give her my thanks and congratulations," I said, rising from my desk. "I'd enjoy seeing your friends again, very much. But . . ."

"But you want to be alone with your scroll," said Iris. "Still. Are you sure you'll be safe here?"

"The thief won't be back," I said. "Everyone in the neighboring villages knows that there isn't anything to steal here anymore. I'll be fine." I handed her some letters, one with news for Aunt Margaret, telling her I wouldn't be returning to America; one for Professor Wilson, telling him I'd join him in Rome during the off-season; and several containing inquiries about excavation opportunities for the following year. As much as I loved Calliopolis, I doubted I'd be invited to return. I wasn't sure that I wanted to. "Thanks so much for going to the Thomas Cook office for me. They'll travel much more quickly from there."

Normally, Rubi took our mail to Beni Suef, but I wouldn't risk having him see the names on my letters. He would recognize Mr. Maspero, at a minimum. Iris, I knew, would hold my secrets. "It's no trouble," she said. "I always stop in at Thomas Cook when I'm in Cairo. You run into the most unexpected people there. I usually get at least one decent invitation out of it." For a moment, I could see Iris in another life entirely, the kind my aunt wanted for me. A more comfortable, conventional life. "I . . ." she said, and then stopped. "I have news to tell you before I go, but I do not think you will want to hear it."

My chest hurt. He had asked her, then. "Is it about James?"

She looked shocked. "We have been so discreet," she said.

"You have," I assured her. "He spoke to me about his plans."

"He has not proposed yet," she said. "He wants to speak to Mr. Drake first, and we will have to arrange for a visit this summer to Toronto so that he can ask my father."

"But you've given him reason to think he should make that visit."

"I have." She finally met my eyes. "You liked him before." Her voice was pleading. "I'm so sorry you've fallen out, Helen. He won't tell me why. You are such a dear friend to me. Can you not repair what has broken between you? I want you to be happy for us."

"I will be happy for you," I said. "I promise."

She embraced me with tears in her eyes. "Thank you, Helen. You will see it is good news. I will be able to make a life out here, a useful life. James wants me to be with him during the season, the way Mr. and Mrs. Petrie do."

"You do not love him," I said.

"That is not for you to say," said Iris, a note of warning in her voice.

"You are right," I told her. "Forgive me. Do not let me spoil one moment of your pleasure. I wish only the best for you."

I prepared to go to bed, but when I stretched out I found that I couldn't calm my mind enough to sleep. Engagements could be broken and often were. Nora would do what she could. I hated the idea of Iris married to James, but I understood the dream of being an excavator's wife. I didn't want to deprive her of the opportunity to stay in the field.

What if there were another way: an excavation team made up solely of women? The diggers would be male, of course, but what if they were directed by females? Could the men be made to listen to us? With fair wages and decent conditions, I thought they could. I had seen the inner mechanics of a dig site here, and there was no magic to it; in truth, between the tantrums and drinking, I saw no reason why I could not manage an excavation at least as effectively as Emmett had done, if not considerably more so. I would need Iris, who had the political acuity that I knew I lacked. And I would need a funder.

There were women who might take a leap with us. Mrs. Hearst, for example, was keen on papyri, and there were other wealthy widows in England and America who followed the archeological news. I was sure Nora would help with introductions. My mind raced, its visions increasingly ambitious. Why not follow Amelia Edwards's example? If we could cement our reputations as pioneers in a man's profession, we might encourage subscriptions from women across the United States and Britain, as she had done. And there would be an audience for our lectures and tours, because I had a discovery in this very room that would draw crowds from Rome to London to New York City. Hermione Grammatike had loved the poetry of the tenth Muse, and that admiration had preserved for us a priceless work of art. Why should the find be claimed by Emmett, who needed no further accolades to advance himself?

I would not steal the scroll; I was no thief. But I could keep it to myself until I was ready to publish my findings. I doubted that Mr. Drake even remembered the linen bag under Hermione's head, and I could wait to reveal it to Emmett until after his departure. I would tell him that I needed assistance with the translation, and take it to Rome where Professor Wilson could assist me with the publication. I was sure that my mentor would be willing to write an introduction for the article. That all this could occur exactly as I imagined it seemed not only possible but inevitable, even preordained. I could trace its beginnings to that evening, fourteen years ago, at the Brooklyn Academy of Music. Was it not time for me to step onto the stage myself, and bring my sisters with me?

I spent the weekend buried in my translation of Reverend Banks's papyri. The first document proved simple, for it was familiar. It would mean a great deal to the Reverend, I knew, and would confirm one of his favorite theories about Calliopolis. The second document, the letter, took longer, not because the language was unfamiliar or flowery, or even because the translation required any particular art; the Greek letters were formed in a strong, clear hand, and the message was plain. It was that I wanted to be absolutely certain of my findings before sharing them with the Reverend. He had been my teacher and would want to check every word, and I thought he might need some time to absorb the contents.

On Sunday morning, I sent a note to the excavation site inviting the Reverend to join me for tea in the afternoon. He arrived promptly, radiating excitement. "Miss Gardiner," he said. "I cannot thank you enough for your dedication to the cause. It will mean a great deal to our supporters around the world. I hope you have good news for us."

"Come and see," I said. "And let me pour you some tea." I had set out the teapot and two cups and saucers on my desk. Iris had brought them from home, and we rarely used them, preferring the rough pottery from the village.

"Thank you," he said. "Perhaps after we discuss the papyri?" He walked over to the long table where I had laid out the two papyri. I had left one covered with blotting paper; I had not had the time to mount it properly, and the text was on one side only. The other I had preserved between two glass sheets, so that the Reverend—and the many who would come after him—could examine both sides. He was not unskilled in Greek translation, and his eyes scanned the document. "Your preservation technique is exceptional, Miss Gardiner. Now, please, do not keep me in suspense."

I walked over to join him, abandoning the teapot. "Your answer is right here," I said, and I touched the glass in three spots, two on one side, and one on the other. "You will recognize the name, I think."

He paled. "Can it be?" He gripped my forearm.

"Are you not well?" I thought he might fall, and I realized, belatedly, that I did not know the Reverend's age. I pulled a chair around behind him and helped him to sit. "You must not exert yourself. Let me get you a glass of water."

"No." He shook his head. "I was overcome for a moment. His blessed name. A fragment of the Holy Book." There were tears in his eyes.

"Yes," I said. "I'm certain. It is one of the Gospels. Even if we did not have Jesus's name, there are other identifiers in the text. You see here?" I indicated another line. "It says: 'The sheep of the flock will be scattered.'" I moved my finger to the next line. "And here: 'Before the rooster crows, you will disown me three times.'"

"Matthew," he said. "It is Matthew."

"Verse 26. Yes," I said. "Reverend Banks, it seems you were right. There *was* a community of Christians here, and a very early one. I am not an expert in dating biblical papyri, and there will be no shortage of attention paid to this scroll once it is revealed to the public. I can suggest an appropriate expert for you to consult in Rome. But to my eye, the style of the hand is consistent with the late second century or early third, which would make it one of the earliest known New Testament fragments. And it is in excellent condition."

The Reverend folded his hands, moving his lips in silent prayer. I turned back to the teapot to allow him privacy to compose himself, and poured two cups. When I turned back, he was wiping his face with a handkerchief, and he accepted the cup and drank it down. "I never lost hope, Miss Gardiner," he said. "I felt God's hand over Calliopolis. I knew he had led me to this place." He paused. "You may be sure that I will include your name in my publications on the subject. You will have made a name for yourself here as well."

"That is most generous of you," I said. I was pleased. Reverend Banks was a man of his word, and it would only assist my plans for a female-led excavation to have my name circulated widely and attached to a spectacular biblical find.

"And now you have achieved what you intended," he said. "You have participated in a discovery of great significance. You will be able to return to your aunt and uncle and take your place in society."

"I do not understand what you mean," I said.

"Your family has taken me into their confidence," he said. "They worry about you, your reputation, your future."

"I'm well aware," I said. "I'm surprised it is a matter of concern to you."

"They hoped I might be able to exert some influence on their behalf. I had hoped to speak to you before now, but I have been preoccupied with my excavation, and the timing was never opportune for a private conversation. But now, happily, I can discharge my duty. I can add my voice to theirs and, as a teacher and I hope a friend, encourage you to return to America at the end of the season. You'll be leaving at the pinnacle of your success."

I had not been aware of the Reverend's connection to Aunt Margaret and Cousin Clifford (for I could not think of him as my uncle). I did not blame him for his intrusion; my cousin knew how to get his way, and the Reverend would not have been a match for him. But I was irritated by his assumption that my passion for papyrology would be sated by a mention in one of his articles, and that my success had peaked with a translation of Matthew. There were other fragments of Matthew; my Sappho was unique in all the world. "I have already written to my aunt to tell her that

I won't be moving to Boston," I said. "Iris took the letter to Cairo for me, in fact."

A flash of anger passed across his face, vanishing behind a false smile. "Another letter can follow," he said. "It is no great shock for a woman to change her mind."

At this, I found my patience at an end. And so I was less politic than I might have been when I said: "There is more to understand about the community here. It is not entirely as you imagined. Let us not get ahead of ourselves." I put on my gloves and removed the blotting paper from the second document. "It is a letter of introduction," I explained. "It was carried by Mersis himself when he arrived here."

"You waited until now to share this? Documentary evidence of Mersis's holy presence on this site?" He chortled. "You have indeed surprised me, Miss Gardiner. An introduction from whom? To the city elders? Asking for permission to establish a center of worship here? This is a day of miracles!"

"The writer is identified as John of Alexandria. He writes to ask that the community admit Mersis as a resident and confirms his bona fides as a Christian. It proves that he came here, yes. But not that he founded the community of worshippers. That had already been established by the time this letter was written."

The Reverend rose and walked to my desk, where he set down his teacup. "I beg your pardon."

"Please come and see for yourself. The translation is not difficult; you will be able to read much of it. John addresses the leader of the existing community of Christians. It seems that he knew her."

"Her?"

"It is a woman. He refers to her as Amma Sarah. He also says that he has told Mersis that she is a female of rare holiness."

"You are mistaken."

"I am not," I said. "It is right here for you to read, if you will only come and see."

"I will do no such thing," he said. "It is obviously a counterfeit, manufactured to taunt me. Did you put it there? Or Mr. Dunn?"

"Reverend Banks," I said. "You forget yourself."

"There was no Desert Mother in Calliopolis," he said. "That is impossible. You cannot make such a claim publicly. You will destroy your scholarly reputation. The church was founded by Mersis. I have it on good authority that the Pope himself believes this. If you publish your lies, you will cheat Mersis of the renown he is owed. You will set back the cause of his supporters by decades, even permanently. You cannot. I will not permit it." He picked up my letter opener from the desktop, knocking his teacup sideways. It toppled off the edge and smashed on the floor. He did not glance at it.

"You must calm yourself, Reverend," I said. "There is no reason to make any decisions about this today. We will show the papyri to Mr. Drake and to Emmett and take their advice. I have no wish to hurt you or your cause, I promise."

"We will destroy it," he said, as if to himself. "Yes, that is what we must do. It cannot be allowed to ruin our plans." He stalked over to the table and reached for the sheet of papyrus.

"You must not, Reverend," I said, sliding between him and the table. "It is a legitimate document. It alters the history we thought we knew, but that is why we excavate, is it not? Please. You are not yourself."

He sliced the letter opener past my shoulder, trying to reach the papyrus. He meant, I saw, to cut it to ribbons. I placed my hands on his chest and pushed as hard as I could. He staggered backward, but caught his balance, adjusted his weight, and charged, still holding the blade. I put an arm out to block him and he twisted his left shoulder away from me, while his right hand punched at my breastbone, stealing my breath.

There was a long, frozen moment before the pain rushed in. I saw the Reverend's face floating further and further above me, rigid with horror. The letter opener was still in his hand, but streaked now with blood. I felt the ground beneath me, as if pinned to it. *I am not angry*, I tried to say, but the words would not come.

"Helen, Helen. I am so sorry. It was an accident. I did not mean it." He moaned aloud, and recited the Lord's Prayer. "What have I done? God forgive me."

I felt terribly cold. And then I felt nothing at all.

THIRTY

CAIRO, 1904

Rubi stands on the ridge above Calliopolis as the sun rises. He is always here at this hour, before the village men arrive to begin work, before the foreigners stumble out from their tents. Nothing that happens on this patch of land is a secret to him. He sees much, hears the rest from people who owe him. Most people here are in his debt one way or another. He is comfortable with this.

Today, though, he is troubled. No: He is afraid. His grandson, Khalid, is in danger. Rubi has many grandchildren, and they are each dear to him, but Khalid is special. There was a time when Rubi counted but one misfortune in his life, which was that he had not been blessed with sons. Later, he counted one more, which was that his daughter Amina arrived in the village several weeks after her wedding, saying that she would never acknowledge her husband or any member of his family again.

What other choice could he have made? He took her in. Her laughter returned and brightened their home. He put her to work, bringing well water to the thirsty men at Calliopolis, at least until he discovered that she was pregnant. After that she stayed at home, so no word of the child's existence would reach her husband. When Khalid was born, Rubi understood more deeply than before the great design in all things. From a young age, Khalid followed his grandfather everywhere he could, begging to hear Rubi's stories about the ancient city on their doorstep. As a child of six, he announced his intention to become an archeologist.

Rubi reflected deeply on this dream of his grandson's. His own plan was to have Khalid take over his position as the headman, but that transition was many years away, and education, he thought, would only enhance Khalid's authority over the workers. Rubi himself spoke several languages—one never knew which country would hold the excavation rights from one season to the next—and he could read and write simple documents on his own. He intended to provide Khalid with at least his own level of schooling.

What would be required to put Khalid in a position to lead his own excavation? It was not entirely outside the bounds of sanity to consider the question. Rubi knew of a man, an Egyptian—Ahmed Kamal—who had labored as an equal with his German counterpart, emptying the royal tomb at Deir el-Bahari and sailing with it to Cairo, where he now worked as a curator at the museum. He had learned about Ahmed Kamal's career from another man, Ahmed Najib, also Egyptian, who was an inspector with the Egyptian Antiquities Service, and who had come to Calliopolis to survey the site under the French concession. Rubi wrote to both men, seeking advice, and was pleased to receive their replies, which mapped out the educational requirements for promotion in the field of archeology.

Rubi kept their letters, sharing them with the tutors he hired to supplement the curriculum at the village school. As Khalid grew, so did his enthusiasm for his chosen career. His teachers gave him glowing reports and recommended that he attend secondary school in Beni Suef. Rubi remembers being pained by the prospect of separation from his grandson during the school term, an emotion that now seems like nothing at all, laughable, when compared to the heaviness of his present burden.

He had been envious of Helen Gardiner. He can admit this to himself. Khalid had danced into the house each night, chattering incessantly about her virtues. Even as he felt grateful to her, Rubi wanted to tell Khalid to beware, that the foreigners had no real loyalty to them, that they would leave without a backward glance. That they would lay blame at the feet of an Egyptian—any Egyptian—before assigning it to one of their own. It gives him no joy to be right. How could it? Helen Gardiner is dead. Precious objects, stolen. His beloved grandson, accused.

From the ridge, Rubi can see smoke from cooking fires rising above the village. The French, the British, the Americans—they have each, in turn, decided that this land belongs to them, bestowed by a piece of paper issued from an office in the capital. Do they not see the faces painted on the walls of the temple? This land belongs to Rubi's people, inherited from their ancestors, and stewarded by the current generation to be passed along to the next. But now the chain is broken. Khalid cannot stay to receive his birthright.

Rubi knows that Khalid is safe; it will not stay that way for long. Favors take you some distance, and he has collected the ones he can. A plan is now unfolding, and he awaits his instructions. He believes that he has put his trust in the right person. He has made his way in the world by having good instincts about such things.

It will all end in death, he expects, likely his own, although this is of little significance to him.

As long as Khalid survives, nothing else matters.

THIRTY-ONE

CAIRO, 2024

Maddie sits by the pool at Mena House, sipping an iced tea. From her seat, she can see the pyramids. Were it not for the other sensory cues—the creaking of swaying palms, the bite of sand that lofts and eddies with the wind and sticks to her sunglasses, the taste of mint and honey in her drink—she would have trouble believing herself here.

Mena House is the most luxurious place Maddie has ever been, and she keeps reminding herself that she isn't paying for it. Her father is footing the bill; he says it is what her mother would have wanted. She couldn't refuse, so she's allowing herself to soak in her surroundings: the intricate wood screens, the mosaic tiles, the carved doors, the lush gardens.

She wonders, idly, if Helen or Iris stayed here as guests. She doubts it. It cost a fortune then too. But maybe they had stopped in for tea, on their way to visit the pyramids. She hopes so.

She feels a drop of water on her arm and looks up to see Gareth standing over her, dripping from the pool. "You were miles away," he says.

"I was a century away," she replies. "How was your swim?"

"Glorious," he says. "I'm running up to get changed. Fifteen minutes to launch?"

"Thereabouts," she says. "Are you sure you want to come? You don't have to."

"I wouldn't miss it," he says. "I owe Helen a lot. I'll meet you in the lobby."

Maddie watches him leave, a smile playing around her mouth, then reaches into her purse to extract the weekend's itinerary. She has all the appointments in her phone, but she finds it easier to believe it's happening when she sees it in print. For one thing, it's on the letterhead of the Grand Egyptian Museum, the greatest archeological museum in the world. There's the reason for their presence in Cairo, in bold letters at the top of the page: DEDICATION CEREMONY FOR THE SLOAN FAMILY DONATION. And finally the events: a cocktail reception and dinner tonight, where Maddie is making a speech on behalf of her family to a crowd of dignitaries and scholars; a private museum tour the next day with Egypt's leading archeologist; and lastly, a symposium in which Rebecca (professor and director of the Center for the Study of Ancient Books, Resurrection College) is giving the keynote address. Maddie knows the talk will be a sensation, perhaps not on the level of Rebecca's paper introducing the lost Sappho poem, but close. Last time, the three of them—Rebecca, Brett, and Maddie—had been interviewed by international press for weeks. This time, Rebecca plans to reveal the contents of the Amma Sarah letter, which is at the heart of an upcoming book about the earliest female-led religious community known to history.

She and Rebecca have speculated often about why Reverend Banks chose to keep the letter rather than destroy it. Rebecca thinks he was torn between his duty to uphold principles of scholarship and his religious beliefs, both of which were central to his identity. Maddie thinks preserving the letter was penance for Helen's death. It's a debate that is unlikely to be resolved.

Gareth and Brett are giving a lecture, too, on techniques for preserving and reading ancient books. She runs her finger over Gareth's title: Director, Alcott Library, University of California, Berkeley. It's strange to think about what's transpired over the past five years. A life-altering pandemic, with a musical chairs of academic appointments as a footnote: Pete's resignation from Berkeley, steps ahead of the discipline committee. Berkeley's offer of the Olsen Chair to Rebecca. Rebecca's decision to reject them in favor of Resurrection College's offer to run the new center for ancient books. Ben Cupul's installation as the Olsen Chair. Gareth's position as director of the Alcott Library, taking the job Rebecca had vacated.

Brett and Rebecca married. And Pete . . . well, his television show on archeological mysteries is exceedingly popular with people who like their history colorful and only somewhat accurate. Maddie streams his episodes sometimes when sleep eludes her.

Maddie stands and makes her way into the lobby. Gareth, fresh from the shower, holds out a hand, and she takes it. Their guide leads them to an air-conditioned sedan. He wants to make sure they understand that it will be very hot this time of day; most tourists prefer to visit early in the morning or toward closing time. He recommends the sunset tour. Over the past year, visitors to Calliopolis have vastly increased. He hears it's because of a popular book, a detective story, but true to life. He has not read it, although he would like to.

"You should," Gareth tells him. "It's excellent." He squeezes her hand, stroking a finger over the ring he gave her six months ago. "It's called *Unearthed*. It's about how the author solved the murder of a woman who worked at Calliopolis in 1904."

"How did she do that?" asks the guide.

"She dug around in a bunch of archives and pieced it all together from old diaries and letters," Gareth says. "It's an incredible story."

"She had some help," says Maddie, smiling at him. Not only from the living, she thinks. She has never believed in an afterlife, but lately she finds herself sending silent messages of gratitude to Iris, to Claude, to Nora, and especially to Helen. Without them, she wouldn't be here now, on the right path at last. An ice-cold-case detective, packing a laptop and a library card. Like Rebecca, Maddie found the experience of being offered the job of her dreams—an assistant professorship in Berkeley's history department—remarkably clarifying. She turned it down to write full-time. Maddie has no regrets. She's working on a sequel now, a history of the women of K'abel through the ages, from the Jade Queen to Maddie's mother, Silvia.

Maddie rummages in her purse and extracts a few sheets of paper, a copy of the letter from Claude's box.

"Are you going to read that to her as well?" asks Gareth.

"I don't think so," says Maddie. "I brought the letter for me. To put me in the right mindset. To remember what happened to her. Do you want me to read it to you?"

"Yes," he says. "I'd like that."

She begins:

Dear Claude,

You opened the box. It is the choice I would have expected you to make. Your sense of adventure matched my own. Perhaps it is why we came to appreciate each other's company despite the many differences between us. I hope when you look back on your life you do not feel that you have been unfortunate. I have tried, where I could, to improve your circumstances.

I hesitate to begin. But you have come here for your story. I will follow my own advice and leap in.

It begins with Calvin Drake. He was not an honest person. I wonder if any truly wealthy people are. I know that I am not, least of all with myself. This quality allowed me to join my life with his for as long as I did.

I'll put it bluntly: Calvin was a thief and a betrayer. He stole from his excavations as a matter of course. He did not think of himself as stealing, of course: He believed the objects belonged to him. He loathed the Egyptian Antiquities Service and had determined that the easiest way to avoid their tariff was to appropriate specimens for himself, a few at a time, over the length of the season.

Usually the lead excavator turned a blind eye. At Calliopolis, though, he encountered a will as strong as his own in Emmett Olsen. Mr. Olsen had a reputation for brilliance but also for drinking, and Calvin assumed that he would be weak and easy to control. (Calvin himself never drank. He had other vices.) He was mistaken about Mr. Olsen; Olsen was a forceful person, and he seemed to feel an obligation to the site itself rather than to Calvin. He kept excellent records, documenting every item that came out of the ground. Helen Gardiner was cut from the same cloth. She could be proprietary about her papyri.

As a consequence, Calvin had to recruit James Dunn to assist him. It was Mr. Dunn who removed the jewelry from the storeroom at Calvin's behest. Your grandfather knew that one of the villagers would be blamed as soon as he heard about the theft. He sent you to his brother's house to protect you, understanding correctly that you would be the first suspect. He then came to tell me that Mr. Dunn had been seen at the village house at the time of the robbery and asked me if I could help you. I imagine he guessed that Mr. Dunn was acting on orders, which is why he did not approach Calvin directly. He said that he would be in my debt.

Around the same time, Helen shared a disturbing rumor with me. I will not repeat it here, but it caused me to consider the depths to which Calvin might sink to satisfy his desires. I spoke to Calvin about my concerns, including my fear that an innocent might be held responsible for the theft. My interference was not well received.

Where Calvin had once shared his thoughts about the progress of the excavation with me, he now kept me at an arm's length, locking himself away in his office with Mr. Dunn. Too late, I realized that his affection toward me depended on my unconditional approval of his actions. I confess that when Helen died, my first thought was that Calvin had a hand in it. But late that night, your grandfather arrived at the steamer with Reverend Banks in tow. He had been found wandering in the desert, covered in Helen's blood, still carrying the knife with which he had killed her. He was raving about his cleric, whom he believed had founded a church at Calliopolis. We did not entirely understand his meaning, but it seemed that Helen had translated a papyrus scroll that disproved his theory and he had accidentally stabbed her while trying to destroy the ancient document.

I injected him with a sedative and placed him under lock and key in one of the staterooms. Calvin was livid. The sensational murder of one foreigner by another would have attracted the scrutiny of the antiquities service and given them a reason to cancel his concession. He insisted that Reverend Banks should be made to disappear and that you should be blamed, not only for the theft, but for Helen's murder. He proposed to conceal one of the stolen objects—a statue of Thoth—in your grandfather's house to draw the attention of the authorities.

I had an acquaintanceship with Dr. Simpson at Luxor Hospital; could Reverend Banks not be ensconced there, quietly, for a time? If he then confessed at some later date, his medical files would serve as evidence of his delusions and he would not be believed. Meanwhile, Helen's body was in cold storage on the boat awaiting an examination by a medical professional. Surely, Calvin thought, Dr. Simpson could perform this service as well. He proposed that I set off at first light; he would stay behind and manage the police investigation.

I will say this: It was a good plan, and I mostly followed it. But I was formulating a plan of my own, to protect my future and yours. I offered your grandfather a great deal of money to help me. You should know that he refused it. I may be wrong, but I suspect that Rubi had his own plans for Calvin before I said a word to him. He simply asked that I ensure safe passage for you to America, along with continued education and future employment.

I agreed. Not long afterward, while we were in Luxor, a band of men on horseback raided the camp and shot Calvin through the chest, in the place where his heart ought to have been.

You should know that your grandfather loved you. It grieved him horribly to let you go. He trusted me to bring you to safety and I believe that I honored his faith in me. I hope you feel likewise.

With my deepest affection,
Eleanor (Nora) Alcott

"We're here," says the guide, pulling off the highway and into a parking lot.

THIRTY-TWO

CALLIOPOLIS, 2024

I was drawn to the ridge this morning. I like it here, in the shadows of the ancient tombs. I remember how we repaired the mummy portraits, Iris and Nora and I, just over there in the stifling heat, the paraffin bubbling and the brushes sticky, and our hair damp with perspiration, the ancient faces illuminated by lanterns.

We don't have many tourists this time of the year, although I notice the crowds are thicker in the morning and evening than they used to be. Even still, I can't imagine that Calliopolis competes favorably with sites that are more extravagant in their charms. In my day, for example, the pyramids were swarming with bodies, as were the temples near Luxor. Calliopolis was always a more refined pleasure. There is not much to see above ground level, except for a few crumbling walls and a temple that didn't merit Miss Musgrave's recommendation even when the decoration was still faintly visible.

Visitors are permitted to descend a ramp and walk a few of the streets where merchants once sold their wares; the area that Emmett excavated as a scriptorium is popular with young women, who wander about with the name Sappho on their lips, before walking out to the ridge to pay their respects to Hermione. There is a reliable stream of Christian pilgrims, also, who wait in a long, snaking line to enter Reverend Banks's church in groups of two, where a security guard permits them one minute of contemplation before they are moved aside for the next pair.

Calliopolis today is much as it was the last time I saw it alive. Instead of tents there is a permanent structure at the entrance, which they call an education center. They have replicas of the mummy portraits there, and photographs from the excavations over the decades. You can see me in the background of one of them, sitting on the edge of a pit with my feet dangling over the edge, writing in a notebook. I was happiest here, when I was alive.

Floating on the ridgeline, I see the car when it arrives. A couple steps out, shimmering in the midday heat. I don't expect them to walk out this far; few have done so recently, most retreating to the cool air of the education center after a blistering tour of the temple and the church. But instead they set off on the marked path to the cemetery right away, winding across the desert without stopping until they reach the rock cuts. They are a man and a woman, older than I was when I died, but still young. They hold hands.

The woman is breathing hard as she sits on a granite slab at the opening to one of the old tombs, and I see her smile as she takes in the view, her eyes shaded by a broad-brimmed straw hat. At dusk, when the tourists leave and the site is laid out before me, I can return to Calliopolis as it was when I knew it, imagining the sound of pickaxes and spades scraping at the dirt, the smell of horses and hardworking men, the electric joy of a find emerging from the earth.

"Helen?" I hear her say, very quietly, surprising me. It has been a very long time since someone spoke to me by name. The last person was Alistair Banks, who sat right where this woman is now, weeping, and begging my forgiveness to lighten the stain on his soul. I could see the madness in him, poor man.

"We know what happened to you. We figured it out, what Alistair Banks did. He tried to make you disappear. He tried to erase you. But he failed." She turns to the man. "This is weird, isn't it? Am I crazy?" I wish I could tell her that she is welcome. People have come here for thousands of years to talk to the dead. And she looks like someone I used to know, though I cannot say who or when.

The man kisses her and says, "Not in the least, Maddie."

She removes a sheet of paper from her bag, holds it in her lap. "I found the Sappho poem hidden in your box," she continues. "I wanted you to know. It's in the national museum here, with your translation. People say it's brilliant. My friend Rebecca did the last lines, the part you didn't get to finish. That's why I came, to read it to you." She clears her throat, and begins to read.

> *You, children, be zealous for the beautiful gifts of the violetlapped*
> > *Muses*
> *and for the clear songloving lyre.*
> *But my skin once soft is now taken by old age,*
> *my hair turns white from black.*
> *And my heart is weighed down and my knees do not lift,*
> *that once were light to dance as fawns.*
> *I groan for this. But what can I do?*
> *A human being without old age is not a possibility.*
> *There is the story of Tithonos, loved by Dawn with her arms of*
> > *roses*
> *and she carried him off to the ends of the earth*
> *when he was beautiful and young. Even so was he gripped*
> *by white old age. He still has his deathless wife.*

It is unusual to feel satisfaction in my current state. I am not much afflicted by emotions now. But I can feel a vibration of pleasing energy around me as she speaks the words aloud. *A human being without old age is not a possibility.* Memory stirs. I was not taken by old age. Was Nora, I wonder? Was Iris?

I look at the woman, Maddie, and now I see Iris there, her face glowing, the sun high in a clear sky, the ancient city beneath our feet. "We remember you," she says.

They stand, and the man puts an arm around her shoulders. They walk back the way they came.

How did I enter their story, become real to them? I won't know the answer, and I am unbothered. The poem was never mine. Nor was it Hermione's. Nor was it Sappho's, truly, once she released it. It became part of everyone who heard it or read it, who saw in it a fragment of truth. The living heard her voice, long after it fell silent.

Not only the Dawn is deathless.

AUTHOR'S NOTE

This book was a great joy to write, and it also took a very long time. Mostly, this was because *City of the Muse* touches on many subjects which are of particular interest to me, and I had difficulty curbing the urge to keep reading. If you are such a person—one, that is, who loves obscure branches of archeology, classical poetry, pioneering women, true crime, and the politics of museum collection—you might appreciate the clarifying details below, as well as the book recommendations that follow.

IMAGINING CALLIOPOLIS

Calliopolis is not a real place, but it is based on settlements which did exist in Egypt during the Greek and Roman occupations (roughly 332 BC to 640 AD), and which were excavated by British, European, and American archeologists in the late 1800s and early 1900s. These towns, some of which yielded the papyrus discoveries described in *City of the Muse*, share an unusual geographical and social history which created the conditions for both the production and preservation of papyrus scrolls; a town's population had to be large enough, wealthy enough, and literate enough to require reams of written material, and the ground sufficiently undisturbed and far removed from the water table to protect the documents over two millennia.

Calliopolis is inspired by the real towns of Tebtunis, Karanis, Oxyrhynchus, and Hawara, located in a region to the south and southwest of Cairo. If you wanted to find Calliopolis on a map, it would be roughly in the location of Herakleopolis Magna (today's city of Ihnasya el-Medina), although I have taken some liberties with the topography, locating my fictional town closer to the existing limestone scarp that defines the edge of the Faiyum basin than Herakleopolis Magna would have been.

The physical characteristics of Calliopolis bear a strong resemblance to those of Karanis, which was excavated meticulously by a team from the University of Michigan between 1924 and 1935, although I've added a temple somewhat like the one found at Qasr Qarun, which was dedicated to Sobek, the crocodile god, during the Ptolemaic period.

EGYPT'S CANAL SYSTEMS

During the Ptolemaic period (when Egypt was ruled by the Greeks), a system of irrigation canals was built to extend the flow of Bahr Yussef—a natural waterway that branches from the Nile—into larger swaths of desert and increase the area available for cultivation of crops. This canal system allowed for the transportation of goods to the rest of the country. In addition to crops, some towns developed specific industries, such as the production of papyrus scrolls that I've imagined for Calliopolis; Karanis, for example, was known as a center for textile weaving.

As the Greek regime faltered, some of these canals fell into disrepair, and population in the desert towns declined. However, once the Romans seized power, they renovated and restored much of the irrigation system, and many of these towns experienced a renewed period of prosperity from 30 BC until around the middle of the third century, when, yet again, a period of civil war disrupted government activities including the maintenance of the canals. From this period on, the cultivated land shrank, the expanding desert dotted with the remains of once-prosperous towns.

FINDING ANCIENT PAPYRUS IN THE DESERT

The most famous of these—at least in papyrological terms—is Oxyrhynchus. It was here, in 1896, that an excavation team from Oxford University uncovered the mother lode of papyrus deposits in what had been a garbage dump. Among them were literary works by classical authors that were presumed lost, meaning works which were known to have existed because they were referenced in other works of the time but of which no copies had survived. Oxyrhynchus also produced the largest collection of New Testament fragments, including early versions of the Gospels. Roughly 90 percent of the papyri found here were neither biblical nor literary, but administrative documents and private correspondence which, taken together, represent the best evidence we have of what everyday life was like in Egypt between the fourth century BC and the seventh century AD.

So much papyrus was removed for preservation during the original British excavation at Oxyrhynchus that in 2011, it was estimated that only 2 percent of the total had been translated to date. Much of it remains in storage at Oxford.

Among the treasures recovered at Oxyrhynchus were fragments of poems by Sappho. They are perhaps the most celebrated finds of Egyptology's papyrus-hunting era because of their rarity: Of the nine books of Sappho's lyrics that were said to have been collected in the Library of Alexandria, only one complete poem and a few shorter quotations survived past antiquity, referenced in works by other writers. Yet during her life and for centuries after her death, she was hailed as one of the great poets of her time, the "tenth Muse." The Sappho translations credited to Helen Gardiner in *City of the Muse* are by Anne Carson, a legend in her own right.

If you are interested in reading more about the intricacies of papyrus preservation and interpretation, you should have a look at Roger Bagnall's magisterial work, *The Oxford Handbook of Papyrology*. I have returned to it over and over again, and it seems to reveal a new bit of useful information each time.

SOME PEOPLE AND PLACES

Most of the characters in *City of the Muse* are fictional, but a few real people appear on the fringes of the story. A few others deserve mention for inspiring characters in the book.

Emma Andrews: A philanthropist and archeologist, she (along with her partner, Theodore Davis) spent eighteen seasons on the Nile aboard their luxury boat *Bedawin* and funded major tomb excavations in the Valley of the Kings. Her diaries are an invaluable resource for researchers, as she kept meticulous notes of the tomb sites, including maps and lists of artifacts. She and Davis (who was her cousin by marriage) began an affair while both were married to other people; she eventually obtained a legal separation, but Davis did not. Nevertheless, their romantic and professional partnership lasted over twenty years until his death in 1915. The characters of Nora Alcott and Calvin Drake in this book are loosely based on Emma Andrews and Theodore Davis.

Howard Carter: Best known for his discovery of Tutankhamen's tomb in the Valley of the Kings in 1922, Carter was a talented artist who began working on excavations in Egypt at the age of seventeen. He rose quickly in the ranks of Egyptology, becoming an inspector for the Egyptian Antiquities Service. In 1905, however, he suffered a major career setback from the fallout of the Saqqara Affair and was unemployed for several years. (These events are described in this novel, although I have moved them earlier in time by one year.) Eventually, he was hired by Lord Carnarvon and remained in that employ until Carnarvon's death in 1923. The Curse of Calliopolis is somewhat inspired by the Curse of Tutankhamen's Tomb, of which Carnarvon was the first so-called victim.

Théodore de Mayerne: A court physician for James I, Charles I, and Charles II, he is famous in art history for the de Mayerne manuscript, which he compiled between 1620 and 1646. He interviewed many leading artists of the day, including Peter Paul Rubens and Anthony van Dyck, about their techniques; he was particularly interested in the chemistry of pigments. The manuscript contains instructions for the conservation of paintings.

The Desert Fathers: A group of third- and fourth-century Christians dedicated to asceticism, whose experiments with hermeticism and other forms of retreat from the world paved the way for Christian monasticism. Teachings of these early religious leaders were collected by their followers and eventually printed as *The Sayings of the Desert Fathers*. Neither Saint Agapius nor Mersis of Calliopolis are among the true fathers, but they are inspired by them and their writings.

Amelia Edwards: A British writer, lecturer, and cofounder of the Egypt Exploration Fund, she was renowned for her memoir, *A Thousand Miles Up the Nile* (first published in 1877), which described a winter spent touring Cairo and the Nile Valley. Concerned about the danger posed by tourism to ancient monuments, she dedicated herself to lecturing and raising funds for the preservation of these sites. Her US lecture series in 1889–1890 was a massive success that inspired many would-be archeologists. Her descriptions of the Egyptological community in the colonial period—including the see-and-be-seen scene at the famous Shepheard's Hotel—were an invaluable resource.

The Egyptian Antiquities Service (Department of Antiquities): Established in 1835 by the Ottoman governor, Muhammad Ali Pasha, with the purpose of protecting Egypt's cultural heritage and preventing artifacts from being taken out of the country. When Egypt fell under British rule in 1882, the Service became a department under the Ministry of Public Works. It issued permits for excavation and dispatched inspectors to ensure compliance with the regulations, which included rules governing the division of finds.

Ahmed Kamal: The first Egyptian Egyptologist, he trained under the German archeologist Heinrich Brugsch (who led a short-lived school—the School of Ancient Language—created to train Egyptians to work as professional Egyptologists). Kamal was the first Egyptian curator of the Egyptian Museum in Cairo and the author of Egypt's first Ancient Egyptian Dictionary.

Gaston Maspero: The French director-general of the Egyptian Antiquities Service and conservator of the Bulaq Museum during the period in which *City of the Muse* is set. He established the practice of offering lesser artifacts for sale through the museum to raise money for excavations.

Margaret Murray: The first woman in Britain to hold a university teaching position in archeology, she trained many of the Egyptologists of the so-called golden age, and served as a powerful role model for the women who followed her. The pioneering program at University College London where she taught was headed by Flinders Petrie and funded by a bequest from Amelia Edwards.

Ahmed Najib: Another graduate of Brugsch's School of Ancient Language, he worked for the Egyptian Antiquities Service and rose to the level of chief inspector. He published an Arabic history of Egypt.

Flinders Petrie: A British archeologist known as the "Father of Egyptology." His systematic approach to excavation professionalized the field. He worked in Egypt for over forty seasons, and made a remarkable number of significant discoveries, including the mummy portraits at Hawara (which are fictionalized in this book). He was infamous for the spartan living conditions on his digs.

Archibald Sayce: A British linguist, Assyriologist, and priest of the Church of England, who spent many winters in the late 1800s and early 1900s aboard his boat on the Nile and was a fixture in the Egyptology community. He traveled with an extensive library and visited archeological sites in full ecclesiastical garb. Descriptions of his appearance and interests inspired the character of Alistair Banks.

Brent Seales: A computer science professor at the University of Kentucky, who has pioneered technology for reading damaged manuscripts, including papyrus scrolls. The computer modeling methods described in this novel were carefully and patiently explained to me by Brent himself, and I am grateful to him, in addition to being wildly impressed. Any errors are obviously mine. I hope he does not mind my tribute to him and his work in the character of Brett Cooper.

THE ETHICS OF COLLECTING

This is a huge topic, and I won't even attempt to do it justice here. However, I have tried throughout the novel to flag the connection between colonialism and traditional archeology. The questionable collection practices of the past (embodied in this novel by Calvin Drake and Bill Hampton) continue to spark live debate about repatriation in museums today (the Parthenon—formerly Elgin—Marbles and the Benin Bronzes are but two examples). Moreover, the theft of cultural property is ongoing, and supported by criminal enterprises and unscrupulous collectors around the world. *The New York Times* has published an excellent series of articles over the last few years highlighting law enforcement's efforts to curb the trafficking of culturally significant artifacts.

FURTHER READING

Adams, Amanda. *Ladies of the Field: Early Women Archaeologists and Their Search for Adventure.* Vancouver: Greystone Books, 2010.

Bagnall, Roger S. *The Oxford Handbook of Papyrology.* New York: Oxford University Press, 2009.

Carson, Anne. *If Not, Winter: Fragments of Sappho.* New York: Vintage, 2002.

Cline, Eric H. *Three Stones Make a Wall: The Story of Archaeology.* Princeton, NJ: Princeton University Press, 2017.

Cohen, Getzel M., and Martha Sharp Joukowsky, eds. *Breaking Ground: Pioneering Women Archaeologists.* Ann Arbor, MI: University of Michigan Press, 2004.

Drower, Margaret S. *Flinders Petrie: A Life in Archaeology.* Madison, WI: University of Wisconsin Press, 1995.

Edwards, Amelia B. *A Thousand Miles Up the Nile.* London: George Routledge and Sons, 1877 and 1890.

Fagan, Brian M. *The Rape of the Nile: Tomb Robbers, Tourists, and Archaeologists in Egypt.* 2nd ed. Boulder, CO: Westview Press, 2004.

Freeman, Philip. *Searching for Sappho: The Lost Songs and World of the First Woman Poet.* New York: W. W. Norton, 2016.

Gaudet, John. *The Pharoah's Treasure: The Origin of Paper and the Rise of Western Civilization*. New York: Pegasus Books, 2018.

Gazda, Elaine K., ed. *Karanis: An Egyptian Town in Roman Times*. Ann Arbor, MI: Kelsey Museum of Archaeology/University of Michigan, 2004.

Grenfell, Bernard P., Arthur S. Hunt, and David G. Hogarth. *Fayûm Towns and Their Papyri*. London: Egypt Exploration Fund, 1900.

Hicks, Dan. *The Brutish Museums: The Benin Bronzes, Colonial Violence and Cultural Restitution*. London: Pluto Press, 2020.

Petrie, W. M. Flinders, F. Ll. Griffith, and Percy E. Newberry. *Kahun, Gurob, and Hawara*. London: Kegan Paul, Trench, Trübner, and Co., 1890.

Sheppard, Kathleen L. *The Life of Margaret Alice Murray: A Woman's Work in Archaeology*. Plymouth, UK: Lexington Books, 2013.

Sheppard, Kathleen L. *Women in the Valley of the Kings: The Untold Story of Women Egyptologists in the Gilded Age*. New York: St. Martin's Press, 2024.

Snape, Steven. *The Complete Cities of Ancient Egypt*. London: Thames & Hudson, 2014.

Thompson, Jason. *Wonderful Things: A History of Egyptology (Volume 2, The Golden Age: 1881–1914)*. New York: American University in Cairo Press, 2015.

Ward, Benedicta. *The Sayings of the Desert Fathers*. Kalamazoo, MI: Cistercian Publications, 1975.

Waxman, Sharon. *Loot: The Battle over the Stolen Treasures of the Ancient World*. New York: Henry Holt, 2008.

ACKNOWLEDGMENTS

As I mentioned in the previous section, this book has been a part of my life for quite some time. I am grateful to everyone who listened to me talk about my Egypt/papyrus book and continued to say it sounded like something they'd want to read, without asking me when/if it would be done. I appreciate you.

My agent, Samantha Haywood, told me from the beginning that I should take my time with this project. I'm grateful to her for hanging in with it, cheering it on, and providing excellent advice along the way. Her team at Transatlantic is uniformly superb. Cheers to Eva Oakes, in particular, for her assistance in developing a market-ready draft.

Working with a new editor is a real leap of faith, and I've been so fortunate to collaborate with Brittany Lavery at Simon & Schuster Canada. From our first meeting, I knew that she understood where I was trying to go and, more importantly, that she could help me get there. It's hard to explain what a relief that is unless you are likewise a writer attempting something which is, for you, ambitious, but trust me when I say: It's huge. Thank you also to the many hardworking folks at S&S Canada for their efforts on my behalf: Nicole Winstanley, Jonathan Evans, Muna Hussein, Natasha Kempnich, and Maya Price-Baker.

Friends and family read various versions of this book in early drafts. It is quite possible that I've forgotten some of them, and if so, I'm VERY SORRY. I do know that Sasha Akhavi, Bonnie Goldberg, Margo Hilton, and Liz Renzetti stepped in as beta readers and were kind with their praise. Big hugs, all around.

Speaking of praise, I have exceptionally generous and gifted colleagues who agreed—some within minutes of my request—to read galleys and offer blurbs. My deep personal thanks to Cathy Marie Buchanan, Janie Chang, Genevieve Graham, Natalie Jenner, and Bryn Turnbull.

In the course of my research, I cold-called a couple of present-day luminaries of the papyrology world: Professor Brent Seales, the Alumni Professor of Computer Science at the University of Kentucky; and Professor Arthur Verhoogt, the Arthur F. Thurnau Professor and Professor of Papyrology and Greek in the Department of Classical Studies at the University of Michigan, Ann Arbor. Their insights were invaluable in the early stages of planning and writing. In another life, I'd do what they do (but maybe not the computer science part).

The Sappho translations that appear in *City of the Muse* are by Anne Carson. I could not imagine using any other translations—Carson's work is exquisite—so I appreciate being granted permission to use them here. Thanks to Penguin Random House (publisher of *If Not, Winter*) and the Aragi agency for facilitating the process. I don't have a lot of regrets in life, but one of them is missing the opportunity to take a course with Professor Carson while a student at McGill University in the nineties.

Thank you to my beloved female friends who know when and how to show up. Special mention to my fellow travelers in the writing business, including but not limited to Kerry Clare, Chantel Guertin, Bianca Marais, Roz Nay, Liz Renzetti, Marissa Stapley, and Uzma Jalaluddin.

My love and appreciation go out to the extended Akhavi-Hilton-Macintosh-Sullivan clan, members of which have been operating as an indomitable and unpaid PR force for my books for more than a decade now. Closer to home, my kids remind me daily that there are at least a few things I love more than fiction. Special thanks to my stepdaughter, Chaya Akhavi, who created the map of Calliopolis which appears at the beginning of this book.

My husband, Sasha Akhavi, has been a steadfast champion of this book from its inception, even when I brought the *Oxford Handbook of Papyrology* on vacation. He's a keeper.

ABOUT THE AUTHOR

Kate Hilton is a bestselling Canadian writer. In addition to *City of the Muse*, her fiction includes *The Hole in the Middle*, *Just Like Family*, and *Better Luck Next Time*. She is also the co-author, with Elizabeth Renzetti, of the Quill and Packet mystery series: *Bury the Lead*, *Widows and Orphans*, and the forthcoming *Put It to Bed*. When not writing, Kate works as a psychotherapist in private practice, with a focus on personal reinvention and life transitions. She lives with her family in Toronto.